THE FORGOTTEN HORSES

A Sequel to The Horses Know Trilogy & Horses Forever

LYNN MANN

Coxstone Press

In memory of Sidney & Dashel,
they will always bound around me.

ONE

Will

Tania wanders among the horses, as much a part of them as they are of her; only my eyes tell me otherwise.

We both sense slight discomfort in one of the older mares in the same instant. By the time I've acknowledged the issue and decided how to help the mare, Tania already has the situation in hand. I would have resonated my energy with the mare's strained tendon and healed it with intention, but Tania's energy resonates with everything the mare is as a matter of course, and her intention is more of a passing impulse that heals the tendon quicker than most can fathom. She doesn't need to think, and never has. She senses imbalance and discord in those around her as if it is happening to her, and responds reflexively and intuitively in a way that strikes awe into anyone who can keep up with what she has done, and fascination into those who can't.

Immediately, Tania is on the mare's back. She sought neither permission nor invitation from the mare, for she had no need. She uses her body to remind the mare's of how to move in perfect balance now that her injury has been healed and compensation by the rest of the mare's body is no longer needed. Then she's off the mare's back, knowing that the herd has no need to move on just yet from the grassland on which we all stand.

The herd is still Ember's, though not for much longer. The white flecks in his coat and the white streaks in his mane and tail may belie the fire that yet burns in his amber eyes, but they corroborate the stiffness in his gait after a period of lying down, and the decrease in stamina that means he is now included in those to whom the herd energy shifts when he and his family are on the move, so that he is able to maintain his position at the back of the herd instead of being left behind.

He is as Aware of the young chestnut stallion who shadows the herd as are the rest of us, but unlike me, he is unconcerned for his future. I know the young stallion is vital to the survival of the herd – the mares and youngsters need a strong male to keep them following the lead mare, to maintain harmony and balance within the herd and to sire offspring – but my heart aches for the time when Ember will find himself left behind while the stallion takes his family away from him.

As Tania continues to wander mindlessly yet super-consciously between the horses, Ember lifts his head and spits out a wad of some of the tougher grasses he can no longer chew now that some of his teeth are missing. Maverick trots around and around the tall, black stallion, his ears pricked, tongue lolling, happy in his belief that it is he who keeps Ember standing in place. I smile at my dog, believing for a moment that he's really there and that at any moment, he'll abandon his game, race over to me and hurl himself into my arms as he always used to. But then his echo fades and all I see, where I so wanted him to be, is grass. I can't contain the tear that spills over my lower eyelid and slides down my face, even as my sense of Maverick where he is now remains constant. Instantly, he's with me, as much by my side as he ever was, but my heart aches for the fact that I can't stroke his head, I can't see those acorn-brown eyes of his alight with the joy of being alive.

I crouch down in the grass and close my eyes so that my five senses of the physical world can't remind me yet again that the dog who spent sixteen years at my side is no longer physically there. I smile as he shuffles closer to me. I feel his warmth, his devotion, his excitement for whatever is about to happen, and I smile as I remember our time together.

Tania's hand is warm on my shoulder. 'You know this doesn't do any of you any good, Dad, not you, not Maverick and not Ember. Pining for Maverick, even though he's always with you, causes him to worry for you, and fretting about Ember is only highlighting his frailties to him. You know all this, so why do you keep doing it?'

I open my eyes and look up into my daughter's bright blue ones. 'Because I'm human, Tan. Your and my level of Awareness allows us both a different perspective on life from that which most people have, and there was a time when I didn't always appreciate other people's feelings because of it – a fact that your mother frequently pointed out to me. As far as I was concerned, being Aware of all aspects of every situation, and being able to instantly see the perfection in whatever happens, meant that having strong emotions about anything was unnecessary.'

Tania nods her agreement.

'But then Maverick's time here came to an end and I finally understood what your mother meant. I felt a physical hurt that no amount of perspective can take away, no amount of sensing him in All That Is can change. I still do sometimes, because the life I'm living here is a physical one. Maverick changed my life when he came into it. He was with me in everything I did and he was a constant reminder of how to be my best. His final and continuing contribution to the life I'm living here is in helping me to fully remember what it is to be human when the level of Awareness you and I share can cause me to forget.'

Tania squeezes my hand, sensing my anguish as if it were her own. Then she senses the perfection of the life that Maverick shared with me, and its timely end, and again dismisses my emotion as unnecessary. I understand her point of view for it is as recognisable as it is familiar. It is why the horses sense my daughter as one of them; for her perspective on life is theirs.

But Tania incarnated as a human, and I have to help her to fully live as one.

She sighs and stands up from her crouch. 'Not this again, Dad?'

I stand up too and take both of her hands in mine. 'Listen to my words, feel your way around them and make room for them before you dismiss them all over again. Being dispassionate about things that bother us humans is a very healthy way for the horses to be; it serves them and they've helped us no end by being that way. But were you meant to be as much like them as you are, you would have incarnated as one of them. You chose to incarnate as a human, and as such, there is room within you for more compassion.'

'Indulging in unnecessary emotion? I disagree. Humans are moving forward, and that means letting go of aspects of ourselves that don't serve us,' my daughter says. I sense her reaching inside of me for my hurt at Maverick's physical loss and Ember's imminent fate, highlighting where it is lodged in my heart, so that I can recognise and release it.

I hold on to it. 'I'll let it go when I'm ready, Tan. Without it, I'm in danger of going back to how I was. When I'm confident I can remain more compassionate without it, I'll let it go.'

She raises her eyebrows as she always does when she thinks I or her mother should listen to her.

I try again. 'It's great that you're drawn to correct imbalance in the same way the horses are, but as a human, you need to do it with compassion so that others can relate to you. You'll learn the lesson in your own way. I'm learning it in mine.'

Tania looks at me levelly in the exact same way that Ember often does. She opens her mouth to say something but then smiles. We both turn towards the bushes of the nearby scrubland at the same time, knowing who is approaching. By the time three dogs come hurtling around a bush, I'm smiling too.

Ash, grandson of Lia's beloved dog, Breeze, is proudly holding the rabbit that the three of them scented, his eyes bright against the dark grey of his coat. Maverick's great-granddaughter, Rebel, is equally proud of the rabbit whose scent she caught whilst on the trail of Ash's kill, and whom she carries with her head held higher than normal as if afraid the tiny animal will drag on the ground. Rebel's sister, Chase, runs alongside the other two, empty mouthed but excited to have taken part in the hunt.

The three stop just short of us, and Ash and Rebel begin to tear into their kills. Chase watches them avidly until Ash shuffles backward slightly with the larger part of his meal, leaving the remainder in a bloody pile. Chase advances slowly towards the pile, and when neither Ash nor Rebel object, takes some of its contents gently between her front teeth and drags them slowly, carefully, to what she deems a respectful distance from the other two before tucking in.

Tania glances at me, Aware that I know exactly what she is

thinking; I can view the dogs ripping into beautiful animals that only a short time ago were living their lives as members of families, with the same level of dispassion against which her mother and I frequently counsel her. But I know the rabbits incarnated as such knowing that at some point they would be prey for a predator, and that when the time came, they would leave their bodies and be free to reincarnate at another time of their choosing, maybe as a predator if that would afford them the experience they required. Everything has happened as it should.

In this instance, emotion on our part won't help either the rabbits or the dogs, I point out.

Yet you think it helps other humans, Tania observes.

Excess emotion for the sake of being emotional, no. Sympathy and sorrow for one who is stricken with misfortune, absolutely, I tell her.

By way of response, my daughter opens herself up to as much of All That Is as the shield that I hold in place around her allows. She experiences herself as one life in a vast, never-ending sea of lives that includes all of the other lives she's lived so far, and experiences everyone and everything else in the same way.

But you're living this lifetime, right now, I tell her. *You chose to be here, living as a human, for a reason just like the rest of us.*

Which you shield me from knowing, Tania retorts.

Your soul may be eternal but your personality is twenty years old and still has a lot to learn. Look for where you're resistant to something instead of focusing all your energy on the things that come so easily to you. That's where your learning will start.

I'm here to bring balance where it's needed, just like the horses are, that much I know, Tania replies stubbornly. She looks over to where the horses are grazing, and allows her sense of them to become all of her like she always does when she doesn't want to listen to me or her mother.

I sense Lia's amusement along with her thought. *Who knew that someone with your level of Awareness, combined with openness that comes from never having been closed to anything, and a will as strong as yours and mine combined, would result in a person who resists us with even more ferocity than you resisted everyone around you at her age?*

I narrow my thought so that it is as insubstantial as Lia's and reply, *At least while she's with the horses and arguing with me, she isn't throwing herself at the shield I have in place. Are you enjoying the break?* I already know the answer to my question, but I also know that it will help to relieve the pressure that has built up within her if she tells me.

It's the same whenever you take her away for a while. I enjoy the rest from monitoring and shielding her for a day or so, and then I miss doing it and I can't remember what else there is to do in life when a large part of my attention isn't with Tania.

When you figure it out, let me know!

Oh, come on, Will, you take your turn at keeping her out of mischief while doing a hundred other things in your Awareness at the same time. If I weren't so keen to be as much a part of our daughter's life as you are, I'd just leave her to you completely.

It helps that I know where she's heading with all this.

I wish I knew too. There is a hint of sadness about Lia's thought, but she quickly adds, *I know, it'll just be one more thing I'll have to keep her shielded from and I can only just about contain her as it is.* She knows most teenagers' parents drop their shields by the time they're eighteen, and she's two years past that and getting more and more frustrated.

She also knows her Awareness far surpasses anyone's except mine, and that we've shielded her to protect her. She may not like it, but she knows her mind, even as strong as it is, would have reeled from being exposed to too much at once, and has needed to *be allowed to adjust to what she's been able to sense as she's matured.*

Amarilla thinks we should let go more, Lia tells me as if I don't know. *She thinks our protectiveness over our daughter is clouding both our Awareness and our judgement.*

I consider, as I have a hundred times before. This time, I admit, *She's right. I think it's time for us to take the final step back and allow Tania to experience her Awareness to its full extent. We've prepared her as well as we can. Now would be a perfect time to do it, while she's with the horses. What do you think?*

I sense Lia's complete trust in me, as constant as it is endearing, warring with her concern for our daughter. While each and every child is shielded from the full extent of their Awareness so that their young minds are only exposed to those things with which they can cope, few children sense their parents shielding them and those that do tend to accept their parents' influence on their Awareness without question. But where the worst from which most children ever need shielding is negativity arising from a difference of opinion between spouses, friends or neighbours, Tania can know all of the horrors of the past, the distractions of the future, and everything in between, all at the same time.

Lia and I have shielded her from everything that would have traumatised her inexperienced mind, and she has fought our guidance and barriers all the way, desperate to know everything she senses is there to be known. We have allowed her Awareness to have more freedom very gradually, but however much we've allowed her, it has never been enough. It has been necessary though – up until a few months ago, that is; having witnessed over and over again in my Awareness everything Tania is here to do, it hasn't just been protectiveness over her that has led me to keep strong blocks in place around the last areas of her Awareness that is still shielded, but protectiveness over Lia, for as strong as she is, the next few years will be difficult for her.

I feel my wife shake herself free of her concerns and make the choice to trust me as she's done so many times already. *Okay, let's do it,* she tells me.

I wish I could warn her about what is to come, but it won't help. Nothing will.

TWO

Tania

─────────

*T*he horses are so peaceful. So wise. So everything that humans aren't. I gather that humanity has advanced considerably in the past century, more than in the preceding few millennia in fact, but I'm not allowed to witness it for myself. My parents allow me to be Aware of how everything around me lives, grows, feels, interacts, but when I want to explore more, to know more, I hit the barriers they have in place around me. It's like having the very worst, most irritating itch just that little bit too far out of reach to be able to scratch. I know how much more there is of which I can be Aware, I can feel it there, waiting for me to experience it all, to BE it all, but I can't access it.

I've made it past Mum's barriers a couple of times, and she still thinks it was she who managed to take hold of me and pull me back. I could tell her that when I squeezed past her, I found Dad sitting just beyond her on one occasion, and Amarilla and Infinity patrolling behind her defences on the other, but I won't. It would hurt her and, silly as it is to be hurt by the actions of others when they're trying to make you think you're better at something than you are, I won't do it. There. Contrary to popular opinion, I'm capable of compassion. I'd be capable of a whole lot more if my prisoners would only let me out.

I stroke the soft, velvety nose of a young filly who has grazed her way over to me for a scratch. I pick tiny, yellow insect eggs off her chest, and smile at the explosion of knowledge and sensation that I suddenly possess. The fly who laid the eggs also endowed four others of the herd with them. I know the exact position of every single egg, how many attempts to lay further eggs were abandoned due to the potential host's skin shuddering or the fly being dislodged by a swishing tail, how the eggs were formed, created... and I suddenly realise that I also know the ancestry of the fly.

I look over at Dad, wondering how it is that I've been allowed to be Aware of the past, and in the same instant, realising it's because he no longer shields me. He, Mum, Amarilla and Infinity are observing me with interest and in Mum's case, concern. Her worries are groundless, she'll see.

I'm the pasts, presents and futures of all of the horses around me, at the same time. Finally, I know them all in their entirety instead of just the present moments of their current lives. I'm also the dogs, the cats, the rabbits and each and every other mammal. I'm the birds, the reptiles, the fish, the plants, fungi and bacteria. I know when and how they arose and when they will cease to exist.

I sense the awe of my parents as I assimilate All That Is in no more than twenty blinks of my eyes. I know all of them just as I know everything about everyone else... yet Dad is managing to hide something from me. That cannot be.

Yet it is, he tells me.

I go after the forbidden knowledge, following the thinnest thread of it to where I know the rest resides in Dad's mind. I am distracted for the tiniest fraction of a second by a nudge to my mind, and when I go back to the thread, it has gone. No, not gone, just moved behind something else. I find the tail end of it and go after it again, but once again, I am distracted just long enough for the thread to move somewhere else. I have it again... and it evades me again.

I'm Aware of the horses' decision to move. They are done grazing for now, and would accompany Dad and me back to Rockwood. I realise that I've been playing cat and mouse with him for hours. I'll continue to play it for as long as it takes.

Forever is a long time, he tells me. I look over to him and he winks at me. I sense Mum's amusement. It has the same flavour as it always does when the source of it is my will contesting Dad's.

Why are you doing this? HOW are you doing this? I ask him as I vault onto the mare who will carry me to Rockwood. As always when I ride, it's a welcome relief to become one physically with one who shares my heart and soul.

I am distracted momentarily by Dad's wistfulness and grief as he glances at Ember from astride the colt who has invited him to sit on his back. Ash, Chase and Rebel bark with excitement as the horses begin to move, and Dad smiles as he watches Maverick's echo hurtle along beside our three incarnate dogs.

He waits until I am alongside him before he replies, *While your Awareness is now fully yours to explore, it's polite to respect other people's privacy and not delve into things they've made clear they wish to keep to themselves.*

I'm frustrated all over again by his insistence on embracing human traits that no longer serve any purpose; if no one bothered with pointless emotion, there would be no need for privacy.

And there would be no need to be human at all, Dad points out. *I'm afraid I'm going to keep telling you the same thing over and over until a glimmer of it takes hold in your mind. You incarnated as a human because of the experience it will give you.*

Resisting your humanity will limit your experience here. Embracing it will allow you to fulfil your life's purpose.

Life's purpose. As soon as I sense his thought, the thread he yet hides from me flares into life and blazes like a beacon. I hurl myself after it, only to find myself distracted yet again by something I can't place for the fraction of a second it takes for him to hide it from me again.

'You're hiding my life's purpose from me?' I say to him, my incredulity shocking me out of mindspeak. Then I realise that it's no big deal, I can know it for myself... only I can't. He's still shielding that aspect of myself from me. I take a breath to rail at him, but he cuts in first.

'Please listen to me and allow yourself to feel the truth of my words through your anger,' he says. He looks across at me and repeats, so softly that I can only just about hear him, 'Just listen.'

I glare at him but wait for him to continue.

'The speed you just adjusted to your – almost – full Awareness was phenomenal, but the remainder will be a little more challenging. I would ask that you be content to continue exploring everything that is new to you while we return to Rockwood. Once we're there, I'll drop the shield entirely. You'll know everything there is to know and I won't keep anything private from you ever again. Deal?'

'What will be different once we're at Rockwood?' I ask, frustrated that I can't find a way to know the answer for myself.

'I'll be able to support your mum.'

'She doesn't need your support, Dad, she's strong and capable of looking after herself.'

'Not where you're concerned, she isn't,' he says quietly.

I know he's right. I wish it weren't the case, I wish Mum would be as calm and sure of herself where I'm concerned as she is with everything else, but she isn't.

'Okay, fine, but you still haven't told me how you managed to hide my life's purpose from me. The shielding I get, but this is something you know, something you've thought a lot about and then buried in your mind so that even I can't access it? How is that possible?'

He grins. 'Just a little trick I learnt from Amarilla. If it's any consolation, she and I are the only two who are adept enough at it to keep anything from you. Everyone else is an open book where you're concerned, but I would still ask you to respect the rules the rest of us abide by, and not delve into something that you can sense someone would prefer remained private. One day you'll do it for your own reasons, but for now, please, do it for mine?'

I sigh. 'Fine.' The mare and I move into canter and I'm immediately fascinated by how, exactly, we came to be capable of moving in such perfect balance. I live the lives of all of the Horse-Bonded ever to have existed, and smile as I come to know everything that has been kept from me about Amarilla and Infinity. But not quite everything, I quickly realise. Just as Dad keeps me from knowing my future, so Amarilla shields me from knowing her and Infinity in their entirety; there's something I'm not allowed to know yet, and the thread I don't even bother to follow has something in common with that which Dad is hiding.

All in good time. It is Infinity whose influence drives the thought from her shared being with Amarilla. Infinity's aloof yet nurturing energy soothes my frustration as they knew it would. As it always has.

Amarilla and Infinity have acted as a bridge between me and the rest of our family on many occasions when I've wanted access to more of my Awareness than my parents, grandparents, aunts and uncles have thought sensible. Infinity has kept Amarilla from being as cautious as the others, and has always been ready to give me sanctuary from my exasperation at being held back, by announcing herself in my Awareness and allowing me to indulge myself in everything that is horse and not human. Amarilla has always taken her lead from Infinity and thrown her weight behind Infinity's inclination to give me more freedom to explore my Awareness than would otherwise have been given. The light knows, without the two of them who are one, I'd probably still only be granted access to the Awareness allowed a child newly into her teens.

There is a sense of finality about Infinity's thought that backs up Dad's assertion that all shields will be dropped when we get back to Rockwood. All of a sudden, I see us and the herd doing exactly that. We're several hours away from the village, yet in my Awareness, we're already there. I'm Aware of my own future! Yet our arrival is all of which I can be Aware. Everything after that is shielded from me. Fine. I'll explore everything else to which I've finally been allowed access, while I'm waiting.

Our arrival is just as I saw it. The people of Rockwood sensed the herd's approach well before the horses spread out in the pasture closest to the edge of the village, and there are already stone troughs full of water arranged at intervals around the outside of it. The horses drink thirstily for they sensed my keenness to be back at the village, and moved at speed without stopping for water. The spring air is cool, but the sun surprisingly warm for the time of year and the horses have only just begun moulting out their winter coats. The colt and mare, who carried Dad and me respectively, are sweating on their chests and where we sat.

Mum appears by my side. She smiles as she kisses my cheek and hands me a bucket of water and sponge. 'There you go, sweetie.' She is trying to hide her anxiety at whatever it is I'm about to find out, even though she knows there's little point.

I put down the bucket and sponge and hug her, whispering, 'Thanks. For everything. I know I'm difficult and exhausting, but thanks for looking out for me all this time. You know I can handle my full Awareness now though, don't you? I'm only a year or two younger than Dad was when he came to his, and I've spent my whole life preparing for it.'

She chews her cheek as she always does when she's trying not to cry, then swallows and brushes my hair away from my face on both sides, tucking it behind my ears. 'I know,' she whispers. 'You're beautiful and you're magnificent, and I'm proud of you.'

I smile. 'I love you too.'

I sponge down the mare and enjoy her relief as she cools in the places where she was hot and itchy. When I've finished, I step out of her way so that she can roll as many of the other horses are currently doing. When the horses are all settled and grazing, the villagers of Rockwood, who have been waiting at the edge of the pasture, sense that the horses will tolerate them moving amongst them, and begin to flood the paddock.

From the youngest child, carried on her mother's hip, to the oldest resident of the village, everyone absorbs the peace, balance and strength that oozes from each and every horse. Some of the villagers are approached by the horses for a scratch, others are content to wander or sit amongst the herd, delighting in its energy and presence.

This was as much as I saw when I witnessed the future, but all of a sudden, I'm Aware of a whole lot more. I sense the change in Dad as he no longer maintains any shield of any type or strength around me. I know the full extent of his abilities; the part of himself that he has never allowed me to see or sense.

I witness all of the times he has allowed his sense of the dog he loved so much to become all of him, giving him the confidence and strength to stop believing in the mental and physical boundaries that enable humans to feel secure in their identities – he can allow himself to exist as energy in its purest form whilst existing in the physical experience! When he does it, and then welcomes the collective consciousness of the dogs into his existence, they are as visible as he is!

I laugh at the reactions of those around him whenever he has been visible as both an echo of himself and all of the dogs who ever existed. He's done it with the horses too – so that's how he helped the horses to reach the Drifters and bring them to Awareness. The Histories I was forced to learn in school, lesson after lesson, when I knew I could know everything that has ever happened in a second if my parents would just drop my shields and let me, miss that wonderful detail out. My frustration is immediately replaced by understanding; few young minds would cope with that information.

Well, I'm Aware of it now, and if Dad can do it, I can do it too.

There's a scream nearby as I become all of the dogs who have ever lived. I'm Aware of children being shielded from me and everything I am, everything I can do, and hurriedly taken back to the village. I'm now also the horses. All of them... and then some of them, one by one. I can not only be Aware of everything and everyone, I can BE whoever and whatever I want to be! And that's not even all of what I can do, who I can be. While I'm the dogs and horses, I'm also Aware of the last aspect of my dad that he kept from me. I witness him finding in his Awareness one who lived long ago, who needed his and Amarilla's help, and the two of them allowing their attention to be drawn back to the past where they could influence the first ever Horse-Bonded. I can do that too.

I smile as I realise that I know exactly what I need to do – that I know my life's purpose.

Immediately, strong arms enfold me, and Dad's thoughts – so narrow, so insubstantial that no one except Amarilla and Infinity is Aware of them – enter my mind. *Focus on me and remember who I am to you. Who you are to you. Focus on the mental and physical boundaries that enclose your soul and allow yourself to be Tania. Tania,* he repeats. *Tania.* His hold on me softens as I settle back into myself. *Well done. Stay within the physical boundaries you've just remembered, and let the horses help you to readjust.*

I feel the herd enclosing me physically as well as with their energy. I feel the heat of their bodies and I hear their snorts. Their energy swirls around and through my being, reminding me that I am who I am. That I am now Aware of my life's purpose.

You see it now, Dad tells me. *Hide it, like this, quickly before anyone picks it up from you.* He directs me to the knowledge I now have as to how he buried my life's purpose in his mind, and how he distracted and confused me whenever I came close to discovering it. Now that I have, I understand why he kept it from me – why he, Amarilla and Infinity have kept it from everyone. Mum is going to freak.

I hide it instantly and no one is any the wiser, which is a good thing as I'm Aware that all those maintaining a vigil over me are already awestruck by my exploration of everything I can now be.

'It's a good thing she's as strong-willed as Will and Lia combined, she'd never have been strong enough to re-centre herself so quickly otherwise,' one of Dad's sisters whispers.

'And it's a good thing you whispered that, Tully,' a familiar voice points out not altogether unkindly, 'it's not like Tania already knows everything that has ever happened and anyone has ever said.'

I grin and pull away from Dad slightly so that I can see Ace's head of silver hair over some of the horses' backs.

She nods at me, raises an eyebrow and says, 'Impressive.'

Victor tilts his head closer to hers and lifts a hand to me in greeting. 'Looks like we timed our visit to see Prime and Ivy perfectly, I'd have hated to have missed that.'

I wave at them both.

Granny Kat is the next to speak. 'Right, well I think that's more than enough excitement for one day, let's get back to the village and be about our lives, shall we?' Her arms encircle Mum's shoulders as she holds her close.

I nod, blow a kiss to Mum, and begin to walk towards the village, Aware that Granny keeps Mum from rushing to my side.

Dad walks on my right and Amarilla appears on my left. They don't speak because they are as Aware as I that they don't need to. They flank me as a silent but constant reminder to keep my discovery hidden for now, to divert my Awareness elsewhere until such time as I am free to explore what I have learnt – what Dad and Amarilla set in motion with their actions before I was even born – without affecting those whom it will distress. I hide the word that arises as soon as I have it; tonight.

As has become custom in the communities of The New since the first children became Aware, Mum and Dad invite our family and friends over for the remainder of the day to celebrate my unshielding.

Everyone contributes food and drink to the long table that has been pushed back against the wall of our kitchen, and everyone hugs and congratulates me on having reached adulthood. No one mentions that I'm two years behind everyone else in my year at school, because everyone, including me, now knows why.

As soon as I have greeted everyone in the long line that snaked its way into our cottage, I am Aware of someone focusing their attention on me, and turn around to see my cousin, Delta, heading towards me. She is Aunt Ivy and Uncle Prime's daughter, and two years my junior. She had her unshielding celebration a few weeks ago and I sense her relief that I'm now considered an adult alongside her. Her dad's purple eyes dominate her face, which is such a pale grey as to appear deathly white. Her hair is the same blond as that which her mother, my father and I have all inherited from Grandad Jack, but is streaked with the silver of her dad's people.

She grins at me as she pokes my shoulder. 'You're hiding something from me.' She brings her face so close to mine that all I can see is the purple of her eyes. Her Awareness isn't as all encompassing as mine, but she has inherited the intelligence of those who dwelt belowground for so long, and the combined power of her brain and Awareness allow her to pick up in me that which all except Dad and Amarilla have missed. She stares into my eyes as if she'll be able to read in my retinas everything she wants to know.

I put my hand to the back of her head and pull her even closer so that our noses touch. 'Maybe,' I say.

How are you doing that? No one can keep anything from me now I have full Awareness, she tells me.

Don't you know it's polite to respect other people's privacy and not delve into things they've made clear they wish to keep to themselves? I reply, repeating the advice Dad gave me earlier. We both giggle.

'You're no fun at all,' Delta says and pulls back from me.

'Actually, cancel that, you're a hoot. Your display out in the pasture was incredible.'

'Give it a go some time,' I say.

Her eyes become serious. 'I'll pass. You were born centred, but I have to work at it. If I drop my physical boundaries, I'll never be strong enough to remember who I am, I'll be swept away by All That Is and I'm having far too much fun in this incarnation to squander it.'

I sigh. 'Just because your brain is twice the size of mine, it doesn't mean you have to overthink everything. Give it a go, it'll be fun.'

She rolls her eyes. 'Just because your will is twice as strong as mine, it doesn't mean you have to be reckless. It's already cost you two years of adulthood.'

I grin as I shake my head. 'I knew you'd bring that up.'

She grabs my hand and pulls me to where Dad and Aunt Mija have kicked off the dancing. 'Come on, let's celebrate!'

I dance with everyone there, even Great-Gran who is well into her eighties. When she trips and almost falls backward, it's Uncle Prime, protective over her as always, who catches her, rights her and kisses her cheek before gently guiding her back to where I'm waiting with my hands outstretched to hold her wrinkled, bony ones.

When Mum takes her turn dancing with me, her love and pride flood my Awareness as we hold hands, lean back and hurl one another around in circles until we're so dizzy, we collapse in a laughing heap. Dad pulls us both to our feet, hugs Mum and then takes me in his arms, wheeling me around the kitchen floor in time with the lively tune the fiddlers have just begun playing. Everyone else clears the area and surrounds us, cheering and clapping.

Dad pushes me away from him, and I circle under his arm.

When he draws me back into his arms, he says under his breath, 'Know that I'll always be there for you. Always. You'll have to know it for it to be of help.' He continues to lead me on his wild dance as if he hasn't spoken.

Our cottage is finally silent. Having helped my parents to clean up after the party, I'm tired but in no mood to sleep.

Rebel whines from the foot of my bed, picking up on my excitement and hoping that whatever I'm planning includes her.

Not this time, I tell her, Ash and Chase, who are responsible for my needing a double bed, since the three of them refuse to sleep anywhere but with me. If Mum and Dad would only stop drawing Maverick and Breeze to them every five minutes, I'm sure they'd be deemed equally acceptable sleeping companions by our three dogs, but as it is, they're reluctant to even enter my parents' bedroom.

I focus on everything of which I became Aware this afternoon. The horses have done so much for humankind. Every single one of them who was bonded and all of those who have helped us since, including Dad's beloved Ember, have been written into the Histories for the benefit of all those whose Awareness is limited, or who prefer to use it sparingly. But I now know that horses were helping humans way before the Horse-Bonded ever existed, and some of them need my help.

It has to be me. There's no one else with the level of Awareness, the strength of will and the degree of self belief necessary to do it. Dad has shown me the way by having already performed both elements of what I must do, but even he has never combined them. It has to be me.

I know that Mum would advise me to become more familiar

with both elements in isolation before doing what I am about to do, so would Dad if he thought I'd listen, but he knows I won't. He and Mum are sound asleep down the hall, as is Amarilla in the cottage she shares with Justin. They're Great-Aunt Amarilla and Great-Uncle Justin really, but they won't be called anything of the sort. They're Justin, Amarilla and Infinity – and it is Infinity who observes me now.

I smile. There is no one I'd rather have with me.

I am all of which I can now be Aware whilst also being Tania, daughter of Lia and Will. I know myself as the individual I chose to be in this incarnation, and I don't need the part of my energy that vibrates slowly enough to be a physical body in order to continue knowing. As I speed it up to vibrate at the same frequency as my mind and soul, I create a net of calming energy around the dogs, who have begun to whine as I gradually become more insubstantial, and eventually fade from their vision altogether.

I could merge with the collective consciousness of the dogs as I did earlier, then slow my energy back down so that all of the dogs who have lived are as visible as I can be. I could, but I don't. I am needed elsewhere.

When I witnessed Dad finding Jonus in the past in his Awareness, then allowing his attention to be drawn there taking Amarilla's with it, I was stunned. I shouldn't have been – it's easy.

Like Dad, I know exactly where I am needed in the past, whose imbalances I can help the horses correct, and in an instant, I'm there. Unlike Dad, I don't leave a body behind because in this instant, I don't have one. But I'm going to need it now that I'm where and when I need to be, so I do as Dad schooled me to do earlier. I remember myself as Tania. I focus on the mental and physical boundaries that will protect my mind and soul while I am here, and I allow the horses, or in this case Infinity, to help me to adjust.

Infinity's discarnate energy swirls around me, holding me together as I gradually re-establish my physicality in The Old. My reformed lips curl up into a smile as I sense her energy being joined by that of some of the horses I am here to help. They know I'm here, and they would help me as I would help them.

I flinch. Their energy isn't as light as that of the horses I have left behind in The New; it's heavy with all that the Horse-Bonded helped the horses of our time to release. I nod to myself. I knew what to expect, for I was Aware of their energy when I was in The New. But being Aware of it whilst the horses expressing it are incarnate, and in close proximity to my newly reforming body, makes it more of a problem for me. As is the fact that rather than merely being Aware of the energy of The Old, I am now surrounded by it. Infused with it. Assaulted by it. And instantly overwhelmed by it.

Infinity, and the horses in whose barn I'm standing, close their energy ever more tightly around me and for a second, it's enough; I remember the words my dad spoke to me as we danced. *Know that I'll always be there for you. Always. You'll have to know it.*

Then the fear, hate and violence that define The Old reach me again. I begin waving my arms around myself, trying to push them all away, but I can't, I'm not substantial enough – I'm not physical enough. I hang on to Dad's words, for they and the horses are all that are keeping me from being swept away.

THREE

Will

_____

*M*y eyes fly open just before the dogs start barking. Tania's done it. She's gone. Lia wakes and sits up, looking around wildly. She throws back the covers and rushes to our daughter's bedroom. She pulls back the curtains so that moonlight floods in, revealing the dogs standing on the bed, looking towards the headboard as they continue to bark in confusion. I sense the remnants of the net of energy my daughter placed around them, and strengthen it. The dogs whine, circle around a few times and then lie down, looking up at Lia and me.

Lia turns to me, her eyes wide and staring. 'Where is she? Why can't I find her in my Awareness? When I woke up, she was just… gone.'

I put my hands on her shoulders. 'It's okay, she's alright. You can find her, she's just a little scattered at the moment, that's all.' I bring our daughter's situation to the forefront of my Awareness. 'Here she is.'

'What? Where? How? Oh, nooooooooooooooo.' Lia sinks to her knees as understanding sweeps through her. 'She should never have attempted that. You've never even done it, how could she possibly have thought she could when she's only just come to full Awareness? Will, you knew this would happen, how could you have let it? I trusted you.'

Ash slides from the bed to the floor on his belly, then slinks to Lia's side and snuggles up to her, licking her face. Chase and Rebel watch me, their tails wagging uncertainly.

I drop to my knees beside my wife and put my arm around her. 'You know our daughter. Do you think I could have stopped her any more than anyone could have stopped either you or me had we been in her situation?'

'We should have kept her shielded for longer,' Lia moans.

'We shielded her for months longer than was necessary because I wanted to spare you this for as long as I possibly could, but it was at Tania's expense. She's just doing what she has to do.'

'But she's not strong enough,' Lia wails, putting her hands to her face. 'It was hard enough for you to adjust to the energy of The Old, and you were only there in your Awareness, plus you had Amarilla and Infinity with you and your body back here to return to so that Maverick and the horses could ground you. Tania's taken all of herself there, and the energy of The Old has overwhelmed her before she can reform her body to protect herself. She'll be carried away by it any moment as if she never existed.'

'No, she won't. Infinity and the horses have got her for now, you can feel they have. They'll keep her together enough that she won't lose herself. I told her to know I'll always be there for her, and she does. She's holding on to my words and when I get back there with her, she'll remember all of herself.'

Lia drops her hands. 'You're going back there too?'

I'm Aware of her desperation for Tania to be alright warring with her terror that I'll succumb to the energy of The Old in the same way as has Tania. 'When you're ready for me to, yes.'

Her motherly instinct wins. 'But she needs you now, you have to go right now!'

'I can leave now, in an hour, next week, and I'll still be drawn to the exact moment she needs me; I'll arrive seconds after she did. I'm not going anywhere until you've had a chance to adjust to what's happening. Please, Lia, know that she'll be okay.'

Lia jumps at a knock on the front door and leaps to her feet, hoping for a desperate second that it is Tania returning home. Then the reality of the situation hits her all over again and she collapses against me, sobbing into my shoulder.

Come on in, Am, I tell my aunt.

I hear the front door creak open, then Amarilla's footsteps on the stairs. The light of her lantern precedes her and makes her white hair appear golden as she appears on the landing. Her blue eyes are as calm as the paler blue ones that look out from behind them. She smiles at me sympathetically and motions for me to turn Lia towards her. When I comply, she steps closer and takes one of my wife's hands in hers.

'Lia, look at me,' she says gently. 'That's it, look into my eyes. Into Fin's eyes. We have Tania. I know you're Aware of it, but see it in our eyes. We have her. She's okay. She needs to do this as much as we, as much as all of us of The New, need her to do it. It won't be any easier for her than it was for me to do what I did, for you to do what you did, or for Will to do everything he's done in order for humanity to be able to carry on existing here, and that's kind of the point; Tania may be capable of much, but she still has a little bit to learn if she's to fulfil her soul's purpose.

'No matter how well you've shielded her, she's always sensed the magnitude of the challenge that awaits her, and she's always been impatient to push on and get started. Now she's

thrown all of that substantial will of hers behind doing exactly
that. It'll be the making of her. You're Aware of her, so sit back
and observe. Watch your daughter as she does what she needs to
do, and be proud of her. There's no need for you to be afraid for
her.'

I sense Lia calming as she stares into the serenity of Infinity's
pale eyes. She begins to nod slowly. 'Infinity has her. She'll be
okay.' She takes hold of my hand and squeezes it hard even as
more tears flow down her cheeks. 'And Will is going to help her,
so she'll definitely be okay.' She turns to me, panic in her eyes
again. 'But what about you? You've never absorbed your physical
boundaries, your body, into your being completely like Tania did.
Will you be alright? Will you be able to slow your energy back
down quickly enough to reform it without being overwhelmed
first, like she's being?'

I grin. 'Of course I will. Maverick will help me, just like
always.'

Lia picks up everything I push to the forefront of my
Awareness, and almost smiles. Then she leans back against the
wall. 'You won't be gone long, will you, the two of you?
Whenever you're with Jonus in the past, you're with him for
hours, days, sometimes, in the time it takes you to blink here.'

I glance at Am, and she and Fin gaze back at me, giving me
the strength to say the words that I know will hurt Lia even more.
'It's only ever my attention that's with Jonus, I'm never with him
physically as I will be when I go to Tania. Once we've managed to
regain our physicality, we'll be subject to physical laws. Well most
of them, anyway, it'll depend a bit on which ones we decide to
believe in, but in order to be relatable to the people of The Old,
that'll need to be most of them.'

Lia's eyes widen in horror. 'You'll be physically vulnerable.
They could kill you both, flaming lanterns, what am I saying,

you're so different from them, they WILL kill you both, then your lives as Will and Tania will be over.'

'If Eminent were here, she'd be the first to assure you that killing me isn't easy,' I say with a grin, 'and she'd laugh out loud if anyone suggested it might be possible to end Tania's life before she's ready.'

Lia sighs and says, 'This is too much.'

'I know,' I reply. 'I'll stay here until it isn't.'

Amarilla turns for the stairs. 'Come on, I think we all need a cup of tea.'

Lia is unable to settle at home, so as soon as it is light, she and I leave our cottage and spend the morning walking through the nearby forest with the dogs, soaking up its newly awakening vitality as the lengthening days and slowly rising temperatures signal that winter has well and truly passed. I am mostly silent as we walk amongst the trees, apart from answering the questions Lia fires at me during the intervals when she stops repeating over and over that which she already knows and can sense, in order to reassure herself that Tania and I will be okay.

When we return to our cottage for lunch, Lia busies herself preparing our meal whilst I feed the dogs. She frowns as we sit down to eat, and says, 'It's too quiet, I still can't bear it.'

'We'll spend some time with the horses this afternoon then, shall we?'

Lia pauses her spoonful of soup on its way to her mouth, looks at me, then continues to raise it. She gulps the hot onion soup down, splutters, then says softly, 'They're still grazing in the pasture right next to the village, and I can't face anyone. They're all Aware of what's happened and I can't talk about it. Not yet.'

I reach for her hand. 'Which they'll also be Aware of. No one will come anywhere near you while they know it's not what you want, you know they won't.'

She sighs and nods. 'Okay, yes, we'll go to the horses then. I can't be here.'

We leave Ash snoring, and Rebel and Chase twitching and yipping in their dreams, on Tania's bed. I put my arm around my wife and hold her close as we walk through the village.

Rockwood has expanded rapidly in the past few decades, to the extent that a growing number of young people have left the village in order to apprentice elsewhere, and many newly married couples have travelled to smaller villages to settle. Those communities have also expanded rapidly – even The Gathering is at full capacity. We are all Aware – even those whose Awareness is limited to sensing their connection to everything – that humanity is on its way to being unable to remain in balance with its environment. It is the reason that Lia and I, like the majority of our generation and that which has followed, have limited the size of our family; none of us in The New need to recreate the patterns of war, disease and starvation that regulated population levels in The Old.

I nod and smile at all of those we pass, drinking in their happiness, their harmony with one another and their surroundings, and their diversity as Kindred and humans of all ancestries live, love and laugh together. Without Tania and what she will do, none of this would exist.

I sense Lia looking sideways at me. 'That should help, I know it should, but it doesn't,' she says.

I hug her. 'Not yet, but it will.'

When Delta approaches, I am Aware that she is desperate to hug Lia and let go of the tears that she is just about managing to hold back.

I wink at my niece and tell her, *Everything will be okay.*

She grimaces and lifts a hand in a tentative wave, then hurries past, unable to bear her sense of Lia's grief compounding her own.

When we reach the pasture where Ember's herd is still grazing, Lia lets out the breath she has been holding. I feel the same way. No matter how Aware we all are of horses and dogs, seeing them, hearing them, being with them always has an instant effect. Where our dogs have spent the morning reminding us how wonderful life is, with their tearing between the trees and leaping over the undergrowth as if they're experiencing the joys of doing so for the very first time, in between bringing us a variety of gifts – mostly twigs and pine cones but Ash was particularly proud of the rabbit bone with which he presented Lia – the moment we are with the horses, we instantly absorb their invitation to be centred and present.

We feel them draw Lia's concerns for our daughter and my concern for Lia to the surface of our beings, so that we can see them for what they are and let them go. Lia's will return, but for now at least, she is afforded relief from her grief and anxiety. We wander over to Ember and when we are almost upon him, he closes the remaining distance between us. He rests his muzzle gently on Lia's shoulder, his fluted ears soft as one of them points towards her and the other towards me. She tilts her head against his cheek and closes her eyes.

I take a step back and smile at the knowledge that Ember and his herd, drawn as ever to any imbalance that their energy can correct, will remain here while I'm gone. Lia is strong in both personality and Awareness, but her maternal instinct to defend her daughter is stronger than both and will pull her off centre every time she senses Tania coming up against that from which she can't protect her. Ember will ensure that Lia can cope with what is to come.

Lia employs Ember's calm strength to bolster her own as she instructs me, *Go to our daughter. I'll be alright. I have the dogs and Ember and his herd. I have everything I need, but Tania doesn't. She needs you.*

I sense the herd energy shift towards her as her fresh thought of Tania's predicament threatens to take hold of her again. Ember rolls an eye in my direction as he draws her pain from her. He doesn't need my gratitude. He's never needed anything from me, yet once again he's given me more than I could have asked of him.

You're sure you'll be alright if I go now? I know what her answer will be, but I want to give her time to strengthen a little more before I leave.

There is barking in the distance, which very rapidly gets closer. Lia almost smiles as Chase, Ash and Rebel burst onto the pasture and surround her and Ember.

I have everything I need, my wife repeats, her eyes tightly closed so that she doesn't have to watch my departure. *Go to our daughter, Will, and when she's done everything she needs to do, you bring her home, do you hear me?*

I grin at the tone her thought carries. That's my Lia. Ember will help her through the next few hours, then the dogs will see her home.

We'll be waiting for her, my parents, Amarilla and the eldest of my six sisters, Mabel, all tell me, their thoughts narrow and delicate so as to not distract Lia from Ember's influence.

I kiss the back of Lia's head and she reaches for my hand and grasps it, her eyes still tightly shut, her head still resting against Ember's cheek. More of the herd energy shifts towards her, and she releases her hold on me and puts her arms around Ember's neck. I'm Aware of her determination to allow the horses to help her so that she doesn't hinder me.

I step away from her and Ember, and sit down in the grass. I watch Rebel, as like her great-grandsire as Chase is unlike him in appearance, pushing her head into Lia's hand, and then as I do so often, I see Maverick's echo trotting circles around Ember, herding him even as the tall, black stallion stands at rest.

I grin and tap my knee, and Maverick bounds over to me, ecstatic at what we are about to do. I sense Amarilla and Infinity waiting for me; They Who Are Infinity will support me even as they support my daughter.

The first time I dropped my boundaries and became one with the collective consciousness of the dogs, it was in order to protect Ember from the wild cats who wanted him for their next meal. I wasn't sure whether I could retain my identity, and it was Am and Fin's belief in me, and the dogs' instinct to protect their pack that drew me past my doubts.

Now it is my love for my daughter combined with my trust in my dog's instincts that will draw me past any doubts I have as to whether I will succeed. I allow my sense of my beloved Maverick to become all of me until I am him and then all of the dogs who have ever lived. We will protect our pack. We will run. Our intention speeds up the slowly vibrating energy of my body until it matches the speed at which Maverick's energy vibrates – at which my soul vibrates. We will protect our pack.

We are with her immediately. In the same instant, my rapidly vibrating energy is assaulted by the insecurity and viciousness of The Old. I recognise it from my time with Jonus and his friends, yet this is different. Where the Ancients made every effort to step aside from the urges and emotions that drove The Old, in order to leave it and start anew, here, fear is accepted as normal and sensible, and violence is viewed as both saviour and protector. The traits that only reared up within the Ancients once they were at their most tired, hungry and doubtful, are embraced and propagated here, and as such they are infinitely stronger.

But so am I.

I focus on everything that makes Maverick and me who we are, and allow the negative energy to pass through us. It weaves itself throughout our essences, trying to take a hold of us and twist us into itself, but try as it might, all it succeeds in doing is being converted to that which it always was. We release the freshly liberated love into the ether as the horses of The New have done for us so many times.

Infinity swirls around us, closing in on us and then coming between Maverick's energy and mine. She holds me together while I do what I must. Maverick's energy encircles hers, protecting me as always. I focus on my forty-two years as Will. I focus on my daughter, barely substantial nearby, and I slow my energy until I am physical once more.

You'll always be here for me. Tania's thought is as frail as is she, as her energy body crouches in the straw, protecting the modesty of the parts of it that she has almost managed to make physical.

I grin at her. 'I see you neglected to think about clothes?'

A flash of indignation strengthens her will as much as does the sight of me.

FOUR

Tania

*H*e's here. He crouches down in front of me and puts his arms around the energy I've just about been managing to hold together with the help of Infinity and the horses who live here.

'Focus on me,' he says out loud, determined to draw me back to my physicality. 'Focus on Infinity. Focus on who you've been for the past twenty years. Come on, Tan, focus on it all, I've got you. Slow your energy down and keep doing it, and while you're there, get a sense of the clothing that will help you fit in here, and divert part of yourself to forming that too.' He doesn't doubt I can do as he says, which makes the doubt with which the energy of The Old is riddled, flinch away from us both. I feel more sure of myself... and more physical.

'That's it,' he says. 'You're Tania, you're my daughter and you're doing fantastically.' The love that explodes from him infuses me, surrounds me and gives me the strength I need.

I hug him back. 'Thanks, Dad.'

'Don't mention it.'

I stand up and brush the straw from the dark green leggings with patches to the insides of both knees that I have created for myself. 'Jodhpurs.' I say the word for the first time, and then repeat it several times so it doesn't feel so strange as it passes my lips.

Dad stands up too and brushes straw and dust from his own black jodhpurs and short-sleeved, fitted top.

'They call it a t-shirt,' he tells me as if I couldn't find that information for myself. He nods at my checked shirt. 'Not so different from ours at home, just a slightly different fabric.'

'What are you, a Tailor now?' I say with a grin.

'I could be if I wanted to, goodness knows, I repaired enough of your clothes when you used to come home with them hanging off you in shreds from following Maverick and Breeze everywhere.'

I sense his instinct to look down to where Maverick would definitely have been if he were here physically, and immediately nod to the horses standing behind him before he can get morose. 'Shall we get started?'

He grins. 'This is your party.'

There are seven horses in the barn, sheltering from the heat and flies of the day. They're a herd and yet not a herd – not in the way the horses of The New are. They aren't related to one another, they haven't always lived alongside one another – they've all come from different places and situations – and since they have all been kept alone in the past with only their people for company, they have far more sense of individuality than do the horses of The New. Yet they are the same. At their cores, they are everything it is to be horse; they are bringers of balance. But their efforts to do so have been misunderstood and ignored at best, punished at worst.

All of the horses here carry injuries that have been inflicted on them by those they have tried to help. Many of the wounds have healed physically and so are invisible, but all are still infected with the fear and anger with which they were inflicted. I sense the welts that once lined a gelding's rump, since the fury of the perpetrator who caused them still roils under the now healthy skin. I sense a mare's long-healed bruises that yet hold the frustration of the rider who repeatedly kicked her. I sense the fear that festers in the apparently pink and healthy gums of another mare, caused by a rider hauling on her bit in terror as she refused to submit to his demands for her to slow down after he terrorised her into bolting in the first place.

Other injuries are still very physically apparent, many having been inflicted by the man who thinks he owns all of the horses who are standing, watching Dad and me. Others are less so, but they scream their existence nevertheless.

The tall, dun horse's pelvis is twisted despite multiple attempts by his many owners to have it set straight. He has held it that way for so long in order to relieve saddle pressure on an old injury to his withers, his body no longer remembers how to be straight. He has been ridden away from health and balance, to a place where misery is all he knows. His discomfort is so great that he rears whenever anyone tries to ride him, but since his parents were both well known for winning jumping competitions, try they still do. The man who now owns him and all of the other broken horses who held me together so that I didn't break, bought him to try and sort him out; not because he cares about him, but because he wants to dominate him into submission and then make a profit on his investment.

The dun gelding's wound is my wound. I sense his momentary shock as I see it so, for he has never truly been seen by a human before. Then he reconciles what he senses from me with what he knows. I heal the wound in our withers during my first step towards him and then begin on our pelvis. I remind it of its healthy alignment and am in place on the back that is both his and ours by the time our pelvis begins to shift. We need to move so that our human body can remind our equine one how to be straight as the pelvis continues to realign. We burst out of the barn into the sunshine, and despite the heat, the other six horses follow in our wake, eager to be included in what is happening.

We are straight and free from pain. We are happy. As we move up to a trot and then a canter, I heal all six of the others who are also me.

A loud bang sends us all into a gallop. Our hearts race as one until seven hearts slow back down at the suggestion of the eighth, for I know who it is who would try to scare me. We canter over to the tall, muscular, middle-aged man who believes the brightly coloured cap on his head makes him look younger and more attractive than he is. His energy is heavy and roils around both within and without his body like a barrel of snakes all trying to escape from one another.

I glance at Dad. The energy that emanates from his physical body and surrounds him like a second skin is bright white as always. I and all of the Horse-Bonded are the same, while all others of The New exude energy in any combination of the colours of the rainbow, including white. The energy emanating from this man is brown with greed and self-involvement. Dad and I can influence it, but we'll need to take it slowly.

I'm Aware of Dad's agreement with my observation as the eight of us who are one halt in a line in front of the man.

'What the bloody hell do you think you're doing, messing around with my horses?' he snarls.

'Healing them,' I say. 'They look a whole lot better now, don't you think?'

The man scowls as he looks from one of the horses to the next, then settles on the dun upon whose back I still sit. 'I should shoot you where you sit. I'll do it too, unless you tell me in one sentence how you made him accept you on his back without throwing you, and with no saddle or bridle either.'

'I didn't make him do anything, he wanted me to heal him and show him how to be straight, so that's what I did.'

I sense the man's confusion a split second before he raises his weapon to his shoulder and points it at me. Dad disables the gun before he fires. The trigger clicks and his cruel smile disappears. His face contorts with anger but I sense the fear that lies beneath. If he can't attack then he can't defend either. He's vulnerable. He hurls his weapon to the ground, clenches his fists and begins to advance on me.

'I'm here to help.' Even as I'm saying the words, we're preparing to move.

We spin on our hocks and canter away. The paddock that confines us is small, but there's plenty of room beyond. We jump the fence, leaving the other horses, the other parts of ourselves who are rapidly remembering what it is to be so, behind. We run. We aren't as balanced as we could be, but by the time we've run ourselves out, we're in a better place than we were. We could keep on running, but we turn back towards the imbalance that calls to us with its readiness to be corrected.

We jump the fence back into the paddock and come to a halt just as the man is exiting his house carrying a replacement weapon. I disable it as Dad moves to stand in front of me, a finger of each hand tucked into the belt loops of his jodhpurs.

'I see you've met my daughter,' Dad says amiably to the man. 'Your horse looks a lot better, doesn't he? He jumped that fence like it was a pole on the ground. Let Tania work for you, and she'll have all of your horses working happily in no time.'

The man almost drops his weapon in disbelief. 'Work for me? WORK FOR ME? She rides my horse without permission, then makes off with him, and you want me to give her a job?'

'Only if you want to make a whole load of money,' Dad says. 'It's just a suggestion.'

Greed is as foreign to me as it is part of the man. He squints into the sun at where the other horses are now milling around me and the dun, waiting for their turns to be ridden and reminded what it's like to move with ease and flow. I slide to the ground, interested as always in the sensation of landing on my own two feet in place of the four that are also mine. I know which of us has the next greatest need to be ridden, and am in position in a heartbeat.

I sense the tension that has been our response to being held in what is deemed a desirable posture by one strong rider after another. Each was drawn to us because our body is beautifully formed and should have excelled at dancing with a rider, yet none who have yet crossed our path have truly known how to dance. We release the tightness, and also the frustration that was trapped in the spot where we were kicked so many times. We are happy and free. We float around the paddock, remembering how we felt before anyone tried to use us for their own ends.

I land on my feet and, in the time it takes us all to draw in a breath, am where I need to be as part of the next horse. I itch to take each of them to perfect balance, but I know as well as they that taking them there, only for them to be ridden back away from it by those they are here to help, would be far from helpful. Returning them to health so that they are ready for the next stage of their lives here is the best I can do for them, and all they require of me.

By the time I've ridden all seven horses back to the health with which they were born, we're all sweaty and thirsty. The man is now leaning back against the paddock fence, his hand over his mouth as he talks to his wife, who leans against the fence from the other side. Her energy is mostly grey with sadness, exhaustion and depression. She's the one we need.

Dad grins as he sits on the top rail of the fence, a sensible distance away from the couple. *Way to go, Tan.*

The pleasure was all mine, apart from the sweating.

Look out, you're about to have company.

I'm Aware too, remember?

He touches a finger to his eyebrow briefly and grins. I smile back and slide to the ground.

The horses all step back, snorting, as the man draws near.

'So, you're looking for work,' he says. He looks over at Dad. 'What about you? Did you teach her to ride like that?'

I was born knowing myself to be one with the horses, but Dad grins and says, 'In a way.' He gives me the ghost of a wink. 'I taught you everything you know, didn't I, Tan?'

I manage not to smile. 'I don't know what I'd have done without you.'

The man looks from Dad to me. 'If you can make the dun take my wife on his back, you're both hired. If you can't, I'll kill you both for trespass and theft.'

'Just as soon as you can get those weapons to work, huh,' Dad says as if he's sympathising with the man over a broken pitchfork. 'I'm Will, and my daughter's name is Tania.'

'Your names won't mean a thing when you're six feet under,' the man replies.

His wife sidles past him and approaches me. She's wearing face powder to cover the bruise on her cheek, and her fractured cheekbone is painful, as are the broken rib that's causing her to wheeze, and the rest of her bruises. The injuries to her body are

the result of her previous attempt to ride the dun horse. Those to
her face are her husband's work.

I smile at her as she falls in beside me to walk to where the
dun is standing, watching the man over our heads with rolling
eyes and flared nostrils.

'I'm Pamela,' the woman whispers whilst trying not to move
her mouth too much. She nods towards the dun. 'He'll kill me. He
tried the last time I sat on him, and I had a saddle and bridle to
help me then.' Through her fear, I sense her resignation to the fact
that at least it would be an end to her suffering if he did.

'He won't,' I say. 'I'll help you onto his back, then you just
need to sit lightly and easily and he'll do the rest.' I sense her fear
and confusion as she replays in her mind her memories of the dun
throwing her, and of him carrying me bareback and bridleless only
a few moments ago.

'I'm not sure I can,' Pamela whispers.

'You've seen that the horses trust me,' I tell her. 'You can too.
I won't let your husband hurt you again.'

Her eyes widen. 'How did you…' Her mouth hardens. 'It
doesn't matter. No one can protect me from him, least of all a
scrap of a girl like you. Don't pretend you care, you just want a
job. You and your dad should never have come here, you'll wind
up dead one way or another.'

'I can protect you. I'm as sure of it as I'm sure you won't tell
your husband that your rib doesn't hurt anymore.'

Pamela's hand flies to the rib I've just healed. She gasps.
'What the hell?'

'You can do this,' I tell her as I stroke the dun's neck. 'Trust
me.' I look into her terrified, brown eyes until they soften very
slightly. 'Trust me and trust the dun. He was hurting even more
than you have been. He isn't now. Be soft and kind, and you'll be

fine.' I sense her glimmer of hope that maybe, somehow, impossibly, I may be right.

She strokes the dun's shoulder with a shaking hand and bends her knee for me to give her a leg up onto his back – onto our back. We stand firm even as she lands heavily. She shifts into position, takes a deep breath and tries to lighten her seat. We move beneath her when we sense she is about to ask us to. We walk, trot and canter around the paddock, always obliging Pamela's intentions to change pace or direction before she has a chance to give us a physical cue. We sense her fear lessening and then turning into something else as she consciously focuses on what she wants us to do, and marvels at our response. When we sense that she's about to ask us to slow down, we oblige and come to a graceful stop near the other horses, as far away from the man as possible.

Pamela leans forward and strokes our ears, whispering, 'That was amazing, and... beautiful. You're beautiful. I'm so sorry for you that you've come to be here.' She swings a leg over the dun's back and lands beside me, even remembering to hold her healed rib and wince as if it still pains her. Then she looks at me. She doesn't know what to say, so I help her.

'You've never felt a connection with a horse like that before,' I say softly, 'and you don't know whether to laugh or cry. There you go, I've just healed your cheekbone so it won't hurt to do either. Thank you for trusting me.'

Pamela glances at Dad and then looks back at me. 'Who are you both? You don't talk like anyone else around here, hell, you don't even walk like the rest of us, and you can... I don't even know what it is you can do. Where have you come from and why are you here?'

I smile. 'We're here to help.'

Pamela's eyes flick nervously to her rapidly approaching husband, and she and the dun both flinch involuntarily.

'Pamela.' She looks back at me, her eyes full of fear again. 'You're exhausted from always being so afraid. Your husband's parents were fearful and cruel, and the only way he can discharge all of the pain that was beaten into him is to beat it into you and the horses.'

Her eyes widen. 'How can you possibly know…'

'Trust me. My dad and I are here to help, as are the horses.'

A large, dirty, callused hand is thrust in front of me. 'Tania, you're hired.'

I turn to the man, smile and shake his hand, taking advantage of the physical contact by sending a stream of light into his body. It disappears into the darkness. 'That's great, thanks, Cliff.'

He scowls and gradually tightens his grip on my hand, waiting for pain and fear to show on my face. 'I didn't tell you my name and I definitely didn't give you permission to use it,' he snarls.

I'm Aware of Mum's panic and Dad's confidence in me even as I smile up at Cliff whilst influencing the muscles and tendons in his hand so that he feels he's squeezing as hard as he can, when actually he's giving me the kind of pleasant, firm handshake of which I know he'll one day be capable. I know it. I see it in him as clearly as I see the pain he has exacted on others through multiple lifetimes until his soul incarnated in The Old in order to receive, when he was at his most vulnerable, that which he had grown used to inflicting, and then clear the pattern in the name of something greater. His eyes narrow as I continue to smile up at him.

'Didn't she do well, love?' Pamela says with a tremble in her voice. 'She worked a miracle with Pebble, I've never felt a horse move like he does now. He'll be worth a fortune, and I bet the others will be every bit as much better than they were when they arrived here.'

'I never asked for your opinion, woman, so keep your trap shut until I do,' Cliff snaps, but he releases his hold on my hand.

Dad arrives by his side. 'Did I hear the word "hired"?'

Cliff's grin is more of a sneer. 'She is. All of a sudden, I'm wondering why I need you.'

'You don't, really. Mind you, between us, we can put more horses right than either of us can alone,' Dad says cheerfully. 'That's more fun for us and more money for you.'

Cliff leans towards him and points a grubby finger in his face. 'You don't get to talk. Keep your mouth shut and you can work alongside her.' He points his thumb back at me. 'Speak when I haven't spoken to you first, and you'll regret it.'

Dad grins and mouths, 'Got it.' It's all I can do to keep myself from laughing.

Pamela looks terrified. Cliff pulls his fist back with the intention of taking a swing at Dad, but finds his arm moving far more slowly than expected. By the time he has extended it to where his fist should have connected with Dad's face, it meets thin air, just short of where Dad stands looking innocent.

Outraged, Cliff tries again... and again and again. I can't decide which is funnier, the incredulous look on Pamela's face, or the man who appears to be trying to assault thin air.

Eventually, Cliff sinks to the ground, exhausted. Sweat drips from his nose and chin, and soaks his shirt. He heaves and gasps as if he's been running for hours.

Pamela is rooted to the spot. She looks frantically between Dad and me, trying to figure out what to do so that none of us will suffer Cliff's revenge for what just happened.

Dad says, 'Right, Tania and I will get on then, shall we?' He claps his hand over his mouth and then continues talking through his fingers. 'I'm talking. Sorry. It just seems a more efficient way of doing things. Anyway, we happened to notice that the barn needs mucking out. We'll get on with that so it's clean and presentable by the time your clients arrive to view the horses, shall we?'

Pamela looks down at Cliff, waiting for his response, but he's still gasping. She nods uncertainly and says, 'I'll get the word out that Pebble and the others are ready for sale, then I'll get us all a drink. There'll be more work done if we're well hydrated.' She holds her wrist up to her mouth and begins talking to it.

Dad puts an arm around my shoulders. *Come on then, daughter of mine, let's get the mucking out done while there's no one around to see us doing it.*

Okaaaaaay then, father of mine, I'll lead, you follow.

He chuckles. *I wouldn't have it any other way.*

I resonate my energy with the piles of horse dung in the barn. Dad adds his intention to mine and we lift all of the dung away from the straw bedding, and out of the far door of the barn to the muck heap. By the time we arrive at the barn physically, we only have the wet straw to lift and add to the dung, which is dealt with in minutes. We watch three large, round bales of fresh straw follow our intentions and move from the loft to the ground, then release the straw from its strings and take a pitch fork each to shake it on top of that which is already down.

The horses wander in, having drunk from the trough outside. We move two hay bales down from the loft in the same way we did the straw, and shake the hay into racks hanging from the barn walls. Then we set about grooming the horses with brushes that were stored in one of the hay racks we have just filled. We destroyed the sedatives and painkillers that were stored alongside them. Cliff may have cared more about having the means to quieten horses and make them presentable for potential clients than about keeping the hay racks full, but, though he doesn't yet know it, that has now changed.

Pamela appears carrying a tray laden with two glasses, a pitcher of water, half a loaf of bread and a chunk of cheese. She stops momentarily and looks around, blinks, then continues over to where Dad is grooming Pebble and I'm grooming a light bay mare.

'Any minute now, I'm going to wake up and find this has all been some weird and wonderful dream,' she says as she puts the tray down in the straw next to the wall. 'Cliff says you're only to be fed basic rations, so this is nothing fancy, but I crammed as much of it on the tray as I could.'

Dad and I drain the pitcher and then set about the bread and cheese while Pamela tells us everything of which we're already Aware. 'By the time Cliff could stand, I'd managed to get two clients booked in to come and see Pebble and Clicka.' She nods at the dancing mare. 'He got excited, thank goodness, and joined in contacting people on our books who've been waiting for us to find them suitable horses – everyone just wants a guaranteed safe ride nowadays – and now all seven horses have potential buyers coming to see them. We told them the horses can be seen ridden without tack, and they couldn't get here quick enough.' She looks at her wrist. 'The first will be here in just under an hour. Cliff's already rubbing his hands together. You won't let him down, will you? You'll ride the horses bareback and bridleless, so their buyers can see they're safe?'

We both nod and I say, 'We will. It's unlikely that the horses will be as relaxed with other people as they are with us, but it's all good, they're all within an hour's travel from here, so they can bring their new horses back for lessons.'

Confusion sharpens Pamela's face. 'You can't possibly know where they live.' Then her eyes blaze with a greater fear. 'Anyway, Cliff won't want you teaching them. He'll want you both sorting out all the horses he's intending to buy once this lot have been sold.'

Dad grins as I explain, 'Cliff will learn that he doesn't own us any more than he owns these horses. We're all here to help him, and you, but there are other people who need our help too.'

Pamela frowns as she looks around at the horses. 'The horses are here to help Cliff and me? That's just dumb. We bought them to sell on, pure and simple. And you might think you're helping me, but you'll either move on before Cliff kills you, or he'll kill you and I'll be right back where I was. That's if this is even all real and not, as I'm beginning to believe, a dream.'

I leave Dad to answer her – I know how he loves to be cryptic.

'It's both real and a dream, isn't that fantastic?' he says, his smile assuring her that it is while all she can do is look at him as if he's both terrifying and crazy. She picks up a brush and begins to groom Clicka, every now and then stopping and turning to where Dad and I have resumed grooming Pebble and the bay mare as if she's going to say something, then shaking her head and returning her attention to Clicka.

All seven horses are gleaming with health and vitality with minutes to spare. We are sorting out which saddles and bridles we will use for the different horses as Cliff's voice drifts into the barn from across the paddock, extolling Pebble's virtues to the gelding's potential buyer. Pamela looks pleadingly at me and Dad.

I smile at her and say, 'Don't worry, everything will be fine.'

You ride while I play at being groom? Dad asks me.

I'd thank you, but I know you're itching to adjust those saddles and bridles so they're comfortable for the horses. Sure, I'll ride.

Cliff appears in the barn doorway accompanied by a young woman with streaks of pink and purple in her long, brown hair, which she constantly tucks behind her ears and then liberates, strokes and tucks behind her ears again. She has painted her face heavily in order to try to hide her exhaustion with life, and wears a hopeful smile that flickers in and out of existence.

Cliff smiles as he says, 'Tania, show Miss Kelford, here, what

Pebble can do, if you please?' His smile doesn't reach his eyes and his energy remains brown and heavy. Miss Kelford's is grey, flecked mainly with the black of imminent death for which she is heading, but with tiny hints of blue as the sensitivity with which she was born fights for continued existence. She needs Pebble desperately if she is to exist in this incarnation for much longer – and exist she must, for we need her.

FIVE

Will

Sophie Kelford believes that having a horse who can win jumping competitions will make her feel better. The twenty-year-old is scared of the life into which she has been born, and is destroying her body with the drugs she takes in order to escape it. She wants to feel safe and strong, but she wants a horse to give her those feelings rather than finding her way to them on her own. The good news is that she's sensitive to her soul's urging to find the horse who will help her, even if not for the reasons she currently believes.

I stand back as Tania vaults onto Pebble's back and rides him out of the barn. Cliff and Sophie follow them with Cliff repeatedly pointing out how very obviously safe the horse is for Tania to be riding without any tack. Pamela follows. I pick up the saddle and bridle to be used when Sophie rides, and, as Tania foresaw, it gives me great pleasure to resonate my energy with that of the component parts of both saddle and bridle, and adjust them according to what I can feel through Tania as she rides the dun gelding, so that he will be comfortable.

Sophie is mesmerised as Tania and Pebble move around the paddock together in walk, trot and canter, experimenting with a wide variety of manoeuvres within each pace. She stops replying to Cliff's continuing efforts to try to get her to agree how safe the horse is, and even stops fiddling with her hair. When Tania and Pebble sail over the horizontal poles that rest on barrels at intervals around the paddock, Sophie gasps.

Cliff's smile widens. 'What did I tell you? Safe as houses, and with a pop on him like that, he'll make jaws drop. Want to have a go?' He doesn't give Sophie a chance to answer, but turns to me and says, 'Will, get Tania off Pebble and tack him up.' He turns back to Sophie and continues to talk at her.

Tania and Pebble arrive in front of us all without my having said a word. Tania slides to the ground and takes the saddle from me, along with the two saddle pads I've selected to use together in order to give Pebble more cushioning than he has been used to. I've widened the saddle considerably so it won't pinch him, and softened and flattened the panels so they will distribute his rider's weight more evenly and comfortably.

Pebble stiffens when the pads and saddle are placed on his back, then relaxes as he senses Tania's confidence that he will be comfortable, and feels the evidence for himself.

Pamela does a double take at the bridle I hand to my daughter. The pieces of leather designed to limit his ability to express himself are no longer in evidence, and the bit has transformed into one whose function is confined to providing support to Pebble should he need it, since I am Aware that Sophie doesn't yet know how to support him with her legs, seat and core alone.

Pamela glares at me and hisses, 'Where did you get that bit? I've seen her ride before, she'll never hold him in it.'

I grin. 'Today is a good day – it's the day she discovers that the bit isn't there as a means of control.'

Pamela's eyes fill with the fear from which she's been enjoying a reprieve whilst Cliff has been so cheerful. 'If she doesn't buy Pebble, we'll all suffer. If he hurts her and she sues Cliff, we're all dead.'

'What will be, will be,' I say.

Pamela groans under her breath. 'You're crazy.' She pinches herself and whispers, 'Wake up, please wake up.'

Tania has never held or even seen a bridle before – neither have I for that matter – but she knows exactly how to ask Pebble if he will accept it, and how to adjust it so he is comfortable. He chomps on the unfamiliar bit, and looks around at Tania, who smiles and rubs his forehead. Then she turns to Sophie and says, 'Okay, you're up. Want a leg up?'

Sophie shakes her head. 'I'll get on from the mounting block.'

'Good idea, much more ladylike than leaping on from the ground,' Cliff agrees. 'Tania, help her.'

Tania turns towards a set of steps with a wide, flat top and Pebble follows her. Sophie hurries to catch them up.

Cliff frowns as he sees Tania talking too softly for him to be able to hear, and glares at me. 'She'd better not stuff this up, for both your sakes.'

I nod as if he's just told me something with which I agree, then turn back to Pebble and the girls. As soon as Sophie is in the saddle, all pretence that she is coping with life falls away. She visibly shakes as she takes up the reins, shortens them and takes a firm hold on Pebble's mouth. He snorts and tosses his head.

Pamela takes in a sharp breath and Cliff growls – actually growls – and says, 'I'm warning you, Will.'

'Noted,' I reply. He takes a step towards me. Without turning to him, I say, 'Just watch them. Tania knows what she's doing.'

Tania reaches up and takes hold of Sophie's hands, sending

light through their connection while she talks to her. When Sophie relaxes her fists, Tania pulls the reins through them until they are of a length for Sophie to merely feel Pebble's mouth and any information he sends up the reins to her. She shows Sophie how to relax her body so that her hands can follow the dun's movement without restricting him in any way, then she stands back.

Sophie nudges Pebble with her heels far more sharply than is necessary and he leaps forward. Immediately, Sophie shortens the reins to where she had them and hangs onto them as if they are all that are keeping her from certain death. Pebble stops. Tania talks to Sophie again and she gradually releases the reins back out and finds the same contact with Pebble's mouth that she had before. Then she closes her heels slowly and carefully to the dun's sides. The dun takes a hesitant step forward, then another, then stops. Sophie looks as if she's going to cry. Tania puts a hand on her leg, again sending light through their connection, and smiles as if everything is going brilliantly – which it is.

'What the hell are they doing?' Cliff snaps, then yells, 'Just show him who's boss, Miss Kelford.' Then he turns to his wife. 'Go and get spurs and a whip.'

'They won't be necessary,' I say, Aware of exactly what the implements are and what Cliff means for Sophie to do with them.

'Didn't I tell you not to speak unless you're spoken to?' Cliff says, trying not to shout and draw Sophie's attention.

'You absolutely did. That doesn't change the fact that Tania knows what Sophie really wants from Pebble, and she's helping her to find it. If you want to sell the horse, leave Tania to do exactly what she's doing.'

Cliff advances on me, takes hold of the front of my t-shirt at the neck, and twists it. 'That's the last time you dare to tell me what to do on my own property.'

I send a blast of light through the physical connection he thinks he has forced upon me, but for which I have been striving. It finds that which Tania transferred to him during their handshake and rapidly expands. Cliff's eyes widen and he lets go of me. The thud of hooves on the ground behind him makes him turn around, staggering as if he's drunk.

Pebble is walking a large circle around the paddock. Tania is walking at his side, talking constantly to Sophie, who is beginning to relax despite having to clench her fists so hard around the reins to prevent herself from shortening them that her knuckles are white. Following Tania's instructions, she asks Pebble to trot and then uses her seat and legs instead of her reins to slow the tempo of the trot. By the time the leggy dun is cantering, she's smiling.

Tania lowers the jump over which she took Pebble and instructs Sophie to include it in the circle she's cantering, as if it's merely a pole on the ground. Pebble and Sophie fly over the jump and canter away with no change to the rhythm of the canter, and Sophie lets out a whoop. She brings the dun to a trot and then walk, and directs him to where we are standing.

'I'll take him,' Sophie says. I sense her shock at what she's achieved by riding so differently from how she always has before, and her desperation to have the same connection with Pebble that she witnessed between him and Tania. I know my daughter has promised to help her achieve it.

Cliff stares at her as if he's never seen her before, then grins. 'Like I told you, he's twenty-five grand. I'll throw in the saddle and bridle for another five.'

Sophie takes her feet out of her stirrups, leans forward and jumps to the ground. She strokes Pebble's nose and he whickers to her. Delight spreads across her face and she says, 'I'll pay full price if I can bring him back here for lessons with Tania.'

Cliff looks from her to Tania, then at me, wanting to object. When avarice wins, he says, 'Lessons are fifty. Sixty if they run over the hour.'

Sophie nods and scrapes the arm of her blouse up to reveal a purple spot the size of my thumb nail, set into the skin of her wrist. Cliff twists his wrist to reveal a black spot, which he moves towards Sophie's. When both spots light up, Sophie says, 'Transfer thirty thousand.'

Both spots flash and Cliff grins. 'It's been a pleasure doing business with you. Tania will be free to teach you tomorrow morning at eight.'

Sophie nods. 'We'll be here.' She turns to Tania. 'Would you help me load him onto my trailer?' She's expecting Pebble to resist her as all of the other horses she's had before have done. She wasn't ready to correct her imbalance then. She is now.

Tania smiles and says, 'Sure. Let's untack him, wash him down and let him have a drink first, shall we? The trough is just over there.'

Sophie smiles back and begins to lead Pebble over to the trough.

Cliff grabs hold of Tania's arm, pulls her close to him and says, 'You nearly cost me a sale. You'd better do a whole lot better next time, or you're dead, do you hear me?'

Tania burns with the light she sends through their physical contact and when I step between them and put my hand on his chest as if to push him away from her, I do the same. Pamela, as brave as she is frightened, grabs Cliff's shoulders and tries to pull him away from us both. I put my spare hand on hers and blast light along our connection. Both Cliff and Pamela look as if they've been struck by lightning, then their expressions soften.

It would be so much easier and quicker if Tania and I could

send continuous flows of light to the man who wants to use us and murder us in equal measures, and his wife, but neither are ready to cope with seeing our light settling around them, so for now, we comfort them in the only way we can, limiting our light transfers to when we can orchestrate physical connections.

Cliff releases Tania, who runs to catch up with Sophie and Pebble. I stand back from him and Pamela and say, 'Okay, so who's next? Clicka, is it?'

'Erm, yes, Clicka. Miss Hadley will be here in about...' Cliff frowns and then blinks. He looks down at the spot on his wrist. 'In about twenty minutes.'

'Okay, well that'll give Sophie plenty of time to get Pebble watered, washed down and loaded, and it'll give me and Pamela time to give Clicka another going over. We'll need to sort out another saddle and bridle as well, now that Sophie's taken hers. Come on, Pamela.'

Cliff frowns slightly again and nods. 'Yes. You do that.'

Pamela silently falls in beside me.

By the time we reach the barn, she's coming back to herself. 'I can't seem to wake myself up, so I'm just going to have to go along with all this craziness. Who are you and your daughter, exactly, just so I can try to make sense of what my subconscious is trying to tell me when I eventually wake up? And where are you from? She won't tell me. Oh no, don't tell me, you're from outer space, aren't you? It would be just like me to throw that curveball into a dream that's already maxed out on weirdness.'

I chuckle. 'I can assure you that while we're from out of town, we're not from outer space. It's more a case of being from inner space.'

You just can't help yourself, can you, Dad?

It's true. I really can't.

'Inner space, riiiiiiiiiight,' Pamela says, nodding.

'Anyway, we'll get Clicka's tack together and cleaned, shall we?' I say. 'Since Cliff's intent on selling everything about the place?' I nod to where the white mare is lying down, snoozing, having rolled in the straw. 'And when she gets up, I'll get the dust and straw off her.'

Pamela lifts her hands and then allows them to fall again. 'Sure, why not, and if she turns pink in the meantime, I won't be even remotely surprised.'

Tania is on a freshly gleaming Clicka's back by the time Belinda Hadley enters the paddock. She's twenty-four and wearing white jodhpurs, a tight, white t-shirt, a black waistcoat despite the heat, and long black boots. She's looking for a horse who will make her look as good a rider as she wants to be but suspects she isn't. In a world where peer approval is everything, she has fitted her soul's urging to keep looking for the horse who will help her to know her own worth, to her wish to be admired. She really just wants to dance, she just doesn't know it yet.

Clicka does. As soon as Tania asks her to move forward, she glides around the paddock as lightly as any horse of The Old is capable. Belinda isn't the only one to see it. For once, Cliff is silent as Clicka's beauty, lightness, willingness and connection with her rider reach even him.

When Clicka glides to a halt in front of us all and Tania is back on her own two feet, I place the saddle I've just adjusted to be comfortable for Clicka on her back, while Tania bridles her. Cliff still can't find anything to say as Tania leads Clicka and Belinda to the mounting block. Pamela looks from one of us to the other with her eyebrows raised, waiting for one of us to explode into a cloud of multi-coloured stars.

She nudges Cliff and says, 'Isn't this great?' When he scowls at her, she laughs and says, 'Your face, honestly, small birds could perch along that brow line. Smile, Cliff, this is a great dream!'

I grin at her. 'Isn't it? I'm always telling everyone that.' Tania's sigh reaches me from the mounting block.

When Clicka moves off looking every bit as stiff and unsure of herself as is Belinda, the woman is devastated. Her fear that she will never be good enough turns to anger and she reaches down and pulls a thin, black stick out from down the back of one of her riding boots. She never gets to hit Clicka with it. I keep my face completely straight as Tania resonates her energy with that of the stick and separates its components until Belinda is left with a handful of soft, limp fibres.

Pamela laughs delightedly and slaps her leg. 'Outstanding! This just keeps getting better and better.'

Tania smiles as she relieves a stunned Belinda of her burden whilst commenting on the lack of workmanship these days, using the contact between their hands to give the woman a burst of light. Then she explains what Belinda needs to do to allow Clicka to move more freely.

As Clicka moves closer to where I'm standing with Pamela and Cliff, Belinda says, 'I just want a beautiful horse that knows its job. If this isn't it, I'll get off.'

Tania puts a hand to her leg to hold her in place, saying, 'Wait a moment.' The light she sends through the physical contact takes her words with them so that they reach the part of Belinda that the young woman doesn't yet know exists. 'Clicka is beautiful and elegant, and believe me, she knows what she's about, you saw that for yourself. She wants a partner, and that partner is you. She's willing to give all of herself to you if you'll give her the same back.'

Belinda glares at her as Cliff stiffens beside me.

'Let me help you be the partner she's looking for, then you'll have the partner you're looking for,' Tania says, driving the words into Belinda with even more light.

'Partner.' Belinda mouths the word as if it's new to her. It takes hold within her. She nods and relaxes in the saddle.

'There you go,' Tania says, 'now gently ask her to move forward.'

Within minutes of Clicka's departure with Belinda, a heavy set man in his thirties arrives to see dark bay gelding, Photon. Unlike the two women, he isn't one of those for whom the horses, Tania and I are looking.

'You'll ride this time,' Cliff tells me. 'Fetch the horse and get on with it.'

Tania nods towards the barn and attempts to wink at me. *Off you toddle.*

I grin and do as I am told while telling her, *Still haven't given up trying to wink, huh? I'm clinging to my assertion that the idea is to close only the one eye.*

I absolutely did just close one eye.

You closed each eye once, I'll give you that.

Hurry along, Dad, Cliff is waiting.

The man who has come to view Photon has a permanent sneer on his face as he watches me ride bareback and bridleless. When Tania approaches carrying the tack she has adjusted, he waves her away. 'That won't be necessary.'

The moment he is astride Photon, the gelding snorts and takes off across the paddock with the man shouting and bouncing around on his back, only stopping in the far corner in order to expedite the departure of his passenger. Cliff kicks the fence upon which he was leaning and storms over to me.

I smile at him as I catch his fist, sending a blast of light through our connection to quell both his terror of being held responsible, and his fury at me. 'He had no intention of paying anywhere near your asking price, and he would never have committed to coming back for paid lessons as the rest of your buyers will,' I say. 'It was his decision to ride with no tack. I'll send him on his way.'

I leave him standing, staring after me as I walk over to where the man has just managed to sit up.

'Here.' I offer him my hand as I heal his collar bone. I pull him to his feet and use the physical connection to send him a burst of light to ease his humiliation and temper. 'No harm done. Now we've seen your ability, we'll give you a call if we have a horse more suitable. Have a great day, goodbye now.'

He walks away, scratching his head and occasionally looking back at me with a frown as if he's forgotten something he wanted to say, before continuing on his way. I turn back to the others to see that Photon has returned to the shade of the barn, and Pamela is doubled up with laughter.

The next three to arrive are exactly whom we need, and their horses give them all a sense of the connection that their souls are pressing them to find.

Chloe Carter's need for a safe, gentle horse who will give her sanctuary from all of the people in her life who are as ambitious and aggressive as she is timid, is met by Minerva, a delicately built, dapple-grey mare who isn't as meek and obliging as the impression she gives when Tania and then Chloe ride her through her paces. Now that Minerva has given Chloe a sense of the connection they can enjoy, and Chloe has committed to the mare, she'll be everything the slight seventeen-year-old with the hunched, self-protective posture needs, as will Tania when the teenager returns in the morning for her first lesson.

Clare Regan's desperate search for a horse who will make her parents – who accompany their twenty-four-year-old daughter to the viewing – see her as less of a failure, is thwarted when Maple, the light bay mare she has come to see, goes beautifully for Tania riding tackless, but is flat and lacklustre as soon as Clare is on board with a saddle and bridle.

Having failed at school and at every job they have found for her, Clare readily agrees when her parents insist she try riding the mare without tack as Tania – with whom her parents are extremely impressed – did. The result is the same to begin with, yet as Clare rides the mare around the paddock, the mare's warmth seeps into her. She begins to believe Tania's assurance that rather than trying ever harder to be what she isn't, she should relax and allow the mare to respond to whom she is.

When Maple begins to soften, Tania and I are both Aware that Clare is beginning to break. Tania encourages Clare to the ground, where she wraps her arms around Maple's neck as if she's afraid the mare will disappear if she lets go, and I distract her parents with my assurance that lessons with Tania will have their daughter doing everything that mine did, in no time. Maple leaves with her chosen human shortly afterward.

When Samuel Thomas arrives and, despite having been invited to view Hector, a sturdy chestnut gelding, demands to try the much larger and more impressive looking Photon instead, I see my daughter's mouth twitch. I am Aware of Cliff's intention to demand that I deal with the slim, handsome twenty-two-year-old, and step in front of my employer.

'He'll react better to her than to me,' I say quietly. 'She's already sold three of your horses, she'll sell another if you let her.'

Cliff's rapidly improving finances cause him to forget his instruction to me to not speak unless I'm spoken to. His eyes brighten with avarice and he nods and leans back against the fence.

I know as well as does Tania that Photon and Hector will do what is needed to begin to help Samuel. They all sense the man's terror that he is neither strong nor clever enough to survive in a world that is rapidly selecting as its survivors those who display both qualities. They perceive his need to beat everyone at everything, to have the best of everything, as a transparent veil that does nothing to hide his fears and they would have him see it the same way.

Unlike Photon's previous rider, Samuel wants the powerful dark bay gelding tacked up, and with the best saddle and bridle we have. It makes no difference. Photon knows exactly for whom he is waiting and deposits Samuel as rapidly as he did the last man who thought to use the horse to enhance his image.

'Just wait,' I urge Cliff as he turns and punches the fence rail. 'You want to sell Hector? He'll buy Hector.'

Cliff picks his gun up from where it has been resting against the nearest fence post. 'He'd better.'

Pamela smiles at me and salutes, now totally convinced that she's dreaming the weirdest and best dream ever. I'm looking forward to the moment she realises she always has been.

A thud of hooves diverts our attention to Hector, who is making his way over to where Tania is sitting on the ground next to a dazed Samuel, her hand on his shoulder. Photon grazes nearby as if nothing has happened. Hector stops in front of Samuel and lowers his huge chestnut head. He nuzzles the man's temple and without thinking, the man raises a hand to stroke the big horse's chin. It is a minute or so before he realises that Hector is free to go anywhere in the paddock, yet is choosing to be near him. I smile as I feel him reach out to the gelding with his mind, unaware that is what he is doing even as he responds to the urging of his soul to find the connection the horse is offering him.

Samuel gets to his feet at Tania's suggestion and refuses her offer to ride Hector without tack for him to see; the horses may have lifted the veil behind which he hides, but only at its lowest edge. Samuel's desire to be better than anyone else isn't ready to be shattered by seeing that which Tania is offering to demonstrate. I lift off the fence the saddle and bridle I have adjusted for Hector, carry them over to where the big horse is standing patiently by the human for whom he has been waiting, and tack him up. I remove Photon's tack and pretend not to see Samuel's shudder as the tall, dark bay wanders back to the remaining few horses.

As soon as Samuel is astride Hector, he adjusts his position, gathers his reins and nudges the gelding's sides firmly to ask him to move forward. Hector remains where he is. He half closes his eyes, which remain so even when Samuel kicks him hard. He would have been prepared to allow Samuel to go to the most extreme lengths to prove to himself that the way he deals with people around him in his day to day life is not the way to reach his horse, but Tania has no intention of allowing that to happen. She reminds Samuel of how he felt when he was on the ground and Hector offered him what he needed.

Photon tosses his head and trots back to Hector, passing close by him and Samuel before spinning on his haunches and trotting back past them on their other side. Samuel shudders involuntarily again at the reminder of what he thought he should want, and looks down at the ears he suddenly knows he does want. Hector walks forward without the need for a physical cue. A broad smile makes Samuel even more handsome.

His confusion is apparent as he repeatedly glances at both Hector and Photon whilst discussing the price he will pay for the chestnut who has stolen his heart, then holds his wrist close to Cliff's and speaks the agreed amount. When Cliff invites him to bring his horse back the following day for a lesson with Tania, he nods without thinking about it and then frowns in even more confusion.

Tania grins. 'Come at eight, Samuel. It'll be a group lesson with others who have bought horses today.'

Immediately, Samuel's expression clears and brightens. A chance to compete. Then he looks back at Photon longingly. Photon kicks at a fly and bucks on the spot, and Samuel flinches and glances back to Hector. His face softens and he smiles again. 'Eight. Fine.' He takes the rope attached to Hector's headcollar from Tania, hitches his tack on his hip and says, 'We'll see you then.'

'That's the first I've heard of it being a group lesson,' Cliff says, his delight at Hector's sale preventing him from growling the words.

'It's the best way,' Tania says with a bright smile. 'I can teach them all within an hour, then we can get on with the rest of our work.'

Cliff nods slowly. 'I like your thinking, girl. Maybe this will work after all.'

'I expected to see the horse tacked up and waiting for me,' a loud voice says from the other side of the fence.

We all turn to see a short, broad young man standing with his legs slightly apart and his hands on his hips.

'Ah, you must be Philip Thatcher,' Cliff says, extending his hand.

The man merely looks at Cliff's hand with distaste. 'I want the horse I've come to see standing in front of me within the next sixty seconds.'

'I doubt it will be quite that soon, Philip,' I say with a grin.

The man scowls and makes a show of taking out a gun from a holster attached to the belt of his jodhpurs, inspecting it and then replacing it. Cliff immediately reaches for his own gun again.

Tania rolls her eyes and says, 'Melody's ready for you, she's just inside the barn, out of the sun. I'll get on and ride her for you now.'

A click accompanies Philip's quick draw and cocking of his gun. Pamela darts behind Cliff, who glances down at his own gun, knowing it has already refused to fire once today, with terror on his face. But it is my daughter at whom Philip's gun is pointing. I move to stand between her and it. 'It's hot today, isn't it. Would you like a glass of water while you watch Tania ride Melody?'

Philip scowls and lifts his gun so it is pointing in my face. Despite her belief that no actual harm can come to me, Pamela lets out a squeak.

'Or maybe some lemonade?' I turn to Cliff. 'You have lemonade, don't you?'

Cliff looks at me as if I'm a lunatic and gives a brief nod. I turn back to Philip. 'So, what is it to be, water or lemonade?'

'One more word of disrespect and I'll blow your head off,' Philip snarls.

I grin at him. 'No you won't. Your need to feel completely in control of the situation is understandable given your family's standing and your terror of them all, but your attempt to achieve it is a little excessive and you know it.'

Philip's hold on his gun loosens and his face reddens. 'Wh... what? What do you know about anything?'

Cliff raises his own, long-barrelled gun to his shoulder and growls, 'Get off my property.'

'There's no need for that, Cliff,' I say. 'Philip's here to see Melody and I'm confident he'll like her, so we'll just carry on as if the last five minutes haven't happened, shall we?' I turn back to Philip, put my hand atop his and gently lower the gun. His eyes widen a fraction as I send a strong burst of light through our physical connection. 'Contrary to the image you feel the need to portray, you're a very nice, very sensitive young man,' I murmur, 'and you have the potential to be an extremely good rider. Melody will help you with that, so please, consider letting her? Tania will help you.' I release his hand and stand aside so that Philip has a clear view of where my daughter is now moving as one with the bay mare.

Philip's mouth drops open at the sight. He snaps it shut and I'm Aware of him fighting to regain his former persona. His family rules the city, their substantial wealth controlling the governors as easily as their hired muscle and reputation controls the criminal underground. Philip is expected to grow into the role his parents have carved out for him, and he's doing his best to fulfil their expectations... yet he's never been able to stay away from horses. Where his family own them, bet on them and expect the riders they employ to win on them, Philip hears the voice within him that just about manages to make itself heard, and rides them himself. As far as his parents, aunts, uncles, brothers, sisters and cousins are concerned, he can ride any horse, however big, however powerful, however much of a handful, and make them do as he wants. Their approval boosts his position above some of his older brothers and sisters, yet it isn't just that which ensures he continually adds to the horses in his stables. He is here, today, because we all need him to be.

I rest a hand on his shoulder as Tania brings Melody over to us, saying, 'Okay, you're up,' and use the contact to send him another burst of light, stronger than either Tania or I have transferred to any of the others. He can take it.

His soul begins to unfurl from the tiny pocket within which he has kept it confined for most of his twenty-four years. The bay mare whickers to him and moves closer. He rubs her nose as she sniffs his face. When she nuzzles his shoulder, he chuckles and ever so gently strokes her cheek.

Tania quietly saddles Melody, then hands her bridle to Philip. He blinks and flushes red as he remembers that he isn't alone with the mare. He bridles Melody more roughly than is necessary, and she reprimands him with a nip on his arm.

Tania, Melody and I are all Aware of his immediate fury. Melody snorts and steps back from him as he pulls back his arm ready to punch her.

Tania puts her hand on his arm and sends him a burst of light every bit as strong as the one I gave him as she says, 'Let her help you. She wants to. She knows what you need and she can give it to you.'

'She bit me,' Philip says. 'No one gets to touch me without my permission.' He frowns in confusion as he notices Tania's hand on his arm. 'And no one gets to hurt me.'

Tania keeps sending him light and says softly, 'She bit you so you'd feel the discomfort you just inflicted on her by being rough with her. She'll always show you back to yourself. The good thing is, she knows how powerful you'll be when you really connect with how you feel inside. Connect with her that way, and the two of you will be unstoppable.'

'Connect?' Philip says the word as if he's never heard it before.

Tania nods. 'Connect. That's all you have to do. Will you let me help you?'

Philip puts his foot in the stirrup and springs lightly into

Melody's saddle, his expression a mixture of warm excitement and cold calculation at the thought of being more powerful. 'So then, help.'

I wink at my daughter. Having helped Philip to connect his soul's purpose with that which she knew would motivate his personality, she has opened the way for Melody to solidify the connection that has flared into existence between the two of them.

An impressive sight follows as Philip, a naturally talented rider, follows each and every suggestion Tania makes so that in the space of twenty minutes, he has softened from the harsh, demanding rider he has always been, to one for whom Melody moves almost as well as she did for Tania. I am Aware that her exhilaration at teaching such an able student almost matches his as he feels his mare responding more quickly and exactly to his gradually softer and more respectful requests. I smile to myself. When he can respond in kind to her, he'll be the person we all need him to be.

Cliff is in such a jovial mood by the time Philip has driven his lorry away with Melody on board, having almost begged Tania to let him return the following day for a lesson, that he has completely forgotten the rule he made forbidding me to speak. When the nervy young man whom Pamela called as another possible buyer for Photon turns up and introduces himself as Jimmy Smith, Cliff agrees with my suggestion that I take the lead so Tania can have a break.

I am Aware of Jimmy's relief as he watches me ride Photon with no tack, judging the gelding to be the safe ride for which he is yearning. He is keen to get into the saddle but he takes the time to introduce himself to Photon first, offering a trembling hand to be sniffed, then stroking Photon's nose and neck before accepting a leg up from me. Photon reacts to Jimmy's nervous disposition immediately by shying at some birds that begin squawking in a nearby tree. Jimmy hauls at the reins and clamps on with his legs as the stirrups swing wildly. I reach a hand out to Photon, who instantly relaxes and sidles back to my side.

'How did you do that? How did you calm him down?' Jimmy squeaks.

I grin up at him. 'I didn't. He calmed himself because I didn't give him a reason to be fearful.'

'But neither did I, it was those birds in the tree.'

'Photon has heard plenty of birds in his lifetime. Their squawking made him jump this time because he was expressing the fear inside you. He'll help you to work through that if you'd like to feel differently.'

Jimmy clamps his jaws tightly shut and grinds his teeth. Then he says, 'How can I not be afraid? How can any of us not be afraid when the world is going mad all around us? They want us all under their control, you know that, don't you? They're making it harder and harder for people to live out in the country, so more and more are moving into the city where they can be watched and controlled more easily.' He nods to the open space behind the barn, that Tania and Pebble explored earlier in the day. 'That'll be covered in high rises or food factories in a few years' time, you can bet on it. And they're provoking more rioting and using the unrest as an excuse to recruit more police. Did you get that pamphlet about informing on your friends and neighbours if you see them doing anything unusual?' His voice rises almost to a squeak. 'Unusual? When the government is acting insane? I don't even have friends to inform on any more, those I had have all gone as mad as the rest.'

I hold my hand up to him. 'I'm Will. You can count me as a

friend.'

He blinks. Then he shakes my hand uncertainly. His eyes widen and soften slightly; unlike any of those Tania and I have touched before him, he feels the light spreading through his body.

'You're right,' I say, 'we're surrounded by insanity, and that's why those of us who see it need to work together. The horses will help us. Are you in?'

He gives the slightest of nods, still holding my hand.

'Okay, so the way to not feel the fear that's erupting all around you is to refuse to take it on as your own. Observe it but leave it where it is. Photon will help you. Feel him moving beneath you, responding to you, and be fascinated with the connection you have with him. Respond to him as he responds to you. Ask him questions with your body and listen to his answers, then be prepared to answer the questions his body will ask of yours.' I release his hand. 'Are you ready?'

'I'm not sure,' he whispers.

'Close your eyes. Photon won't go anywhere. Just close your eyes, and tell me which parts of his body are moving.'

'Well, he's, um, he's standing still.'

'So, his legs aren't moving. Which parts are?'

'His, er, his nostrils? I can hear him breathing so they must be.'

'Feel him breathing.'

Jimmy pauses. 'His lungs are moving.' His voice becomes stronger. 'His heart is moving, I can feel it under my knee.'

'Very good. Where else?'

'He's moving his tongue, I can feel it at the end of the reins. And his ears. I swear I just felt him move his ears.'

'Now you're doing really well,' I say. 'Keep your eyes closed and squeeze your heels gently against Photon's sides to ask him to walk on. As he moves, keep telling me exactly which parts of his body are doing what.'

I walk around the paddock with Jimmy and Photon for some time. Jimmy has a smile on his face as he gets more and more absorbed in, and fascinated by, that which he can feel from the horse who has waited twelve years to be found by him.

When I finally say, 'Okay, open your eyes,' it is a few moments before he does. Photon shoots forward a few steps and then turns sideways, nostrils flaring, searching for the cause of the noise that startled him. Jimmy manages to stay in the saddle, but I feel the crushing disappointment that accompanies his fear as his view of his surroundings instantly bring him back to his life.

'Stand back from it all, Jimmy,' I remind him. 'Look at Photon's ears in front of you. Feel him underneath you. He's still there, exactly as he was before.'

Jimmy stares at me and then looks at Photon's ears. The fear drains out of his face. 'What just happened?'

'When you had your eyes closed and focused on your connection to him, you weren't afraid and he was free to react to his surroundings in his own way. As soon as you opened your eyes, you forgot your connection with him and he responded to the fear that is so habitual for you, as if it were his. Let him help you to be less afraid, he wants to.'

'He does? How can you possibly know that?'

I grin. 'He won't compromise, he wants you or no one. He dumped the last two people who tried to ride him shortly after they got on, then carried you around with your eyes closed as if you and he were the only ones who existed.'

Jimmy smiles and strokes Photon's neck. 'It was amazing.'

'You can bring him back here as often as you want, Tania and I'll help you to get that feeling again.'

Jimmy nods slowly. I feel him make his decision. Photon does too, and turns to nuzzle his foot.

Seven horses and riders will be returning in the morning. The young riders all believe they have their own reasons for doing so, but in truth, they are the same; they are looking for a way to resist the insanity that surrounds them and they know, deep down, that it is their new horses who will provide it.

SIX

Pamela

*C*liff puts one arm around me and the other around Tania, and pulls us both to him. He doesn't see Tania wrinkle her nose at his body odour, he's too busy congratulating himself on his eye for a good horse and his ability to make good decisions. It's as if he never tried to shoot Will and Tania dead only this morning – but then he didn't really, did he, because this is just a dream. It has to be. I've never had such a realistic one before – where I can smell horses and sweat, where I can feel so much pain, where I can be so moved by the strangest events as they unfold in front of me – but I can come up with no other explanation for how Tania healed me and every single one of the horses; how she and Will have managed to completely change the behaviour not only of my husband and the horses, but of each and every person who visited our yard; how one so young and beautiful can have so much talent and confidence, yet be so unaffected by the effect she has on those around her, particularly the young men; how I feel as if I can do anything when she and her father are around. I have no idea who they are, with their total lack of fear and wrist safes.

Everyone has a wrist safe. It's the single fact to which I keep returning every time I feel myself hoping that maybe, just maybe, this isn't a dream after all. But it has to be. Wrist safes have been mandatory for twenty or so years. Tania would have had hers implanted before she began school at five years of age, and her parents, like all parents, would have been as glad of it as of their own; no child can ever go missing with a computer chip in their wrist since not only are they instantly trackable, but everyone with whom they come into contact is too. That was how the idea was sold to us all in the beginning; the feeling of always being safe, in addition to having a secure, theft-free way to pay for everything we're told we want, made everyone rush to have their wrist safes implanted.

Most people still feel more secure for having them, but I don't. It doesn't stop my husband beating me and I've never believed that having my location, transactions and phone calls constantly monitored by the governors can be a good thing; having power doesn't make them good people.

I glance again at both Will and Tania to confirm that which I have already observed; their wrists are unmarked. I relax into my husband's side, confident all over again that I'm dreaming. I even put an arm across his chest and hug him back. If it's my dream, I can do anything I want. I can ride horses who normally scare me. I can pretend my husband is the man I thought I was marrying. I can be happy.

Will catches my eye and winks. 'It's been a great day, hasn't it?'

Cliff releases me and Tania and holds his hand out to Will. 'It sure has, it was a good decision to allow you and Tania to prove your worth. Unlike my wife, you can both sell and ride.' He glances at me as Will shakes his hand. 'Get yourself in the kitchen, Pamela, and cook us all a celebratory dinner.'

'Do you know what, my darling, I might just do that,' I reply with a smile, 'because it's been more than a great day, it's been a stupendous one. We've had happy, healthy horses leave here with happy owners, we have two incredibly strange new staff members, and you've even cracked a smile. Dinner will be ready in an hour, so don't any of you be late.'

Tania smiles at me. Will chuckles, still shaking Cliff's hand, and Cliff looks stunned. His eyes begin to narrow as they have so many times before. I would normally shrink back into myself and apologise for whatever I could possibly have done to annoy him, hoping to escape his fists, but I smile even more brightly and say, 'Try cracking another smile, dear, it suits you.' I even laugh at the amazement on his face.

I turn away from my husband as Will says to him, 'Before Tania and I go and clear the barn and paddock of dung ready for tomorrow, may I ask how many horses you're planning to bring in for us to work with? Just so we can make sure we have enough hay in the racks, and a big enough area bedded down?'

'Um, yes, right, horses coming here tomorrow to be sold on,' Cliff says. 'Two so far. Why are you still holding my hand, man?'

I smile as Will's voice floats across the paddock. 'I just felt as if you needed me to. I'll let go now.' Cliff will be feeling better for having been in contact with Will, just like we both have every time it's happened. How I wish there were people like him and his daughter in my waking world.

We sit down to eat dinner exactly an hour later. Will and Tania look hot, but strangely, every bit as clean as when they first arrived, despite their exertions of the day. I glance down at myself and am chagrined to find that I am as grubby as Cliff. It's my dream. I close my eyes for a second and imagine I'm in a set of clean clothes. I open my eyes to find myself as dirty as before.

'It doesn't work while you still believe in all the rules of physicality,' Tania whispers.

I jump and then smile at her. 'Of course it doesn't. Help yourself to rice and curry, I didn't make it very hot as I wasn't sure how spicy you both like your food.'

'It sounds great, thank you,' Will says.

Cliff slams a bottle of beer down in front of him, flips the lid off with his thumb, then does the same for Tania. I go to the fridge to get my own, but Cliff snarls, 'Not you, woman, you don't deserve one. Will and Tania have done all the work here today.'

I almost return to the table but then I remember. I can do anything I want. 'I do deserve one, and I'm having one. In fact, check me out, I'm having two.'

Cliff scowls at me and clenches a fist.

'Cheers,' Will says, clinking his bottle against Cliff's. 'To a successful day and many more to follow. Thanks for having us to dinner, this looks wonderful.'

Cliff visibly relaxes and I note that Will has contrived to ensure his fingers are in contact with Cliff's as their bottles touch. It must be my subconscious reminding me that all the while I'm dreaming, Will and Tania will make sure Cliff can't hurt me. I relax too.

I hold meaningful conversations with all three of the others, even Cliff, whom I catch looking at me strangely every now and then. I laugh and smile, I even manage to block out the noise from the television that Cliff insists on having set to the news channel so that it constantly blares messages of doom and gloom. It's only when Cliff nods off to sleep, his chin resting on his chest, that I realise all of the food has been eaten, Cliff has drunk even more than normal without lifting a finger to me, I know absolutely no more about Will and Tania than I did before we all sat down, and the news channel is giving out news that I'm not sure I would have made up in my happy dream.

My heart lurches as the newscaster reports even more rioting in the city. So, the farmers have had the last of their subsidies withdrawn. Now that crops and animals can be farmed in the gigantic, sterile, climate-controlled, disease-free warehouses built specifically for the purpose, the governors have decided that there is no longer any need for food to be produced that is susceptible to our erratic weather patterns, disease and vermin.

The television screen shows the army razing the rioters' farms to the ground both as punishment for their actions and to eliminate the diseased produce we are assured they have been cultivating. I doubt the rioters will be seen or heard of again other than to be held up as examples of what happens when people resist the governments' attempts to provide "safety and comfort" for the rest of us.

I glance over at Will and Tania, who are also watching the news report, and say, 'The farm dwellers who haven't rioted will be forced to move to the city for food and water. They'll be given apartments in the high rises that seem to be going up everywhere, put to work in menial jobs and sucked into the system with everyone else. The government wants us all where we can be easily controlled, that's what Cliff says, and for once, I think he may be right. I don't know how long we're going to be able to hang on here.'

Will looks sideways at me and grins. 'However real it seems, it's all still a dream. Sometimes it might feel like a nightmare, but you've already realised that once you're aware you're dreaming, you can experience it however you want to.'

I aim the remote control at the television and it winks off. I sigh with relief. 'Thanks for the reminder. This is wonderful, I wish I didn't have to wake up.'

Tania has a mischievous glint in her eyes. 'How do you think you'll feel when you wake up and realise that what you thought was a dream is real, and what you thought was reality is a dream?'

'I'd love it, but you're tormenting me now. I suppose that's my subconscious telling me I believe I should always be punished? My shrink said that's what I believe, before Cliff found out I was seeing one and made sure it never happened again.'

'I'm not tormenting you. I'm telling you the future,' Tania says and grins her father's grin.

'Of course you are,' I reply, and start to laugh. I don't think I've ever laughed in this house before, and even Cliff's snoring doesn't make me want to stop. When I eventually do, I say, 'You'll both stay here for the night, or however long my dream lasts, obviously?'

'Dreams can last a long time,' Will says. 'We'd love to stay here while we're needed. Thank you.' He gets to his feet and begins gathering plates and dishes into a pile.

'We'll just have time to clear away and wash up before the horses arrive,' Tania says.

'They aren't due here this evening,' I reply. 'Cliff arranged for their current owner to deliver them from mid-morning onward tomorrow.'

'What can I say, the man on his way with them now is desperate to be rid of them,' Tania replies. 'Cliff barely offered him anything for them anyway, and he's so relieved not to have to pay to dispose of them, he's planning to dump them here and be on his way before Cliff can change his mind.'

'And you know this because…'

'It's all a dream,' Tania finishes for me. 'Come on, let's get this lot done, then we can go and play.'

Sure enough, the second Will shuts the drawer on the clean cutlery he has just placed within it, a horn hoots from outside. Cliff jumps in his chair and snorts, then settles back into his rhythmic snoring.

Tania and Will wait for me to go out of the door before them, and follow me out to the yard where a lorry is waiting with its engine still running. A man wearing stained jeans, a brown vest and a cap that looks as if it was orange before it got covered in filth, has already lowered the ramp and is leading a brown and white gelding down the ramp. He hits the horse with the lead rope to try to make him walk faster, but he's so lame, all he can manage is a hobble.

Tania runs to take the lead rope from the man, who thrusts it at her and hurries back into the lorry. I can hardly bear to watch the horse trying not to fall on his knees as he slowly, painfully teeters down the ramp. Then he takes a better step. Tania immediately looks back at the man, but he's busy pulling at the lead rope of a huge bay mare with a wide blaze down her nose. Tania strokes the gelding's neck and he takes another step. It's tentative, but even more sure than the last.

Will hurries past them up the ramp, and takes the bay mare's lead rope. He holds his hand out for her to sniff, which she does slowly and carefully.

'Get her out now, I haven't got all evening,' the man snaps.

Having already witnessed the abilities with which I've somehow managed to endow Tania and Will in my dream, I know what they're doing now. I can help by distracting the repulsive specimen who has brought the horses here.

'How much was it that Cliff offered you?' I call up to him. 'He's not here at the moment, but I'm his wife, I'll pay you.'

His eyes light up and he rushes down the ramp, his hand outstretched. His fingers and palm are callused and he almost crushes my hand in his grip, just like Cliff does when he's trying to intimidate someone from the outset. But he isn't in control of this situation, I am – it's my dream. I squeeze his hand back hard, and don't let go when he tries to.

'It's a pleasure to meet you, Mrs Taylor,' the man tells me while his eyes promise me it's anything but. 'Cliff agreed to pay a round four grand for the two of them.'

Tania has moved the now sound gelding away from the bottom of the ramp, and is standing with him, stroking his face and talking softly to him while her father leads a now very willing mare down the ramp to join them. I can't let the man turn around. If I can't be a hero in real life, at least I'll get to know what it feels like by being one now.

'One of them can barely walk and the other is as intractable as they come,' I tell him, still gripping his hand. 'I'd be surprised if you weren't happy to give them away to save yourself the cost of disposing of them.'

His eyebrows shoot upward and his eyes widen before he manages to get a hold of himself again.

I smile. 'I'll give you a grand for the two of them. Say the word, and I'll activate my account right now.' I maintain my grip on his hand so that my wrist safe is close to his.

'Done,' he says.

'Transfer one thousand,' I say. Both of our wrist safes flash to confirm the transaction. 'Now, get off my yard.'

The man smiles nastily at me, then turns back to his lorry to find its ramp already raised and secured in place. He glares at Will and Tania, who are standing with the two horses, then back at the ramp. It would have been fun to cause him to turn and see the ramp rising into the air by itself, but I just wanted him gone without a fuss. I close the yard gate behind his lorry and it belches out a cloud of blue smoke as it accelerates away.

Will and Tania take the two horses to the paddock and remove their headcollars. Both horses immediately turn and trot away. The skewbald gelding holds his dung-encrusted tail up in the air as he pushes himself up into canter and rips around the paddock as if his life depends upon it. He's magnificent. I've never wanted to ride a horse as much as I want to ride him. I blink. I'd normally be terrified at the thought of riding a horse I don't know who is so very obviously athletic and powerful – it's only my greater terror of Cliff that makes me do it when the situation arises.

'But in a dream, you can be anyone and do anything you want,' Tania says as she appears by my side. 'He'll be back in a minute, when he's explored everything his body can do now. He'll need me to ride him for a few minutes, but then he's all yours.'

'He's all mine.' I breathe the words, knowing that they're true.

I barely glance at Will riding the bay mare, even though when I do, it's every bit as breathtaking a sight as when he and Tania rode the other horses earlier today. My attention is with the gelding.

He glides to a halt in front of Tania. His eyes are a lighter brown than I have seen on any other horse, and hold an intensity and vitality that sing to me as if they're tunes I recognise, though I've never in my life felt anything other than weak and helpless.

Tania vaults onto his back and I'm mesmerised as his raw power and athleticism are gradually softened and refined into a picture of potent elegance, as his body responds to hers. By the time he canters over to me, I can't wait to get on his back.

Tania slides to the ground. 'You're everything you see in him, you know. You just need to let him help you believe it. Up you get.' She bends down and cups her hands to give me a leg up.

'I can't ride him without a saddle and bridle. I'm nowhere near as good a rider as you and your dad.'

'So, dream yourself into being a better one,' Tania replies. 'Look into his eyes again, feel what you just felt and then be that person. It's as easy or as difficult as you want it to be.'

I look into eyes the colour of autumn leaves as they stare back at me, daring me to be someone I've never had the courage to be. What the heck, if I fall off and break my neck, Tania will just heal me like she did before. Hell, this is a dream, I'll probably just bounce.

I accept Tania's leg up and by the time I land on the gelding's back, I feel more sure of myself, as if Tania's hands on my knee somehow squeezed strength into me. I can do this.

'Just ride him as you did Pebble.'

'You were helping me do that, I know you were. How do I slow down or stop by myself without a bridle?' I ask.

'The same way you slow down or stop with a bridle,' she says with a grin. 'By using your seat and legs. Slow or stop the movement in your seat, close your thighs and gently pull back, then increase the pull until you get the response you're looking for. Try not to though, if you can help it; you'll get the most out of this experience if you just go with him wherever he wants to go.'

'But he could do anything. He could go anywhere.'

'Exactly,' Tania says, stroking my mount's neck, 'and it's up to you whether you decide to go with him, it's your dream.'

I look at the white ears in front of me and remember again what I saw in the gelding's eyes. I nod to myself. 'It's my dream.' I take hold of a clump of his mane in each hand and touch my calves lightly to his sides. When he moves off at a canter, I go with him. I don't doubt for a second that I can follow his movement as he speeds up so that everything around us is a blur, then slows down as he approaches the fence. I stiffen as I wonder whether he'll stop, veer away from it or jump it, then remember that it doesn't matter. In my dream, I can take whatever challenges come at me, in fact I can throw myself into them. As my horse checks his stride and then gathers himself together, I go with him and we clear the fence with feet to spare.

I've never been allowed to ride anywhere but the paddock, and instantly, I realise what I've been missing. We're free! I feel my horse's heart thumping near my left knee, his muscles pumping beneath me, his hooves pounding on the ground, and I urge him on even faster. I feel his delight as he gallops onward, only diverting from his course when trees block his way. Eventually, he slows to a canter, then a trot and a walk. He snorts to clear his nose, his rib cage heaving. I slide to the ground and walk beside him. It's my dream, he won't leave me.

He drops to the ground and rolls, grunting with delight. When he's back on his feet, he looks at me. I decide that in this dream, from which I never, ever, want to wake up, I know what he's thinking. He wants me to get back on. I've never vaulted onto a horse before, but I should be able to sprout wings and fly if I feel like it, so I can do this.

I'm on his back in a heartbeat. My heart sinks when he heads for home, but when I think of asking him to turn away, I remember Tania's words. *You'll get the most out of this experience if you just go with him wherever he wants to go.* He wants to go back, not just because he's tired, but because it's where we need to be.

My horse canters slowly back the way we came. We jump the fence with less speed and more style than on our outward attempt, and Will claps as we land. 'Very nicely done on all counts,' he calls out. 'How do you feel?'

'Like I'm scared to go to bed even though it's getting dark, because when I wake up, this dream will be over. You, Tania and this amazing horse will all be gone, and I'll be back in hell.'

'Assuming that the dream still exists when you wake, what will you call him?' Will nods to my horse.

I barely have to think about it. 'Zeal.'

'Nice. Tania's on her way to help you wash him down.' He looks down as one of the barn cats entwines herself around his leg, and says, 'Well, hello, little one, so the nightlife is waking up, is it? Looking forward to a night's hunting, are you?' He crouches down and the black cat jumps onto his knee and rubs her face against his.

I land on my feet next to Zeal, rub his neck and tell Will, 'She's one of the feral cats we put food out for to help keep the mice and rats down. I wonder what my subconscious is trying to tell me now, with her behaving like a pet with you?'

'Why wonder when you can know, like you did with Zeal out there in the pasture?' Tania says, dumping one of the buckets of water she's carrying at my feet and handing me a sponge. She reaches out a hand and strokes the cat's head.

I stare at her for a moment and then look back at the cat. 'She's never met anyone like you two before. She knows you're not like the rest of us, just like I know it. She knows she can trust you in a way she can't trust any of us.'

Will nods. 'While you're about it, and while Zeal is right next to you reminding you that you can, remember what you know about your husband.'

I dunk the sponge in the bucket and then squeeze it over Zeal's back. As I rub his sweat away, I say, 'He's a violent bully. He wants to love me but he doesn't know how.' I frown to myself. 'Is this the point of my dream? To realise something that doesn't help me at all?'

Will stands up and grins. 'You've realised a whole lot more than that.'

A curtain of water appears over the top of Zeal's back and hits me full in the face. I gasp and splutter as I blink water out of my eyes. 'Better?' Tania says, crouching under Zeal's neck. 'I finished his other side and thought you looked a bit hot.' Her eyes twinkle as she grins at me and I can't help but smile. I pick up my own bucket and she ducks back behind Zeal. 'I'm not hot!'

I manage to laugh. 'You definitely won't be when I catch up with you.'

By the time we're both soaking wet, the sun is the merest crescent on the horizon, and Zeal and the mare have disappeared from sight. I send Will and Tania back to the house ahead of me with directions to their rooms, and head for the barn. I pause in the doorway, watching the two horses pulling hay from one of the full racks. I wander over to Zeal, my eyes drinking in every detail of him in the hope I can re-create him in my future dreams. I stroke his shoulder and then put my forehead to it. I breathe in his scent and warmth, then sink into the straw at his feet. If I'm going to have to leave him here in dream world, I want to drink in as much of him as possible before I go.

When I come to, my nostrils are full of the scents of straw and horse dung, and my neck and back hurt. I open my eyes to find myself in the barn, underneath the hay rack from which Zeal was eating in my dream. I'm propped up against the wall and I have a rash on my arms from the straw. I sit up, rub my neck and back, and frown. I must have been sleep-walking again.

Aside from several large piles of dung nearby, there are no signs of any horses. I sigh. The seven we took in a week or so ago must have spent most of the night grazing out in the paddock. Clearing all of the piles of dung from out there will take twice as long as if they had huddled in the barn as they normally do. I'd better get started before Cliff gets out here. Hopefully, if I look busy, he won't make me get on Pebble again.

I get to my feet and frown again as I move my jaw and then touch my face. No pain. Nor is there any when I breathe. My hand goes to the rib that has been causing me so much trouble, and I prod all around it. How can that be?

'Morning,' Tania says, poking her head around the barn door with a smile. 'We've cleared up all the dung out here, refilled the water troughs and groomed Zeal and the mare. You're a bit stiff, let me help you with that.'

I barely notice the discomfort receding in my neck and back as my heart leaps within my chest. 'Zeal is real? You're real?' I hurry to the paddock and put both hands over my mouth when I catch sight of the horse of my dreams enthusiastically grooming the bay mare who arrived with him yesterday. In my dream.

Tania puts a hand on my arm. 'Breathe, Pamela. You'll pass out if you don't. Come on, with me. Breathe out, then breathe in. You're not ill, you're not going mad and you're no more asleep than you were yesterday. Out, and now in, that's it.'

It's not just the breathing that is calming me down, I know it. I feel it now. Tania's hand is warm on my arm, but it's more than that. It's an instrument of calm, of strength, of hope, I know it as surely as I knew what Zeal was thinking yesterday. I feel like I did when I was riding him. When I thought I was dreaming.

'It's liberating, isn't it, knowing that nothing can hurt you,' Will says from behind me.

I turn to him. 'But I don't know that. I believed it because I thought I was dreaming, but if I wasn't, I could have been killed. I pushed Cliff way past where he would have done it in the past,

I rode Zeal as if I was brave and strong and the world's best rider, and I did a deal with that foul man who delivered the horses last night without knowing what he and Cliff had agreed, who he was or what he was capable of. I don't know how I got through yesterday with my skin intact, but I know I won't do it today.'

'The only difference between yesterday and today is that you no longer believe you're dreaming,' Will says. 'Believe it again, know it to the centre of your bones, and every day will be like yesterday.' Another of the barn cats stalks up to him and rubs her head on his leg. I've only ever seen her from a distance, yet here she is, bringing yesterday into today.

I shake my head. 'I don't understand. How can you two be here for real? You can heal as if by magic, you know what people are thinking, you make people feel different so they forget what they were going to say, what they were going to do, who they've always been, even. You can transform horses from being mean and dangerous to being... like I've never known horses to be before. And neither of you have wrist safes. No one escapes those, not now. You can't be real, you just can't be.'

'When I asked you how you'd feel if you woke up and realised that what you thought was a dream is real, and what you thought was reality is really a dream, you said you'd love it,' Tania says. 'So love it. Embrace it. Find the courage to live as if you're dreaming until you know for sure you are.'

Immediately, I picture Cliff finding out about the deal I did last night. 'I don't think I can.'

'Zeal knows you can.' Tania nods over to where my horse – my horse? How could I have been so stupid to think he could ever be mine? – has stopped grooming with the mare, and is watching me with those pale brown eyes of his, so full of passion. I think back to when I rode him yesterday. I remember my complete lack of fear, my willingness to embrace his power, my certainty that I knew what he was thinking.

'You know what he's thinking now,' Tania whispers. 'You've discovered your intuition, so use it. This is still the dream, Pamela.'

I want to believe her more than I've ever wanted anything. I begin to run to Zeal, then slow my steps and approach him more politely. I don't allow myself to think anything. I'm back in the dream. He sniffs my hand and I stroke his nose and then vault onto his back. He instantly moves away from the mare. I trust him. I can hardly believe it, but I do. Completely. And he trusts me, I know it. He trusts me to care for him, to look out for him, to protect him, and I trust him to do the same for me. Where yesterday I followed his movements and desires, today I feel I can ask him to follow mine... and he does without question. The dream is real.

'What the hell do you think you're doing, riding without my say so?' Cliff yells from the porch of the house. He's hopping around, trying to pull on one of his boots while holding up his jeans since he seems to have forgotten his belt.

I glance at Will and Tania. Tania grins and gives me two thumbs up, and Will winks. I remember the realisation to which they prompted me last night, and look back at Cliff. He wants to love me but he has no clue how. 'I'm doing exactly that, riding without your say so,' I yell back. 'And I'm doing a bloody good job of it too. For goodness' sake, find your belt.'

SEVEN

Tania

This is fun. Where yesterday, Pamela's energy was mostly grey, the flecks of red, orange, blue, indigo and violet it contained have expanded and are now pulsing as if they would expand further. When she stands up to Cliff, the red flecks of strength and passion, and the orange flecks of courage and optimism, flare and expand. When her attention is with Zeal, it is the blue energy of sensitivity, the indigo energy of vision and clarity, and the violet energy of intuition that expand. We'll help her to develop all of the aspects of herself that have been compressed by the depression and exhaustion that have dominated her life.

Cliff's energy is still brown but has changed from the dull, muddy brown that it was, to a rich brown that is on the verge of giving way to red. He finally pulls his boot on and stops hopping, then yells at his wife. 'Don't you think I tried to find my belt? I woke up by myself without a clue how I got to bed, only to find you hadn't put any clean clothes out ready for me, and my belt was missing. And now I find you out here, riding as if you don't have a care in the world. You get over here right now so I can remind you of your place.'

Pamela retorts, 'I'm in the only place I want to be right now. This is Zeal, I bought him last night while you were sleeping off all the beer you put away. He isn't for sale, by the way, he's mine. Watch what we can do.'

Dad and I wander over to meet Cliff as he marches to the paddock, holding up his jeans, full of his intention to drag Pamela down from Zeal's back if he has to. Last night, we bathed him in light as our energy and intention carried him to his bed. I hid his belt to give Pamela the time she would need with Zeal this morning, while Dad removed his outer clothes and made sure he was comfortable. We left him sleeping within a net of calming, soothing energy and as a result, he slept soundly and peacefully; we've prepared him well for what is to come.

'Morning, Cliff,' Dad says, 'all of the chores are done, and there are still two hours to go before our students get here for their lesson. Pamela and Zeal look great together, don't they? Have them doing that when future buyers arrive and the rest of your horses will be sold before they've even been viewed.'

'You and Tania can do that,' Cliff growls.

'Well, we won't necessarily always be here, but Pamela will,' Dad says. 'Thanks for the board and lodgings by the way, we were very comfortable in our rooms, and had a great night's sleep.'

Cliff reaches the fence and scowls as he tries to remember asking us to stay.

'It meant we were straight out here to work at first light too, instead of having to lose time travelling,' Dad continues. It's overkill; Cliff will be well past caring what we do by the end of the day, but Dad likes to be polite.

Cliff rallies. 'I'll be taking your living expenses from your wages, like we agreed.'

Dad nods. 'Of course.'

Zeal comes to a sliding stop in front of Cliff, who is forced to take a step back from the resulting cloud of dust.

'That horse is for sale to the highest bidder,' Cliff says, his eyes bright with anticipation of Pamela's distress.

Pamela gazes evenly at Dad and then at me. She trusts that we won't let her come to harm every bit as much as she trusts her horse. She says to Cliff, 'And the highest bidder is me. Now that I have Zeal helping me, I'll pay you with the work I'll put into future horses we take on to sell. I'll pay you with all of the money I earn teaching others to connect with their horses now I know how. And I'll pay you with the standard he and I will set, which will place this yard above any other. He's mine.'

Cliff smiles nastily. 'He can stay until someone offers me a price I can't refuse. Then he'll be gone and you'll carry on doing everything you just promised, because it's your job.'

'So that's settled then,' Dad says with a hint of a wink at Pamela. 'What do you fancy for breakfast, Cliff? I do a mean omelette.'

Cliff sneers at him. 'Call yourself a man? Tania and Pamela will sort it.'

'While you and I light fires and beat our chests?' Dad says with a chuckle. 'I'll do it, Tania's omelettes are indistinguishable from scrambled eggs, and Pamela needs a little more time with Zeal.'

I nod. 'Harsh but true.'

'Come on.' Dad claps a hand to Cliff's shoulder as the taller man scowls and opens his mouth to make a retort. 'Prepare to taste the best omelette you've ever tasted.'

Cliff's scowl softens as Dad's light encourages his greedy, selfish brown energy further towards red. 'You'd better not be exaggerating,' he mutters but allows himself to be guided back to the house.

I grin at Pamela. 'You two are looking great. Don't miss breakfast though, Dad wasn't over-egging his ability with a frying pan.'

Pamela shakes her head as she smiles back. 'Over-egging? Seriously?'

'It made you smile.'

She nods. 'That it did. Thanks, I won't be late.'

'See you in a bit then.'

'Tania?' I turn back to her.

'I have no idea who you are or what's going on here, and that scares the hell out of me, but at the same time, I know that whatever it is, it's good. I know you and your dad are good.' The indigo and violet flecks in her energy flare larger and brighter as they gain strength. 'Thank you.'

I smile at her. 'You're welcome. Hurry up now or your breakfast will be cold, and that's no yolk.'

Pamela laughs. 'It's a good job you're such an amazing rider, your jokes are as bad as it sounds like your cooking is.'

'As it happens, I'm an eggscellent cook.'

Pamela laughs harder and puts her hands over her ears. 'I can't hear any more, go!' Yellow flecks of joy appear in her energy.

She's doing well. Infinity and Amarilla know they are stating the obvious as well as they know that I welcome their communication.

Isn't she? I'm going to enjoy today. Give Mum a hug for me, won't you, Am?

Of course. Have fun, we'll be there when you need us.

I have a spring in my step as I continue on to the house.

'I don't think I've ever been up so early on a Sunday,' Cliff says with a yawn. He doesn't cover his mouth, which still contains the remainder of his third and final omelette. 'Pour me another coffee, Pamela.'

He has just spent the last hour or so regaling us all with tales of horses he's owned in the past, how he turned them around and how much he got for them.

'So why don't you ride now, Cliff?' Dad asks, though he knows full well.

'I don't have time for that any more, I'm the brains behind this outfit. If I left business matters to Pamela, we'd be dead in the water within weeks.'

'It's because the last horse you rode – Tinker, wasn't he called? – threw you,' I say. 'You broke your pelvis and you've had trouble regaining your confidence.'

Cliff's mouth – thankfully now empty – drops open. He clamps it shut, slams his fist on the table and gets to his feet. I feel the fear roiling around in his stomach as if it were my own as he glares at me. 'How the hell do you know…' He shakes his head. 'It doesn't matter.'

'No it doesn't, not really,' I agree. 'It's just a good time to bring it to the surface. When you can let it go, you'll feel a whole lot better.'

Dad sits back in his chair and grins at me. Pamela has forgotten that she was just about to put a forkful of omelette in her mouth, and watches me over the top of it.

'I'm not afraid of any horse,' Cliff says. He leans over the table and points at me. 'And you need to learn to watch your mouth.'

'Your pelvis is healthy and strong now,' I say, 'you'll be able to get your confidence back. I'll help.' I glance at Dad and Pamela, then back at Cliff, whose mouth is open again. 'We all will. Anyway, our students are beginning to arrive. Come on, you don't want to miss this.' I get to my feet and hurry outside.

I raise my hand and wave to everyone milling around in the car park.

Samuel immediately waves back with a bright smile as he leads Hector down the ramp of his trailer, as does Belinda, whose jodhpurs and t-shirt are once again as bright white as is her mare. Philip nods to me before returning to grooming Melody, whose ears twitch constantly and occasionally flatten at the horses tethered to the trailers and lorries around her. Clare's mum waves at me even as she continues barking orders at her daughter, while Clare hurries around Maple's legs, affixing protective boots the mare doesn't need. I know Chloe has seen me, but the youngest of my students keeps her eyes down as she attaches a haynet to the outside of her trailer for Minerva.

Jimmy mutters constantly to himself as he adjusts the position of Photon's saddle, and Sophie looks as pale and washed out as her streaked hair is vibrant. She's taken more of the drugs that are killing her, but the black flecks in her mainly grey energy are no larger than they were yesterday, and the blue speckles that make her sensitivity as visible to me as it is obvious in my Awareness, have been joined by those of indigo and violet. She strokes Pebble constantly as she moves around him, taking off his travelling boots, bringing him water, brushing him and then tacking him up.

I wander over to Chloe. The exhaustion that results from living in The Old makes the majority of her energy as grey as everyone else's, but again like everyone's here, it is flecked with blue. Like Pamela and Sophie, she also has the tiniest specks of indigo and violet, but unlike anyone else, she also has pink flecks. Her desperation for genuine friendship has kept her looking for the horse who she has a feeling will give her that which no humans she has ever met have been able to.

'Morning, Chloe,' I say.

She smiles but barely meets my eyes. 'Morning.'

'Don't worry about everyone else during the lesson, just focus on yourself and Minerva, and you'll barely notice them.'

She nods. 'Okay.' She isn't convinced. She thinks they'll all ride at her and frighten her horse.

'No one will ride at you. You and Minerva will be fine.'

Chloe looks at me in shock. I stare back at her with a smile. Her violet flecks increase a little in size as she decides she trusts me. 'Okay. Thank you.'

'Don't mention it. Be ready in ten, okay?'

She nods.

'It's going to be another hot one, isn't it?' Samuel calls out to me. He has the biggest lorry in the car park, and its silver paintwork is sparkling in the sunshine.

'It's summer, it's always hot,' Philip snaps from beside his own lorry.

Samuel looks Philip's horse and lorry – both smaller than his – up and down and then looks at his own. He smiles and shakes his head.

Philip is beside him in a flash, the red flecks in his energy swelling almost enough to equal the grey. 'You dare to dismiss me?' The menace he hurls at Samuel is so potent, even I am disturbed slightly for a moment.

Hector pulls back on the rope with which Samuel has tied him to the lorry, his eyes almost as wide as his human's.

I settle Philip's aggression into the context of the situation. He's just perfect. I smile and put a hand on both his and Samuel's arms. Both take as much light as I can send without it being visible, as I say, 'We're starting in eight minutes. Do either of you want a hand?'

Philip blinks and takes a step backward. 'Of course not, I can get my own horse ready.' He glares at Samuel and then stomps back to where Melody is patiently waiting for him.

'How about you, Samuel?'

'It's Sam. Call me Sam,' he says. I'm Aware he's feeling shaken and would like my help tacking Hector up, but there's no way he'll let me help him when Philip has declined my assistance. 'And no, I'm f...fine. I'll be ready on time.'

'Tania, would you mind checking that Clare's put Maple's tack on the way you had it?' Clare's mother shouts from across the car park. As I make my way over to the three of them, she shouts almost as loudly, 'She gets everything else wrong, I'd be surprised if she's managed to do it properly.'

'It's perfect,' I tell Clare and then turn to her mother. 'There's no such thing as wrong, Mrs Regan. Clare's done everything absolutely perfectly her whole life in order to make sure she ends up here at this precise time, as have you. You can relax in the knowledge that you're both amazing. Can you and Maple be ready in six minutes, Clare?'

The slender twenty-three-year-old, who looks much younger whenever she is near her mother, looks at me incredulously for some time, then nods. She doesn't understand yet, but she will.

I leave them and wander over to Belinda, who has taken Pebble's bridle from Sophie and is showing her how to put it on the dun gelding. 'You see, if you put the reins over his head first, they don't hang down in front of his legs. It's just a safer way to do it.' She looks at Sophie expectantly. Sophie stares at her.

'Is Clicka ready, Belinda?' I ask her.

Belinda looks over her shoulder to where the white mare is saddled but still wearing only a headcollar. 'As good as, it won't take me a minute to bridle her. Sophie just needed my help.'

Sophie continues to stare at her and Belinda begins to panic at the thought that her attempt to get the admiration of one of her fellow class members has had the opposite effect.

'Right, well now Pebble has his bridle on comfortably, I'll leave you to it then,' she says. 'I'm right over there if you need me.'

Sophie sighs and mutters, 'Interfering know all. I don't know what I'm doing here, being patronised by the likes of her.'

'You know exactly what you're doing here,' I say. 'You feel it every time you touch Pebble, every time you look at him. Trust yourself, you're exactly where you need to be.' I give her a wink that Dad would be proud of, and move on to where Belinda is now hurriedly bridling Clicka.

'You were up early to get her that clean,' I say. 'It wouldn't have mattered, you know, had you both turned up covered in poo stains.'

She pauses for a moment and then continues feeding a piece of leather through its keeper. 'It would have mattered to me.'

'It's exhausting, living life around a need for approval.'

Belinda spins around. 'You're very blunt, aren't you?'

I look around at the other six who are getting ready to ride their horses. 'This session is going to be difficult for you if you can't put your need to impress to one side. To get the best from Clicka, you're going to need to listen to her like you did yesterday.'

Belinda looks around too. Her anguish over what everyone

will think of her is quickly replaced by the pattern to which she always reverts when she's worried. She glares at me. 'She'll do as she's told, like any well-trained horse should. If she doesn't, I'll know who to blame.'

I nod slowly and leave her be.

Jimmy is standing by Photon, whose dark coat is gleaming in the morning sunshine. The gelding is tacked up and ready to be mounted, but Jimmy is having a heated conversation with Sam.

'A wall though?' Jimmy says. 'How can they possibly expect us to go along with having a wall put up all around us? They say it's to keep us safe, but it isn't, it's to keep us under control.'

'If they go ahead and provide us with cars that drive themselves as they're promising, they can build anything they want as far as I'm concerned,' Sam replies as he tightens Hector's girth.

'Oh, for goodness' sake, their plan's working, isn't it?' Jimmy retorts. 'They promise you a comfortable apartment with clean air and a constant temperature no matter what the weather – which has only reached the extremes it has because of their policies, by the way – cars that perform tricks, a constant supply of screens to stare at, and the "safety" of almost as many police as there are citizens, and you let them do anything they want.' He looks at me. 'I'm surrounded by morons.'

I grin. 'Thanks.' I glance over at Sam, who is unsure whether to leave Hector standing untethered while he breaks Jimmy's nose. 'All ready to get on? Great.'

'I didn't come here this morning to be insulted,' he tells me.

'No, you came here to have a lesson with Tania,' Pamela says from Zeal's back as he clatters into the car park. Her indigo and violet flecks flare again as she asks me, 'Okay if I join in?'

I grin. 'Of course.'

Instantly, Sam forgets all thought of exacting revenge on Jimmy as he takes in the sight of Pamela riding bareback and bridleless. He can't be the best rider in the group while she's doing that. His competitiveness blocks out the fear he felt at doing it when he tried Hector yesterday. 'I can ride without tack too,' he says.

'Ride with tack or without, it doesn't matter,' I say loudly so that everyone can hear. 'What does matter is that you can support your horse while they learn to carry your weight without strain or injury. All of you, remember how you felt yesterday when you knew, somewhere very deep inside, that your horses are the ones you've spent your whole lives waiting to meet. That feeling is more important than anything else.' I look around at each and every rider. 'Everything else will come as a result of knowing that.'

Sam hesitates, looking between Zeal and Hector, then shrugs and mounts his sturdy, chestnut gelding. Jimmy is only a few breaths behind. One by one, the others mount their own horses – Clare is given a leg up by her mother.

I open the gate to the paddock and the horses march in, eager to help their riders move closer to balance. My eyes confirm everything of which I am Aware.

Philip ensures that he and his beautiful bay, Melody, are the first to pass me. Philip's need to dominate has been brought to the fore by the presence of the other riders, and he has lost a good deal of the sensitivity and softness he achieved yesterday.

Sam and Hector are next, although the gap between the two is rapidly increasing as Sam's frantic nudging of Hector's sides only results in Hector slowing down as he resists his rider's need to be the best.

Belinda is right behind them and rapidly becoming annoyed that Clicka is being prevented from striding out in her best and most attractive walk by Hector's large rump moving so slowly ahead of her.

Having seen Pamela and Zeal, Clare's mum has talked her into riding bareback and bridleless again, but whereas yesterday Clare had the opportunity to focus solely on her horse and relax, today she's nervous about riding amongst others in case she falls short. She's stiff and as a result so is Maple.

Chloe looks as if she would rather be anywhere than here, on her finely-boned grey mare. She craves the sense of connection that she found with her horse yesterday and doesn't believe she'll find it again without my help, but she's intimidated by the strong characters who surround her and she doesn't feel anywhere near as safe astride Minerva as she did in our last session. She sits with a stiff, rounded back and hunched shoulders as Minerva jogs into the paddock behind Maple.

Sophie holds Pebble firmly in check, convinced that if she doesn't keep her reins short and a tight hold on her horse's mouth, he'll get over-excited amongst the other horses and take off with her. Pebble begins to dance on the spot just inside the gate as a result of being given nowhere to go and Sophie bounces up and down in the saddle, as rigid as she's causing him to be.

Jimmy and Photon are the last into the paddock. Jimmy is breathing in and out so quickly, he's almost panting as Photon leaps first to one side and then the other in his attempts to get past Pebble. He too holds tightly to his horse's mouth in the belief it will increase his safety, but all it's doing is causing him to feel more vulnerable.

'You're going to need to close your eyes again, Jimmy,' I say.

He looks at me as if I'm crazy. 'With all this going on? No chance.'

I step forward into Photon's path and hold my hand out to him. Instantly, he calms and stands still. 'Close your eyes and tell me which parts of your horse are moving, just like you did when you rode him yesterday. Trust him to take you apart from everything that's going on around you. He's the only one who can.'

Jimmy looks at me desperately, then blinks and strokes his horse's neck. He keeps blinking, then closes his eyes and holds them tightly shut. 'His ribs are moving with every breath,' he tells me. 'His skin is shuddering just behind me, there must be a fly on him.' He smiles. 'He just looked to the left.'

'That's great going, Jimmy. Now ask him to walk forward and keep saying out loud which parts of him are moving. I won't always be as close to you as I am now, but I'll know everything you say.'

Photon walks calmly around Pebble and joins the other horses as their riders guide them around the paddock.

I turn my attention to Sophie. The black flecks in her energy are steadily growing as she thinks of getting off and giving up on the horse on whom she has pinned all of her hopes to make her feel safe. Talking to her won't help at the moment. I put my hand on her leg, repeatedly stepping aside from Pebble as he dances around beneath her, and transfer a strong blast of light until the black flecks hold their size and then begin to shrink. It's today or never for Sophie.

'Let go of the reins,' I say to her, still sending as much light to her as I can to support her without disturbing her ability to think for herself. 'Sophie, Pebble can help you to know what safety feels like when it comes from inside of you. It's already there, you just have to notice it.'

Sophie looks at me in disbelief, but it's enough. I see her soul looking out of her eyes as surely as I feel it. I increase the amount of light I'm sending to her and her eyes brighten as her soul reaches out to me. The black flecks shrink almost to nothing. Almost.

'Let go of the reins.'

Sophie does as I say. Immediately, Pebble relaxes and walks calmly forward.

'Well done,' I say as I walk beside them. 'I'm going to go and stand over there, and I want you to walk a large circle around me while focusing on feeling exactly as you do now.' I move away and leave the two of them to continue alone.

Tania, that was... Dad can't find the word he wants. He knows he doesn't need to; I feel his pride in me, which is unnecessary. *You drew her imbalance to the surface, you drew her soul out from where it was trapped, just like the horses do. Knowing what you would be capable of doesn't compare with seeing it in the flesh.*

I've only set the process in motion, the horses will still need to do the rest. Ready, Fin? My question is more of an observation to us all that the time has come; Infinity and Amarilla are always ready.

Even so, Amarilla replies, *Ready when you are.*

I grin at Dad, who is leaning on the paddock fence, talking to Clare's mum but within easy reach of Cliff, should the yard proprietor need him. I feel his anticipation as he grins back.

I turn back to the riders and call out, 'Okay, everyone, please ask your horses to walk a large circle around me, like Pebble's already doing.'

I smile to myself and am Aware of Amarilla doing the same as the eight horse and rider partnerships fall in together. Eight. The symbol of infinity and a constant flow of energy and power. When Infinity adds her energy to that which the eight horses and riders have generated by their very existence, the energy of The Old won't stand a chance of maintaining its hold on them.

'Jimmy, you're doing brilliantly,' I call out. 'Keep your eyes closed and focus on Photon's movement. The rest of you, I want you to listen to Jimmy for a moment and then do as he's doing.

With your eyes open or closed, it doesn't matter, notice every single movement your horse makes beneath you. Start at their tails and work forward, or with their ears and work backward, whichever works for you, but notice everything, however small.'

Within seconds, Pamela, Sophie and Philip are every bit as focused on their horses as is Jimmy. Sam focuses for a few moments at a time in between glancing at Philip and Pamela, whom he considers his main competition. Belinda does likewise in between peering around at everyone to see if they're watching her. Clare is doing a little better, but whenever Hector slows in front of her due to Sam's loss of focus, she loses her own and looks at everyone else to check she's measuring up. Chloe keeps her eyes locked on Minerva's ears and waits for the ordeal to end.

Minerva shies suddenly and Chloe squeaks and comes back to herself a little more. Minerva's sudden movement causes Clicka to shy and buck. Belinda, who was looking over at Philip at the time, is unseated. Clicka bucks again and Belinda flies over her head and lands heavily on her shoulder. I've healed it by the time Clicka takes her place back in the circle as if nothing has happened.

Sophie tries to bury her soul back where she had it confined, so that she can revert to her tried and trusted pattern of feeling unsafe, but I reach out to her and draw it back out, noting Dad's fascination as I do so. Pebble joins his energy to mine and we hold her steady as she manages to focus on his movement again.

I help Belinda to her feet, healing her bruising as I do so.

'I want my money back, that horse is dangerous,' she says, her face bright red with mortification not only at having fallen off, but at the bright green grass stains on her shoulder and hip that are evidence of the fact.

'What was she saying to you just before you fell off?' I ask her.

'Saying to me? Don't be ridiculous, she wasn't saying anything, she's a horse.'

'Who was communicating with you via her movement. What was she telling you?'

Belinda scowls at me. 'How should I know? You tell me, you're the teacher.' I feel her nausea that is fast turning to a feeling that she will actually be sick as a result of shock and utter mortification at being in the middle of her worst nightmare. She shoots a quick look around at everyone still riding, prepared to lash out at them now that she deems it impossible they will admire her.

'Clicka was very stiff throughout her body. She was telling you that she needed you to stop trying so hard and relax so that she could relax too. Had you listened, she wouldn't have reacted to Minerva.'

'What a load of rubbish, I told you I would know who to blame if she didn't do as she was told.'

I nod. 'You did.' I put a hand on her wrist and say, 'Belinda, you wanted me to help you find the connection you found with Clicka when you rode her yesterday, when no one else was here. When you forgot about trying to impress anyone.' The burst of light I send through our contact finds the pattern my words have carved out for it, and lifts it from where it has resided since she was a small child. Belinda's eyes widen and she claps a hand over her mouth as she heaves. I put my hand on her back and rub it as Clicka wanders over. When the beautiful white mare reaches us, she lowers her head and blows hot breath on the back of Belinda's neck.

'What's she telling you now?' I say softly. 'You know the answer, Belinda. Tell me without thinking, just the first thing that comes into your head.'

Belinda gags and coughs. 'She loves me, which is weird, because she just dumped me.'

'Love her back, listen to her above everything that's going on around you, and she won't need to dump you again. Want a leg up?'

Belinda stands up straight and wipes her mouth on the back of her hand. Clicka nuzzles the shoulder I've just healed. 'Um, okay.'

When Belinda and Clicka take their places back in the circle, I call out, 'You're all doing brilliantly. Keep going for a few minutes longer, then we'll move it up to a trot.'

I walk over to where Chloe is almost curled up on Minerva's back in her attempt to make herself as small as possible and protect herself from anything else that might happen. I feel the fear she's always had of horses that, while significant, has never been enough to keep her away from them, from riding them, from searching for the one she believes will be the trusted friend she has never managed to find in human form.

'You're one brave, tough girl,' I say to her. She looks at me out of the corner of her eye in disbelief as I walk next to Minerva. 'Most people run away from what frightens them but you've always trusted yourself and walked straight towards your fear. You've listened to your soul even when it's terrified you, and as a result you've found Minerva. She's everything you've always known she'd be, Chloe, you just need to trust yourself for a little bit longer and you'll prove it to yourself.'

Chloe looks directly at me. 'She… she is? She scared me.'

'You scared you. She just showed you your fear of everyone here so you would have something tangible to turn away from. Turn to her, find her the way you've been trying to your whole life. What's her left hind foot doing right now?'

'It's, err, it's in the air, now it's landed. And landed again…
now.'

'Good, now focus on her right hind as well as her left, and
when you know exactly what both of them are doing without
having to think about it, add in her front feet, her rib cage, her left
stifle and then her right, her head, her ears, even her eyes. Each
time you add another part of her body to the list of those whose
movement you can pinpoint, sit up a little straighter, okay?'

Chloe nods and within seconds unfurls a little.

I walk back to the centre of the circle. 'Okay, everyone, please
ask your horses to trot. Jimmy, you're doing well as you are, so
please keep your eyes closed.'

All of the horses move into trot immediately except for
Hector. Sam looks around anxiously and rates himself and his
horse as being at the bottom of the group. I feel his fear; winners
get ahead in The Old, losers fade away to nothing.

Maple trots past Hector with Clare bouncing around on her
back as she becomes stiffer and stiffer in line with her increasing
certainty that she isn't good enough, that she'll let her mother
down, that she'll embarrass herself like she always does, that she
shouldn't have let herself be talked into riding bareback when she
isn't as good a rider as those riding with tack. But all the time that
her fear is rising in concert with Sam's, the energy generated by
the eight riding in a circle is building and beginning to swirl above
them. Infinity has begun to swirl with it, and slowly, she speeds
it up.

Hector begins to trot and Maple slows hers and softens so that
Clare's bouncing lessens. The horses, more aware of their
individuality than any in The New, rejoice as their energies, their
identities, merge like droplets of water into the clearest pool. The
energy of the eight, the infinity energy, swirls even faster and
unbidden, the horses all move up to a canter. The energy of the

horses combines with that of both infinity and Infinity, and with the power of the circle, and blasts away the energy of The Old.

All eight riders are pulled far away from their fears, from the experiences they have lived, and into their partnerships with their horses. As they connect, soul to soul, with the horses who have endured so much to find them, the warmest, most gentle breeze blows within the circle. The horses canter on as each of their riders opens to the fact that there is something far greater, far more powerful than anything The Old can throw at them.

Jimmy grins and opens his eyes, no longer afraid to see what his world is coming to. Sam is completely absorbed in his horse as Hector responds to his rider's subtlest suggestions. Clare follows Maple's movement easily and confidently. Sophie laughs out loud as she rides with her arms out to either side, her dependence on her reins forgotten. Philip smiles in delight as Melody canters slowly but powerfully beneath him. Chloe's eyes are bright as she sits up straight on Minerva's back, blissful in the knowledge that her search is over for a friend she can trust. Belinda is so captivated by the horse who carries her body and soul, she is allowing Clicka to dance. Pamela sits Zeal's canter as if she has always been so sure of herself.

It is time. 'Everyone, your horses have done enough for today,' I call out. 'Slow your movement as you close your thighs around your horses, and gradually pull back until they come to a stop. Hop off, wash them down and then let them move around and roll as much as they want to before you take them home.'

All eight of the horses lift in front slightly as their riders support them into a halt. I'm Aware that the horses have no thought of being helped to achieve perfect balance, even though they are every bit as Aware that Dad and I could get them there in no time. That isn't why they are here; they incarnated into their current lives in order to work with the humans with whom they have so successfully connected. What I can do, is teach their riders how to support them, how to help them balance their rider's weight so that they won't suffer the kinds of injuries from which I have already healed them.

All in good time, Infinity tells me as she withdraws from the circle.

I nod. *All in good time.*

EIGHT

Will

---

*T*he eight who dismount from their horses in front of me are very different people from whom they were when their feet were last in contact with the ground. Their horses are different too; they have come out of themselves and reconnected with one another more now that they are no longer with humans who would restrict them to being a fraction of all they can be, and as a collective they are stronger.

Further, the vitality that Tania awakened in the horses only yesterday has been magnified a hundredfold as a result of them having connected, body and soul, with their humans. Their eyes are bright, their coats shine and they are practically bursting with energy. Tania was right to call the session to an end, for their muscles would have been pulled and strained long before their vigour waned.

It isn't only the eight horses and riders who have been dramatically altered by what has just happened, either. When the energy of the eight combined with that of Infinity and the circle of horses to drive all negativity from its vicinity, Clare's mum and

Cliff were left without the fears that have shaped them too. Both of them fell silent. In the absence of her expectations borne from anxiety, Clare's mum finally saw her daughter's inherent worth and beauty for the first time. And Cliff saw Pamela, not as the weak, snivelling wretch he has always felt proud of himself for taking in, but as the strong, confident woman she is. He found himself admiring her and wanting her to admire him. And he found himself wanting to ride as he has been terrified to ever since losing his confidence.

'The bay mare who arrived with Zeal is ready and waiting for you to ride her, Cliff,' I say, nodding over to where she is wandering over to us both from the barn.

'How did she... I mean, I put the bar across the door to keep her out of the way of the lesson, she must have broken through it.'

'Don't worry, she hasn't damaged it, I just caused it to move out of her way,' I say. At Cliff's confused frown, I add, 'Of all the things that have happened in the last twenty-four hours, that's hardly the most surprising, is it?'

He looks back at the mare, then at Pamela and all of the others chattering and exclaiming in the paddock, and begins to laugh. Then he bends double and laughs until he cries. He's exactly where the mare wants him. I put a hand on his back and send him a burst of light just as she reaches him and nuzzles the top of his head until his cap falls off. She stands on it as Cliff straightens and looks at her, his greying brown hair standing on end. She nuzzles his face and he frowns again, unsure what to do.

Tania appears with the saddle and bridle I adjusted for the mare yesterday evening, and says to Cliff, 'I'll just tack her up for you, then you can have a little play together.'

Cliff looks past her to where two of the horses are rolling while their adoring humans watch them. 'I can't ride now. Not in front of that lot.'

'Sure you can,' Tania says. 'Dad can help you remember anything you've forgotten, but after what's just happened, you won't need him, your soul will make sure you remember.'

'Of… course… it… will,' Cliff murmurs. He looks at me and begins to laugh again.

Finally, the man is going to be good company and I won't have to miss Levittsson so much. I grin as I sense my Kindred friend's feigned outrage.

Cliff claps me on the shoulder. 'You're a strange pair, you and that girl of yours, in fact all of this is so far beyond strange, I don't even know where to start trying to make sense of it, so you know what? I won't bother. I need to ride me a horse.'

'She's all ready to go,' Tania says. 'You might as well get on from the fence, I'll hold your other stirrup.'

Cliff looks at me and rolls his eyes like a hen-pecked husband. 'Well, I guess I might as well just do exactly as I'm told.'

I sense the uncertainty that washes over him as he climbs the fence, but then he catches sight of Pamela standing with her arm over Zeal's neck as she chats to Belinda. His uncertainty is replaced by determination and he mounts the mare.

Tania leans against the fence and flicks her fingers at me. *Shoo.*

I'll just get to it then, I tell her as I say to Cliff, 'Just ask her to walk around the perimeter of the paddock while you get used to the feel of sitting on a horse again. It looks like I'm coming with you.'

Tania shuts one eye fully while half closing the other.

One eye shut, one eye open, I tell her for the hundredth time. *Flaming lanterns, how is it possible that you can do everything in the universe except wink?* I grin at her and she laughs.

As I walk next to Cliff and the mare, I chat to Cliff to keep him from feeling self-conscious, and heal his body where the negative patterns he has released allow me to. I also help his body adjust to riding, assisting him in loosening where he is trying to, and in holding himself in a posture that helps both his and the mare's balance. He was a capable rider in the physical sense when he rode before, but his need to feel in control prevented him from having a partnership with a horse. I sense his hesitancy as his old way of riding now feels foreign to him, and he's not sure with what to replace it. The mare is unsure too. She walks very slowly, as if she'll stop at any moment.

'When you can count the number of times her heart beats in a minute, everything else will come easily to you,' I tell him.

'That's impossible,' Cliff says.

'Like the bar moving on its own so the mare could leave the barn?' I say.

He stares at me. 'Tell me how to do it.'

'Listen for it. Explore the feel of her body as she moves beneath you until you can sing its rhythms, until you know its habits and tendencies as well as your own. Then you'll feel her heart beating, you'll feel it thumping in your chest as if it's yours. Start with her tail. What's it doing?'

'Um, it's moving from side to side, only a tiny bit as she isn't moving the rest of her body much.'

'Perfect. How about her pelvis?'

There is a pause and then Cliff says, 'It's dropping to the left and then to the right, and moving me with it.'

'Okay, work your way through her hips, stifles, hocks, hind fetlocks and feet. Nothing else exists.'

By the time Cliff has worked his way to the mare's rib cage, they are moving at a decent walk. He describes her breathing… and then his face lights up with a smile as he begins to count her heartbeats out loud. He relaxes into his pelvis, sits up straight and softens his rein contact with her mouth. He breathes with her as he asks her to trot without even being aware that is what he's done. His count speeds up and when he eases her into canter, speeds up again.

He forgets about the count. He's completely absorbed in exploring what all of the joints in her forequarters are doing, how she's holding her neck and how deep and easy are her outward breaths. When they quicken and begin to sound a little hard, he thinks about slowing her back to a walk. She's there in five strides without him having done any more than think. It's only then that he looks to see where I am, and realises that everyone, horse and human alike, is watching him.

Everyone except Pamela is smiling. She is standing, leaning against Zeal for the strength that has gone from her legs as she stares at her husband in disbelief. She glances at Tania, then at me. I grin at her and her whole face breaks into a smile. She looks quickly back to Cliff and blinks to make sure she's definitely still seeing what she hopes she did. He smiles back at her.

Tania comes to their rescue. She claps her hands loudly and then waves them both in the air, saying, 'Right, you lot, it's time to get your horses loaded and off home.'

The other seven riders all look at one another, each hoping that someone else will come up with a reason why they need to stay longer.

'You can come back tomorrow but we've got work to do here now, so you need to be on your way,' Tania insists.

'Tomorrow's Monday, so I'll have to work,' Belinda says forlornly.

'So, come here before or after work. You can come as soon as it's light and until it gets dark. Who's in?' Tania says.

'We should all ride together,' Philip says firmly, looking around at all the others with hard eyes, daring them to disagree.

'We should,' Jimmy agrees.

'Absolutely,' Sophie says.

Sam shakes his fist as if he's just won. 'I'm in.'

'Definitely all of us together,' Clare agrees.

Chloe looks around at everyone in disbelief, then nods.

'Shall we be here at zero six hundred hours?' Belinda says.

Everyone nods and Philip says, 'Zero six hundred hours? What are you, a soldier?'

Belinda grins. 'I was just trying to be clear, you know so no one thought I meant six in the evening.'

Clare clicks at Maple to follow her and turns for the gate with a chuckle. 'You didn't think six a.m. would suffice?'

'Suffice? Are you approaching ninety?' Jimmy says, walking along just behind her with Photon at his side.

Clare laughs and Sam says, 'At least she can ride with her eyes open.' He closes his eyes and puts a hand out in front of himself as he walks.

'It worked, didn't it?' Jimmy says with a grin.

'It worked,' Sophie agrees as their voices fade to a murmur.

'I'LL SEE YOU ALL AT SIX O'CLOCK TOMORROW MORNING,' Tania yells at their retreating backs.

They all turn and wave, and Sam calls out, 'On behalf of us all, thank you again.'

'Are you my mother now?' Philip says loudly. 'We all thanked Tania before.'

Sam punches him lightly on the shoulder and retorts every bit as loudly, 'Just demonstrating my superior manners.'

'So, demonstrate them a little more and move Hector away from my ramp? Clicka wants her hay,' Belinda says with a grin, then rolls her eyes as Philip takes Sam in a headlock and ruffles his hair, and adds, 'give me strength.'

'Just demonstrating superior superiority, if you ask me,' Jimmy says and chucks a bucket of water over Sam and Philip.

We all smile at the shrieks and laughter that follow as a water fight breaks out. Tania races over to the car park and joins in.

I'm Aware of Lia relaxing for the first time since Tania and I arrived here, and of her surprised delight that for the first time ever, Tania has put everything she is to one side and is behaving exactly like the seven other young people. It's a welcome break for our daughter to be with people who aren't constantly watching her, admiring her or monitoring her in their Awareness to see what her advanced way of being will lead her to do next, and we're both glad for her.

Cliff has dismounted from his mare and is hugging his wife. Pamela clings to him, scared that he'll revert back to whom he was if she lets go. When she finally releases him, the two of them talk for a while, then make their way over to where I'm sitting on the fence, chuckling at the sight of Tania laughing as she sits in a puddle created by the seven buckets of water that have just been emptied over her head. She could lift the water and fling it back at her seven students, but she won't, and not just because she doesn't want to scare them; she's as happy as she's ever been at being included in their fun and in the sense of kinship that is quickly forming between them all.

Chloe offers her a hand and pulls her to her feet, then flings her arms around my daughter, overwhelmed to not only have found the horse of her dreams, but to have been accepted into a group of friends by others who have also found theirs.

'I know you're not going to answer me, Will, but I have to ask,' Cliff says. 'Who the hell are you and that daughter of yours, to have done everything you've done here in less than twenty-four hours?'

I look down at him as he stands with his arm around Pamela, his final traces of meanness having been drawn out of him and ground into the dust along with his cap, by his horse. I grin and say, 'We're just a father and daughter who have come from a distant future to help those who will ensure the future exists.'

Cliff turns his head and looks sideways at me as Pamela's mouth falls open. She begins to nod slowly, her eyes flicking between Tania and me, but he slaps his leg and laughs out loud. 'I knew it! I think I'll ask you that every day until you eventually run out of weirdness and tell me the truth.'

I chuckle and nod towards the bay mare who is now grooming with Zeal. 'Have you decided on a name for her?'

He turns and watches the mare. 'Heart,' he says softly. 'Her name is Heart.'

Pamela watches me thoughtfully and whispers, 'When you realise that what you thought was a dream is real, and what you thought was reality is really a dream.'

'What's that?' Cliff says, turning back to us both.

'Nothing, just me trying to make sense of life,' Pamela murmurs, still watching me as if expecting the answers she is trying to find to suddenly erupt out of me.

'Well, that was a fine way to start the day,' Tania says, squelching in her boots and walking with her legs apart and her dripping arms out to either side.

Pamela blinks and turns to Tania. 'Um, it was a brilliant way to start the day, but I can see you need a shower and change of clothes. I think we could all do with a nice cold glass of juice while we decide where to go from here, so we'll go back to the house, I'll look you out some of my clothes, Tania, and then when you're comfortable, we can all have a chat.'

Cliff nods as if he's used to Pamela organising his life, and Tania says, 'Great idea,' and follows them both as the first lorry – Philip's – pulls out onto the road. All of the others except for Clare and Chloe have loaded their horses and the sound of engines turning over fills the car park. Chloe gives Minerva a last hug and then leaves her horse to walk up the ramp of her trailer by herself. Clare stands with her mum, their arms around one another and their heads close together as they talk. Eventually, they part and Clare unties Maple from the side of her trailer and leads her up its ramp. As she pulls out of the car park, I say a silent farewell to her mum, knowing that she won't feel the need to come with her daughter again.

I'd love to chat with Lia, but although she has a sense of me, Tania and what we're doing in the past, that is as much as her Awareness allows.

Tania interrupts my thoughts. *So, chat with me.*

And me, Amarilla adds. *I'm with Lia now, so I can tell her what you say.*

That wasn't really what I had in mind.

Am, tell Mum we'll be home in a few weeks, everything is going great, Tania says.

I nod. *A few weeks is about right. Tania, you were magnificent today, as were you, Fin.*

Neither Infinity nor my daughter acknowledge my praise; both of them view it as superfluous. *Be that as it may,* I tell them, *it doesn't change the fact. Am, give Lia a hug from me and also reassure her that her Awareness didn't just fail her and our daughter has indeed just had the time of her life sitting in a puddle.*

Tania and I spend the remainder of the morning outside, making repairs to the paddock fence. Since the property is surrounded by fields, we are unobserved and free to lift the replacement rails into position without lifting a finger, but having agreed that Cliff and Pamela need a break from having to accept any more strangeness, we nail the rails into place by hand. We're Aware that the noise of our hammering reassures the couple of their privacy in their red brick house so that they feel free to begin to get to know one another again, now that their horses have helped them to find themselves.

Just as our stomachs are beginning to rumble, Pamela appears. She waves to us on her way into the barn to see Zeal, then when she reappears, she calls out, 'Come on in for lunch, there's a pile of sandwiches waiting for you.'

I hammer the last nail into the rail that Tania was pretending to hold for me, then allow the hammer to drop to the ground by the fence post and box of nails. When we reach Pamela, she tells us in a low voice, 'Cliff just helped me to make sandwiches for the first time ever, so if there's too much butter or not enough, or the same with the filling, could you just eat them anyway?'

'I'm pleased for you, Pamela,' I reply as we walk towards the house. 'Of course we'll eat them, we're grateful for any food you give us.'

'I'm so hungry, I doubt I'll notice what I'm eating,' Tania says, 'but the fact that Cliff helped you prepare lunch, and you were happy about it, will give the food a lift and make it more pleasing to eat anyway, so I wouldn't worry about it.'

Pamela looks sideways at her and then takes the opening Tania has offered her. 'You both say such strange things in such a matter of fact way that I find myself believing you.' She hurries around in front of us to keep us where we are. 'You said the two of you are from the future, Will. The rational part of my brain tells me that isn't possible, but you appeared from nowhere, you don't appear to have anywhere to live or any possessions, you can apparently heal others by thought, you have a way of making people behave differently around you, you know things no one else knows, and neither of you have wrist safes… it's the only answer that explains all of that. And you said you're here to help those who can ensure the future exists, so you must mean us? Me and Cliff? And the seven who mysteriously bought previously broken horses all on the same day, who all came back here today for a lesson – and, by the way, all paid me without me even having to ask them for the transfer – and all left as completely different people, like Cliff is, and I am?' She waves a hand towards the barn, where Zeal and Heart are sheltering from the sun. 'And my husband and I each have a horse now? I mean, what the hell?' She's breathing hard by the time she runs out of the words she's been desperate, yet terrified, to hear herself say.

Aware that Cliff is in the kitchen, pouring glasses of lemonade for each of us while humming to himself, Tania and I both surround Pamela in a cloud of white light. She looks around herself and then back at us.

'It's just love,' Tania says. 'We had to be touching you to give it to you before so you could take it without panicking, but you can take it this way now. Dad always tells the truth. It might not always be the truth you think you heard – he considers his ability to do that a gift to humankind – but it is the truth. We came here from the future to help you and because without you and the seven who rode with you today, and all of your horses, we won't ever be born. The future is an amazing time to be alive, and it exists because of you all and everything you'll do.'

We strengthen our light flows as her legs begin to shake. Reaching out to hold her up won't help right now, she needs her own space as everything she thought she knew spins around in her mind, becoming entangled with everything that has happened in the past few days and everything she has just learnt. Gradually, her strength returns.

'You're from the future. To help us… save the human race?' she says.

'Exactly,' Tania confirms. 'It sounds scary, but what better reason could there be for being alive?'

'How? How will we do that?'

'By following the path your horses are showing you,' Tania says. 'They're in this with you. Zeal will be with you every step of the way.'

Pamela nods slowly and then stands straighter, stronger as Tania's words sink in and have the effect my daughter knew they would. Then she says, 'What about Cliff? You mentioned me and the other seven who rode with me today, but what about my husband?'

'He'll help you all,' I say. 'He'll be instrumental to the process, but ultimately, it'll be down to the eight of you and those who will follow you.'

'What will be? What's going to happen?'

'Even if we told you, it wouldn't help,' Tania says. 'You'll still need to live through it all and knowing what's coming will just distract you. One of the things the horses of our time have made very sure to teach us is the importance of being present, of living our lives moment by moment so that all of our attention, our intelligence, our energy, our power, is available to us in every single second we're alive. There is literally no time like the present for living your life.'

'That's a bit rich, coming from the two of you,' Pamela says with the ghost of a smile, and we both chuckle. Her face straightens as a thought strikes her. 'The horses taught you the importance of being present? How did they do that?'

Tania smiles. 'In lots of different ways, just like they'll teach you now that you're listening.'

Pamela nods thoughtfully. Then she says, 'Is it just the two of you here, or are there more of you?'

'It's just the two of us,' I say, 'which believe me, my wife isn't happy about.'

'Why isn't she here too?'

'She doesn't have the ability to be Aware of the past and future, let alone move herself to them,' Tania says. 'Dad and I are the only ones who can do that.'

'So, it's all up to the two of you?'

'Nope, we have you, the others and all of the horses,' Tania says. 'That's plenty.'

Pamela puts a hand to her forehead and laughs weakly. 'I can't believe I'm having this conversation. So, what do we do now?'

'We go inside and eat lunch with Cliff,' I say, 'and we divert him from trying to transfer the wages that he's now actually intending to pay us, to wrist safes that don't exist.'

Pamela turns and begins to walk to the house on whose doorstep Cliff has just appeared, his hand above his eyes as he squints into the sun to see where we all are. 'Weird as it feels to ask,' she whispers, 'can't you just magic them up for yourselves?'

'We could give the appearance of having them,' I whisper back, 'but there's nowhere for the transfer to go, we have no need for bank accounts, and it's better that your money stays with you.'

'You could tell him what you've told me.'

'I did, you were there,' I say.

'Come on in, the sandwiches are getting cold,' Cliff says with a grin.

Pamela smiles and flaps her hand at him. 'Clown.' She turns to Tania and me. 'We should get going on the sandwiches, when I said there was a pile, I should have said a mountain.'

NINE

Pamela

*T*his is surreal. I'm sitting at the same kitchen table over which Cliff has hurled abuse at me, lunged at me, even dragged me by my hair on one occasion. I've sat here and cried so many times during the fourteen years we've been married, but now I'm laughing. Not just in pretence of finding my husband's jokes funny, either, but because they actually are, and moreover, because I'm pretty sure I'm on the edge of hysteria.

I just can't take it all in. Cliff having a personality transplant would have been enough to throw me by itself, but all the rest of it – everything that's happened since Will and Tania turned up yesterday, everything that they know will happen and that I can't know until it happens – is too much. I suppose I should be congratulating myself that I'm still sane. If I am.

I think of Zeal, how safe I feel when I ride him and when I'm around him. Except safe isn't the right word; for once in my life, safety doesn't come into it. I feel whole, as if my life up until yesterday was just about existing until my real life – this life, where dreams and reality have merged – was ready to begin. So, then, it must be okay.

I take a deep breath and calm down a little just as Cliff launches into an impression of one of the governors during his last speech on his commitment to ensuring safety and comfort for all of his citizens. Unfortunately for the governor, he has an unusually high-pitched voice for a man of his size and stature, which Cliff, despite also being a big man, manages to take off perfectly.

'We promise safety and comfort for all except those who object to us seizing their land in order to build more high rises and food factories, those who resist being evicted from their farms and forced to work in the city at jobs they hate, those who object to having their locations, calls and transactions monitored at all times, those who have any tendency towards independent thought, and those who otherwise disagree with us in any way.'

We all laugh. 'It's not quite that bad,' I say.

Cliff is suddenly serious. 'Give it a few years and it will be. I don't know how long we'll have fields all around us, Hank was telling me only last week that the fields on the far side of his have been seized now that they're not needed for farming.' He leans towards Tania. 'It was one of Hank's fields you jumped into on Pebble yesterday morning. He's kept a hold of his land so far because he's applied to set up a solar farm on it, but he's worried they'll seize it, build high rises on it and then just put the panels on the tops of the buildings like they've started doing in the city. Give it a few years and we'll barely be able to see the sun for all the skyscrapers towering over us.'

'What about our land? What about the horses? Our business?' I say.

'As long as the business is successful and we pay our taxes, we should be okay for a while yet...'

'So then, let's focus on making the business successful,' Tania interrupts, smiling as she catches my eye. 'Have you got any more horses coming in for us to work with? Eight at a time works well for us.'

Cliff nudges Will and says out of the corner of his mouth, 'Proper little slave driver you have there. Does she get it from her mother?'

Will grins. 'She absolutely does.'

'So, where is she? Your wife? Are you divorced? A widower?'

My heart starts thumping wildly, but I should have known Will would know what to say.

'Happily, I'm neither. My wife's at home with our dogs and horses while I travel with Tania so she can get work experience.'

'Talking of which, I need to pay you both,' Cliff says. 'Fifty a day each on top of your board and lodging?'

'Fine,' Will says. 'At the end of the month is soon enough for us, that gives us three weeks to prove we're worth it.'

Cliff smiles a natural smile as if he's always done it. 'You've already proved that. In answer to your question, Tania, no, my wife and I haven't begun looking for more horses yet, but we'll get right on that this afternoon, and hopefully have more coming for when you finish teaching tomorrow. Is that soon enough?'

Tania rolls her eyes. 'I guess. We'll get back to mending the fence then.'

'I'll come out with you both and check on the horses,' I say.

Cliff nods. 'I'll come too.'

The four of us clear the table and wash the dishes as if we're a family used to pitching in together, then head back out into the heat of the day. Will and Tania head for the section of fence on which they were working before lunch, and Cliff and I head for the barn.

'I'm frightened this is a dream and I'm going to wake up,' Cliff says. 'Or a coma. What if I got kicked in the head by one of the horses, and I'm in a hospital bed somewhere, hooked up to machines while you sit by my bedside hoping I'll die?'

'I would never hope for that.'

'Not now maybe, but you must have done loads of times, I know I have.'

'You've hoped you'd die? Why?'

'Every time I lashed out at you, I hated myself but I couldn't stop myself. It was like I could only feel better if I was making you suffer the way I used to suffer when my old man beat me, but it only lasted for a few minutes and then I felt even worse. And then this morning, when I watched you and the others ride, and then when I rode, I felt better without needing to hit anyone. I still do. I've no idea how it's happened, but I feel good about life even with everything that's going on. I can't lose this feeling. I can't wake up.'

I take his hand and squeeze it as we walk. 'So then, don't, and I won't either. If we keep working with the horses and with Will and Tania, we won't. Why don't you ride again this evening, when the heat lifts a bit? You didn't push Heart at all this morning, she can manage another session.'

Cliff nods. 'Good idea. I'll ask Will to help me, I like the way he teaches.'

'And you'd find it hard being taught by a young girl,' I say. I tense, hoping I was right to trust that I could speak to him that way.

He chuckles. 'Not hard, just strange, and there's only so much strangeness a man can take in any one day.'

'I know.' I pat his arm. 'I know.'

We spend a good hour grooming our horses – I can hardly

believe I'm thinking of them that way – and by the time we leave them snoozing head to tail in the deep, cleaner than clean straw bed Will and Tania have maintained for them, we're both feeling calmer and happier about life.

As the afternoon progresses, we find that we work well together. I search the internet for horses for sale within a few hours' drive, and pass the details of those I select on to Cliff for him to choose those he wants to pursue. He makes calls and by the end of the afternoon has arranged for five horses to be delivered tomorrow, and another three to be ready for him to collect.

He slaps the table and when I flinch, smiles at me and says, 'Eight more horses, just as the lady ordered. Sorry for scaring you.'

My lips begin to tremble and my eyes fill with tears. 'It's okay. Thank you…' I swallow. 'Thank you for your apology.'

Cliff takes a deep breath and blows it out slowly. He comes around to my side of the table, holds out his hand and pulls me to my feet. He hugs me and says, 'I'm sorry for everything.'

I hug him back. 'Thank you.' I lose track of how long we stand so.

Eventually, Cliff pulls back from me, reaches for my apron and puts it on. 'So, what am I cooking for dinner?'

'You? Cooking?' I start to laugh, then straighten my face. It's no good; the last time Cliff put me in hospital, I came home to a sink full of pans of burnt, unrecognisable contents and a pile of takeaway cartons. I laugh harder and Cliff shakes his head and chuckles.

'Can anyone join in?' Tania says from the doorway.

'For the love of us all, please do, Cliff's cooking dinner,' I manage to reply.

'I gather that isn't a good thing?' Will says from behind her.

'Cliff, why don't you and I make a cottage pie, and show Pamela how rude she was to laugh?'

Cliff hands him a bottle of beer from the fridge and chinks it against his own. 'Sounds good to me. If I promise not to drink too much and fall asleep, would you give me a hand with Heart after dinner?'

'You want to ride so you'll be able to carry on dreaming when you go to sleep,' Tania says. 'Good idea.'

'I can say, hand on my heart, that if you're sober and awake, I'll give you a hand with your Heart,' Will says, grinning that grin of his that allows him to say anything.

Cliff looks from one of them to the other and then at me. 'When I said there's only so much strangeness a man can take in any one day, I was wrong.'

I chuckle. 'Don't you have a cottage pie to make?'

I stand with Zeal as he grazes in the cool of the evening, watching Cliff ride Heart. He's a tall, well built man but the mare's height and solid build absorb his size perfectly. I'm transported back to the first time I met my husband, when he was riding a similar type of horse at a showjumping competition. The pair won all of their classes and Cliff was the handsome, jovial centre of attention around the collecting ring. I was at the show grooming for another rider, and was in the stable block, filling buckets of water for my two charges when Cliff swaggered in with a trail of admirers, to check on his horse. I was so flattered when he introduced himself to me and then proceeded to chat me up, I ignored the fact his horse shot to the back of his stable as soon as Cliff approached the door.

Over the months that followed, I steadily ignored anything I didn't want to see, and continued that way until we were married and Cliff turned his violence on me. I've always blamed myself for it, feeling that I deserved everything he dished out to me because I ignored it when he was doing it to the horses. I've stuck around to protect them as much as I can, which hasn't been very much. And now I'm glad I did. Somehow – and I still can't believe it – everything is working out. I'm watching my husband combine all of his physical riding talent with a sensitivity, an emotional connection with his horse, of which I never dreamt he could be capable, and the result is beautiful. And tomorrow morning, I'll be riding Zeal again.

I suddenly feel nervous. What if I can't replicate the level of connection we achieved this morning? What if, by the time I wake up tomorrow, this feeling I have of being strong and capable has vanished and I'm back to being weak and out of control again?

Zeal stamps his foot at a fly, making me jump. I put a hand to his neck and immediately feel better. Even as he stands at rest, calmly watching his stable mate, his eyes hold an intensity, a fervour. He has a mission, I know it as surely as I know my own name. He was crippled when he arrived here, but arrive here he did. Whatever happened to him in his life, he held on until he could get here, until he could get the help he needed – until he was mine. I feel a restlessness, a roiling in my stomach that I've never experienced before, and remember that I have a mission too.

I watch Will as he walks a small circle inside Heart's larger one. He's as relaxed a person as I've ever met, yet things happen around him, as if he's a forcefield around which things can't help but whirl and change. My gaze travels to Tania, who's sitting on the paddock fence, stroking the tail of the barn cat who sits on her shoulder, while watching Heart and Cliff. She's as blunt as the summer days are long, but everything she says has an effect far beyond anything that words should be able to cause. It's as if in any situation, she becomes the problem, the solution and all of the words and actions in between, until no problem exists. And she and her dad are here, with Cliff, Heart, Zeal and me.

Whatever my mission is, I'll succeed.

TEN

Tania

I wave to my students from my place on the paddock
fence as they mill around the car park, greeting one
another and fussing the horses. Cliff shuts the gate between the car
park and the road, then wanders among them all, his intention
merely to exchange pleasantries. He's surprised and delighted
when, as he shakes their hands, each and every student instructs
their wrist safe to transfer funds to Cliff's in advance payment for
their lesson, and in every case, he puts his free hand atop his
client's in a display of gratitude.

The seven are astride their horses in no time. Clare has chosen
to ride with tack today, while Sophie has decided to ride Pebble
without a bridle. No one comments on either change as they ride
their horses towards the paddock gate. I hurry to unlatch it for
them, and hold it ajar as they all file into the paddock to join
Pamela and Zeal.

'Just have a little wander around,' I call out. 'Check in with
your horses exactly as you did yesterday, sense what their bodies

are doing beneath you and how they're feeling, then when you're ready, move them onto a large circle around me. There's absolutely no rush, you need to be in a world of your own with your horse, completely unaware of what anyone else is doing – take yourselves inside the super being that is you and your horse. Jimmy, Sophie, Pamela, that's excellent. You too, Chloe, Clare and Sam. There you go, Belinda.'

I walk over to Philip and Melody; Philip is having a little trouble this morning. I'm Aware that, full of the connection he achieved with his horse yesterday and how he felt as a result, he carried the feeling with him through the rest of his day. To begin with, he brushed off the surprised looks he got from those around him. By the evening, he was beginning to panic that he might have lost the respect of those so used to his normal domineering manner that they seemed uncomfortable by his good cheer. He has to have the total respect and obedience of those around him, otherwise he could lose his standing within his family, and become a target for those who see his demise as necessary for their quest for increasing status and power. He hasn't slept much and although he's relieved to be back here with Melody and surrounded by those with whom he shared yesterday's experience, he's having trouble removing himself from his worries.

I walk at his stirrup and say, 'You know, there are different types of power. There's perceived power, which is what your family relies on. It comes from conning people into believing you're better than they are, and maintaining it needs constant attention, which is exhausting. Then there's inner power, which you achieved when you and Melody connected yesterday. It's always there inside you, no matter what you do, and it's limitless. The more you connect with it, the stronger it gets, and you know what? Everyone has the same inner power, whether they're aware of it or not, and because of that, they recognise it when they see it in others. You misinterpreted the reactions of those around you yesterday. Sure, they were surprised, but they were also confused and more than a little intimidated; there's nothing more terrifying than an opponent who has absolutely no fear.'

'How do you know all that?' Philip barks at me, his throat hoarse as my words bring the slither of fear that instilled itself into him yesterday to the surface, ready for release.

'The question you should be asking yourself is, why are you so certain that I do? How do you know that I'm not just guessing?'

'Because there's something about you. About you and your dad. You both talk like there's no doubt that what you're saying is true.'

I nod. 'That's your inner power recognising ours. Choose it over the perceived power you've been relying on up until now, not just when you ride but in everything you do, just like you did yesterday until you started checking yourself. Choose it and see what happens. Every time you ride, every time you connect with Melody, it'll get stronger until you're unstoppable.'

Philip nods slowly. 'I hope you're right.'

'No, you don't. Be honest with yourself, Philip, even if you can't be honest with me.'

A smile twitches at the corners of his mouth. 'Fine. I know you're right. I'm still not sure exactly how I know, but I kind of do. And it's Phil.'

'Okay, Phil, focus on connecting with Melody, that's all you need to do for your life to feel easier.'

I walk to the centre of where I want my circle of horses and riders to be, and wait. Pamela and Zeal, Jimmy and Photon, Phil and Melody, and Chloe and Minerva join it first. Sam and Hector are close behind, followed by Belinda and Clicka, Sophie and Pebble, and finally Clare and Maple. Clare gave herself as long as she needed to get used to the extra support, but slightly less feel, afforded her by her saddle; she's come a long way since this time yesterday.

'You're all doing really well,' I tell them. Yesterday, you focused on connecting with your horses. Now, we're going to look at how you can help them to carry your weight without causing harm to themselves. The joints in your horses' forequarters, from the shoulder down to the fetlock, are almost in a straight line, resulting in little ability for shock absorbency; in other words, they aren't designed to carry weight when the horse is moving. The joints in your horses' hindquarters, from hip to stifle to hock to fetlock, are arranged in a kind of zigzag, like a giant spring, resulting in a great ability to absorb shock – they are designed to carry weight when the horse is moving.

'When unhindered horses begin to move, they will naturally lift in front and transfer their weight back onto the joints in their hindquarters that can support it, and then balance it there. When we sit on them just behind their shoulders, our weight pushes them onto their forequarters, making it more difficult for them to lift and transfer their weight back to where it needs to be in order for them to balance and move efficiently and without risk of strain or injury. So, you need to help your horses to move as well with you on their backs as they do without you. The first step is to make sure you're sitting up straight. If you're hunched or leaning forward slightly, if even just your head is tilted, your horse will feel more weight on their forequarters.'

Immediately, all eight riders shift their bodies as they check they are straight. Some were already sitting in a good position, others needed to adjust the way they were sitting, but all have a level of awareness of their bodies that arises from being as sensitive as each of them is. They were born for this.

As the lesson progresses and the riders follow my instructions with only the odd reminder to remain connected to their horses, the collective picture they create begins to soften and strengthen. All of the riders are experienced, but this is the first time any of them have ridden with the sole aim of supporting their horse's body so that they can carry their rider's weight without compromising themselves. The horses all respond enthusiastically to their rider's attempts to help, which spurs the riders on to try even harder to feel what their horses need from them, leaving all thoughts of what they need from their horses far behind them.

One by one, the horses' bodies gradually become more connected from the hind feet all the way through to their forequarters. Their ears soften, as do their eyes, which appear to open a little more and deepen so that nothing of themselves is hidden. Their riders can't see what I can, but, deeply connected with their horses as they are, they feel it and become more connected both within themselves and to their roles here.

Even if I weren't already Aware of the roles the eight riders in front of me will adopt, I can see it in their energy. Where all of them still radiate some of the grey energy of depression, sadness and exhaustion that is characteristic of so many in The Old, it is now far from the dominant energy, and the black energy that emanated from Sophie has completely gone.

All eight riders more strongly radiate the blue energy of truth and sensitivity that was previously present only as flecks within the grey.

Belinda, Phil and Clare also now burn with the orange energy of courage and optimism, and the red of grounded strength and passion, as does Pamela, some of whose energy still flares indigo and violet.

Jimmy, Chloe, Sam and Sophie all radiate the green energy of peace and healing in addition to the pink of friendship, the indigo of clarity and the violet of intuition.

I ask the eight riders to halt and dismount. They stand in their circle, patting and stroking their horses in silence while looking around at one another. They don't know exactly what it is they are sensing, but the infinity energy that binds them together fuels the patterns of energy that are developing within each of them, causing them to expand and reach out towards the energy fields of those standing with them. Like attracts like and when the energy fields of Belinda, Phil, Clare and Pamela come into contact, they merge. The four look solely at one another without knowing why, but just conscious of feeling a sudden affinity with each of the other three.

The other half of the group are behaving in exactly the same way between themselves as tendrils of energy extend out from Jimmy, Chloe, Sam and Sophie and entwine around one another, causing the four to connect as easily and readily as they just did with their horses.

'Perfect,' I say. Everyone blinks, and Jimmy and Chloe jump. They all turn to look at me. 'That will do for today, You and your horses have all been completely brilliant. Same time tomorrow?'

They all merely nod, none of them able to find any words to say.

'Great. See you then.'

Pam clears her throat, glances slightly nervously at Cliff and then straightens her shoulders and says, 'Since I think we'll be wanting to ride together most days from now on, future sessions will be subject to a donation rather than a fee. Just pay us what you can afford, okay? Come on, let's get our horses washed down.' She smiles at the round of thanks directed at her, then walks with Zeal to the car park, the others following in her wake.

I'm Aware of her uncertainty about why, exactly, she is going to wash her horse down using water from the tap in the car park when she could do it more easily at the trough in the paddock, and know that she just doesn't feel able or inclined to break up the energy of the group just yet.

Cliff, whose energy is now a deep red flecked with orange, is as confused as his wife. He opens his mouth to call out to her, but Dad intervenes as I climb the fence and sit down next to him. 'I'm not surprised they all want to have a chat about what they just achieved, it was pretty great to watch, wasn't it?'

Cliff closes his mouth and tilts his head from one side to the other. 'I guess. What did they achieve, exactly? I saw their horses begin to move much better, but when they all got off at the end of the session, they all looked spaced out, and then Pam practically offered free lessons.'

'They connected with their horses more strongly and that opened them up to connecting with who they are inside, and to each other. It'll take a bit of processing.'

Cliff rubs his chin. 'You're telling me.'

The two of them continue chatting while I watch the goings on in the car park.

The four with predominantly red and orange energy waste no time huddling together and discussing the lesson, though none of them directly mention the affinity they are now aware exists between them.

The other four are far more circumspect. Sophie is standing with Chloe and Minvera, having offered Chloe the use of her sweat scraper as an excuse to be near her. Jimmy is likewise standing with Sam and Hector, having called out a compliment as to how well Hector responded to Sam in the lesson as an opening for their conversation. When Jimmy goes back to continue preparing Photon for the journey home, Sophie joins him and Chloe sidles shyly over to Sam.

They'll all become more confident about following their feelings as they get more used to having them. Everything is going perfectly.

ELEVEN

Will

---

*C*hloe is the last to leave. I sense her reluctance to return to her life from the oasis of hope and happiness that this place and the people she has met here are rapidly becoming for her. Then I sense her switch her thoughts to the horse who stands patiently in the trailer behind her. I sense her gratitude that the one with whom she has found everything she has ever wanted and more, is with her. Knowing what is to come, I almost feel sorry for her but then I see it as the perfection it is both for her, Minerva, and the rest of us.

That's a relief, for a moment I thought I was going to have to reach after you and pull you out of the quagmire you almost fell into, Tania tells me.

You call it a quagmire, I still call it compassion, I reply. *But let's not go there again, our first two new friends of the day are here.* I nod over to where Cliff, having only just closed the gate after Chloe, is now opening it for a large, yellow lorry to pull in to the car park.

Zeal and Heart both whinny from the depths of the barn, and

are answered by shrill, nervous whinnies emanating from the lorry.

Pamela appears in the barn doorway. When she sees the lorry, she puts the bar up to keep Zeal and Heart inside, then glances over at Tania and me and smiles. 'Let's get today's show on the road, shall we?'

As we've needed to do with so many words and phrases that have no meaning in our own time, we find the meaning of Pamela's suggestion in our Awareness and both smile back to her.

Tania jumps off the fence. 'Absolutely. They're both terrified, but they won't be for much longer.' She jogs to the car park and arrives just as Cliff is helping a woman almost as tall as he to lower the lorry's ramp.

'So I'm guessing that by the time the horses are released in the paddock, they'll be free of any ailments they came with, and ready and willing to be ridden?' Pamela says to me.

'They're free of them now,' I reply as Cliff and the woman each lead a horse down the ramp to where Tania is waiting to take them. 'The grey had a chronically sore back and the chestnut's pelvis was way out of kilter. Neither issue showed up until they were ridden, so Tania's been straight on it. That dealer thinks she's selling Cliff a couple of dangerous wrecks, but in fact they're feeling almost as good as they did before they were ever ridden.'

Cliff and the woman hold their wrists close together, then the woman hurries back into the cab of the lorry before he can change his mind. She wastes no time turning her lorry around, and is out of the car park only ten minutes after arriving.

Tania removes the chestnut's headcollar and then the grey's. She vaults onto the grey's back and jumps him into the paddock, closely followed by the chestnut. Cliff stands with his hands in the air at her not having waited for him to open the gate, but she doesn't care. She is the grey as they canter around together, her part of their body reminding his how he moved before he was forced to compensate for his initial back injury, and then to compensate for all of the subsequent compensations. When his body is free to be that which it was born to be, the chestnut pulls alongside for his turn. Tania shifts from one back to the next and the chestnut soon joins the grey in his relief.

Tania is as Aware as I that Cliff's attention is fully taken by the two horses now cantering side by side around his paddock. She resonates the minutest part of herself with the bar across the barn entrance, and shifts it to one side. Zeal and Heart burst out of the barn at a canter and join the three of them. Pamela and Cliff laugh in delight as the four horses leap and buck like foals, Tania never moving from her place on the chestnut's back. When the two newcomers have accepted their places in the new herd of four, the horses slow to a halt and begin to graze.

Tania slides down from the chestnut and says, 'They're ready and waiting for their people.'

'We didn't get as far as booking viewings for the new arrivals,' Pamela says, 'stupidly, now I come to think of it, having seen you at work before.'

'You don't need to, their people will come here tomorrow of their own accord,' Tania says with a wink.

Pamela stares at her and then nods.

'I need to get off in the lorry and collect the three over at Dinastown,' Cliff says as he reaches us. He nods to the horses. 'I think you'd better get on and contact some more of the folks on our waiting list, Pam, those two look like they're ready for viewings. Good job, Tania.'

'I'm all over it, there'll be people coming to see them tomorrow,' Pamela says. 'You head off, and I'm pretty confident that by the time you get back, the other three due to arrive in the next few hours will be as ready as those two, and we'll have viewings lined up for all of them.'

Cliff salutes. 'Yes m'am.' He turns and heads for the house.

'Well, that's an easy day for you guys then,' Pamela says.

I shake my head. 'We've the fence to finish repairing. Come on, Tan, let's get to it.'

Pamela says, 'You don't need to. You can just relax out of the heat until the other horses get here?'

'No, it's okay, we're quite happy working.'

'This really is all in a day's work for you two, isn't it?' Pamela says. 'You achieve miracles without blinking and then just go and mend a fence?'

'A miracle is only a miracle when it can't be explained,' Tania says, 'so in truth, nothing we do is a miracle. You, on the other hand, have no explanation whatsoever for what you're achieving, you're going with it on trust and feeling alone. If anyone's performing miracles around here, it's you.' She turns and marches over to where we left off replacing the fence rails too splintered to really be called such.

'How is it that at thirty-nine years old, I'm finding myself unable to talk back to someone half my age?' Pamela says.

I chuckle. 'Don't beat yourself up, she's left her mother and me floundering ever since she first began talking.'

'I wish I could meet your wife. What's her name?'

'Lia.'

'I hope Lia is proud of her daughter, because whatever Tania says, the two of you absolutely are performing miracles here. You're changing lives.'

'You might not thank us in the long run.'

Pamela stares at me and I sense her intuition flexing and stretching. She directs it towards me. 'You're a good person and so is Tania,' she says finally. 'I trust you both.'

I can't see her energy for myself, but I'm Aware of what Tania sees in her and I'm pretty sure that very soon, there'll be very little grey energy left in Pamela at all. I grin at her. 'You're a good person too.'

One of the barn cats, a large, grey male with a pointed face and bright green eyes, chooses to reinforce the energy of my statement by rubbing himself against Pamela's leg. She flinches and looks down, then looks up at me. 'He's never come near me before, let alone done that.'

I grin. 'He feels safe around you now and he knows the time has come to fulfil his mission.'

'He has a mission? A cat? Seriously?'

'You don't need to ask me. Look at him, reach out to him like you do to Zeal, and see what you find.'

Pamela stares down at the cat. He turns and leaps up onto the top rail of the fence next to me in a single bound, then leans towards Pamela and stares back at her, his green eyes holding hers. She holds out her hand, and he rubs his face against it, purring loudly. Her eyes light up. She's unaware of the thread that links the two of them flaring to life, but she feels a subtle warmth infusing her body as the cat's protection settles around her. She is capable of holding the negativity of The Old away from herself most of the time now that she has connected with Zeal, but when she's stressed, weary or asleep, he will keep her shielded.

Cliff arrives back at the end of the afternoon with three bays – two mares and a gelding – to join the four horses who were here when he left, and the three – a brown mare with white spots on her hind quarters, a piebald gelding and a chestnut mare – who arrived in his absence. Tania takes the mares and I take the gelding, all three of whom are healed within minutes of the injuries that caused them to be sold, and ridden to complete health within the space of ten minutes.

Cliff stands, hands on his hips, grinning as all ten happy, healthy horses mill around him while the three new arrivals settle into the herd.

'Bottle of cold beer?' Pamela calls out to him.

He lifts a hand and makes his way over to where the three of us are waiting for him.

'I think we could all do with one,' Tania says, wiping her brow.

'Done,' Pamela replies, then turns to Cliff. 'That's eight healthy, happy horses all ready to be viewed tomorrow.'

'You've got viewings organised for them all?' he says.

Pamela hasn't made a single phone call. She looks sideways at Tania, and instantly remembers that she trusts her. 'Um, yes, absolutely. There'll be, er, eight buyers here for them tomorrow.'

'When's the first booked in for?'

Tania comes to Pamela's rescue. 'First thing. We'll get most of the viewings done before it gets too hot, and the remaining few later on when there's a bit more shade in the paddock.'

'Good enough,' Cliff agrees. 'You've made good headway with the fence, just the far side to do. I'll give you both a hand with it in between the morning and afternoon viewings tomorrow.'

'Good enough,' Tania replies in as gruff a voice as she can manage, her attempt at imitating him no less amusing for its failure.

He chuckles. 'Never in my life have I accepted cheek from a staff member.'

'I'm pretty sure if we counted up all of the things we've done in the past few days that we've never done before, we'd either lose count or run out of numbers,' Pamela says, looking down at the cat at her feet, who purrs up at her. 'So we'll carry on in that vein, shall we, and after dinner, when it's cool, take Zeal and Heart out for a ride together? Will and Tania, you're welcome to come with us on two of the others?'

We know that isn't what she really wants. 'No, we're good thanks,' Tania says, 'I'll be washing my hair and Dad'll be painting his toenails.' We all laugh.

Cliff stops laughing when he notices the cat at Pamela's feet. 'He's been around for a year or two and he's never come anywhere near us.'

'He seems to have decided he likes me,' Pamela says and turns for the house. 'I wonder if he'll come inside.'

'I can tell you right now that he won't,' Cliff replies as we all follow her. 'He's probably got worms and fleas, and I have no intention of sharing my house with either.'

Tania and I grin at one another; he thinks he has a choice.

'Don't worry,' I say, 'I checked him over and he has neither.'

Cliff turns to me. 'Whose side are you on?'

'Believe it or not, yours,' I reply with a grin. 'He's claimed Pamela as his, which means you'll have a difficult job keeping him away from her. I just want you to be able to relax in the knowledge that he's the only visitor in your house – although to be honest, it'll soon be his house.'

Cliff puts his hands over his ears. 'I can't hear this.'

We reach the house and the cat stalks in at Pamela's side. She turns to Cliff and grins. 'Just think, we'll never have to worry about mice and rats coming in to the house from the yard…'

'Which wouldn't be there if he and the others were doing their job properly,' Cliff interrupts.

'…and he'll be company for me in the evenings when you're snoring your beer off in front of the television.' Pamela turns and winks at him as we file into the house behind her.

'What are you going to call him, Pamela?' Tania says.

'Why do I feel like I'm invisible?' Cliff says to me.

'Hmmm, let me see.' Pamela heads straight to the fridge and takes out four beers, which she passes around. When she hands Cliff his, she holds on to it and looks him straight in the eyes. 'Shield,' she says with a smile. 'The newest member of our family is called Shield.'

Cliff puts his free hand to his face and covers his eyes. 'I'm going to need more than one beer.'

'That cat is as relentless as the tide coming in,' Cliff says, rubbing his eyes as he appears in the kitchen. His hair is ruffled and he is unshaven.

Tania chuckles. 'I suppose we should be grateful you managed to get dressed this morning. Bad night?'

He squints at her. 'I've been walked on, jumped on, sat on, purred at…'

'And then the cat came in and made it all worse?' Tania says with a grin.

'…and he even sat on my chest to lick his arse at one point,' Cliff continues as if Tania hasn't interrupted. 'I put him outside three times and he found his way back in every single time. I don't know how, I closed windows, doors – he's unstoppable.'

Tania and I smile at one another, both immediately Aware that each time Cliff put Shield down outside, he immediately slunk back in before Cliff even had a chance to turn around. He's adept at using his stealth and colouring to enable him to be wherever he wants to be at nighttime, and from now on, that's with Pamela.

Pamela breezes into the kitchen. 'Morning, everyone. Ooh,

Tania, scrambled eggs, you're an angel. I slept so well last night, I'm raring to go this morning so you'd better do extra for me.'

'You can have my share,' Cliff says, eyeing Shield as he stalks in behind Pamela, his tail straight up in the air with just the tip wafting from side to side. 'Now that little beast is out of our bedroom, I'm going back to bed to get some sleep. Someone wake me before the first viewing?'

'Sure,' I tell his retreating back.

'What's happened?' Pamela says, also watching Cliff's departure.

'Shield's spent the night teaching Cliff the way the land lies now,' Tania says, 'and Cliff's a bit tired and grumpy.'

'I wasn't aware of a thing,' Pamela says, 'I don't think I've ever slept so well. What have you been up to, Shield?' She strokes his head as he sits on the kitchen table licking a front paw. 'I don't think we want you on there, shall I get you some food, huh?' She picks him up and carries him, purring, to the larder.

Tania grins at me as she spoons scrambled eggs onto the three rounds of toast I've just buttered. 'The pieces are all in place.'

I nod. 'Ready for this morning's lesson?'

'I was born ready.'

'No one can argue with that.'

TWELVE

Pamela
___

I have never been a cat person. I would never have wished one harm, I've just never had any interest in them. We always had dogs when I was growing up, and I missed them after I moved in with Cliff but he never let me have one. It was probably for the best – he would either have beaten it or driven it to bite him and the end result would have been the same – but for so long, I yearned for the feeling of safety, of protection that I always felt in the presence of the dogs with whom I grew up.

I never dreamt it possible to have anything like that feeling from a cat, and I don't, not really, it isn't the same. But I do feel something when Shield is near me, hence the name I've chosen for him. And he carries himself with an air of self-importance, of invincibility, as if he will always get what he wants and nothing bad can ever touch him, which almost makes me feel as if I should carry myself in the same way because he's chosen me as his.

I empty a tin of sardines onto a saucer and put it down for him to eat, which he does, hungrily but daintily.

'Your usual portion and your extra portion of scrambled eggs are on the table,' Tania says. 'Cliff was right, Shield is one beast of a cat.'

I smile as I sit at the table. 'He's a big beauty, isn't he? Wonderful, thanks, Tania. You didn't need to get up and do this, couldn't you sleep either?'

She smiles back. 'I slept fine, thanks. We're just always up with the dawn at home, so we're up with the dawn here too. You look so much better,' she adds. 'Who knew that all you needed in life was a bit of Zeal, a grey Shield and a very tall Cliff?'

I laugh with her and then say, 'I wonder if I should warn the others that you're on razor sharp form this morning.'

'And miss the fun of watching them discover it for themselves?' Will says.

'Good point. We'll get this down, then head outside and get the barn and paddock chores done before everyone arrives, shall we?'

'Already done, and all of the horses have been groomed except for Zeal and Heart, we knew you and Cliff would want to see to them,' Will says. 'And before you tell us how wonderful we are, I'll own up to the fact that we barely broke a sweat doing it.'

'That doesn't make you any less wonderful. I'm going to miss you like mad when you're not around. How long are you going to be here for, by the way?'

'A week or two longer should do it,' Will replies.

'Should do what, exactly?'

Tania grins. 'See you lot well on your way. Come on, eat up, your horse is waiting.'

I find myself doing as I'm told, not because I can't escape my lifelong habit of obedience, but because, as is so often the case when Will or Tania speak, it seems like we're having a parallel conversation, where the answer they give me is relevant not only to my question but to a whole lot more besides on which I can't quite put my finger.

The heat is already building when we step outdoors. I look around for Shield and catch a glimpse of him through the kitchen window, already curled up asleep on the kitchen table from which I have removed him several times. For a moment, I feel irritated but then I smile as I remember hearing Cliff describe him as being like the tide coming in. Shield may have claimed me, but he clearly answers to no one, which I find refreshing and also more than a little endearing. I hope Cliff comes to see it that way too.

By the time Zeal is gleaming in the morning sun, and all of the dust he rolled into his coat is stuck to the sweat pouring out of me, the first two trailers have arrived in the car park. I haven't got time to go inside for a shower, so I grab a sponge and douse myself with water from the trough.

I've decided to ride Zeal with tack on today, to see whether I can support him better if I have more support myself from sitting in a saddle, and whether, as Tania was suggesting to those using bridles yesterday, the reins will give me an extra way of receiving feedback as to Zeal's balance and the level of connection through his body. I've dried off a bit by the time Zeal is standing tacked up and ready for me to mount, so I waste no time in doing so.

We leave the eight new horses and Heart eating hay in the cool of the barn, and meander over to the car park where everyone is preparing their horses for our lesson. Interestingly, Jimmy, Sam, Sophie and Chloe have parked in one half of the car park, while Phil, Belinda and Clare are grouped in the other half. There isn't a huge gap between the vehicles of the two groups, but it's definitely there. Even more interestingly, Zeal heads for the section of fence on the other side of which Melody, Clicka and Maple are being tacked up, without me having asked him to. Or did I? Now I come to think of it, I would have headed for them had I been moving under my own steam.

Jimmy calls across the car park to Belinda, who laughs and is rewarded by Jimmy's laughter when she replies. Clare, whose trailer is closest to those of the "other side", asks Chloe a question and is immediately answered in a friendly tone. There is no animosity whatsoever between the two "sides", just an affinity between the four on one side and the three – four including me – on the other.

Tania stops to stroke Zeal's neck on her way past us to open the gate between the paddock and the car park. She grins up at me and says, 'It's all good. Go with it.' She's gone before I can ask her yet another question on which I can't yet put my finger.

I frown as someone I don't recognise jumps down from the cab of Sam's lorry, and another appears beside the ramp. My eye is caught by another stranger appearing from behind Clare's trailer, then by another sitting in the passenger seat of Belinda's car, and yet another with Sophie. All of the strangers help with the horses in the easy way that only those used to being around them can, which makes me smile. It's great that they've come to watch their friends ride, maybe they'll like what they see and bring their own horses here for lessons.

The three for whom I feel a stronger affinity are the first to mount and join me in the paddock, leaving Clare's two friends and the one who came with Belinda watching at the fence. I smile at the three observers, then at Belinda and Phil, and wave to Clare who is just behind them.

The four of us ride our horses to the centre of the paddock and form a circle. Immediately, we all put into practice everything Tania taught us yesterday so that we connect with our horses and begin to help them carry us more easily. I feel an even stronger affinity with the other three. I don't want to break my focus on Zeal to look around at the others, but I don't feel as if I need to; a sense of strength and determination seems to be hovering over us all.

'Okay, you four,' Tania calls out to us, 'move out onto a larger circle until there's enough space between your horse and the one in front for the others to slot in between you.'

I feel a momentary disappointment; I don't want whatever spell is connecting the four of us to be broken. I notice in my peripheral vision that none of the others are moving their horses out immediately either. I take a breath. Tania has got us to this point, we should do as she asks. I put my inside leg to Zeal's side and he moves away from it, making our section of the circle larger. Photon and Jimmy move into place in front of us, and immediately, the feel of the circle changes. It's as if our determination has been watered down with something much softer, yet, strangely, no less strong.

'All eight of your horses are looking so much better than this time yesterday,' Tania says. 'You've all connected with them, you're listening to them and you're responding to what you can feel, really well. Keep going. Keep adjusting your bodies in accordance with what your horses need in any given moment, and keep asking them to adjust theirs if you feel them starting to get heavy in front. I'll call out when I want you to change pace or direction, or if I have any small suggestions for any of you, so when I'm quiet it's because there's nothing happening that you can't figure out and adjust for yourselves.'

I'm glad Tania isn't going to throw anything new at us; my mind is everywhere at once as I try to figure out what is happening between the eight of us, whilst still keeping my connection with Zeal. What is this I'm feeling? Why am I feeling it? How am I feeling it?

'And trot, please,' Tania calls out. 'Remember to maintain your balance through the transition, and to support your horses so that they can keep their weight and yours off their forequarters as they increase their speed. Well done all of you. Now remember to use your legs and seat to keep your horses trotting in a rhythm slow enough that they can keep their balance, but fast enough that they don't drop into a walk. Lovely.'

It's hard work – and yet it isn't. The physical tasks with which my body is occupied are difficult and constant, yet they pale into insignificance as my connection with Zeal gradually strengthens. Every movement, every effort my body makes to support his is amplified infinitely by the power and strength of his response. I'm fascinated and absorbed and I feel… powerful.

'And canter now, please,' Tania calls out, 'all the time supporting your horses exactly as you have been. Perfect. Now focus on everything you feel. You've set your bodies to their tasks using thought, now trust them to carry on supporting your horses from instinct while your minds go where your horses can take them.'

Immediately, I get the same feeling as I did when it was just me, Phil, Belinda and Clare riding together. I'm stronger than I ever suspected I could be, and I'm determined, not just to ride my horse well, but to make a difference in a world that is slowly going mad. I don't need to be frightened anymore. I don't need to feel a victim of everything that is going on around me. I can decide for myself what is right and how I want to live my life, regardless of what anyone else is doing. Zeal picks up his speed a little and I sense that he agrees with me, that he is, as Tania said, taking my mind where it needs to go. He's in this with me. If I ever doubt who I am, how I need to be or what I need to do, all I need to do is find this connection with him and I'll know.

I look around at the others. Clare meets my eyes first and I know she feels the same way as I. Belinda's eyes are bright as she glances at me, confirming she does too. Phil's gaze is steady, confident, as he looks between the three of us while our horses continue to hold us together in our knowing. Without cue or signal, all four of us look around at the others, who all blink from the gazes they've been sharing with one another, and then look around at us. They're different. They have a different role from ours, but the two roles are connected as surely as the eight of us are connected to our horses and to one another. We all know it. We all feel it.

'Brilliant,' Tania says. 'Slow your horses back to a walk, retaining your connection with them, supporting them in every second until your feet are back in contact with the ground. Then give them all a big hug because they're every bit as wonderful as you know and even more amazing than you're beginning to suspect.'

Zeal is weary, I can feel it. He isn't used to carrying a rider's weight in the way I've been asking him to and while it leaves his body unstrained in the most important sense, he's using his muscles in a different way from before, which is tiring for him. They need time to build and strengthen in the same way as do the muscles of my own body and, I am quickly coming to believe, as does my mind.

I hug my horse before I dismount, and then again for some time afterward. Then I hug each of my friends, for that is who they are now. None of us speak because none of us know what to say.

Phil turns to Tania, who is standing with her thumbs hooked

into the top of her jodhpurs, watching us all, and opens his mouth
to say something, then shuts it again.

'When you can't think of the question you think you need to
ask, it's because deep down, you already know the answer,' Tania
says. 'Just keep riding your horses together – all eight of you – as
much as you can, and you'll find your way.'

We all find ourselves nodding at her in agreement about
something we don't understand. I swear that one day, I'll figure
out how she does that.

Tania turns and walks towards the car park, then holds the gate
open for the others and their horses to walk through. Immediately,
the five who have been watching their friends all jump down from
the fence and run, one to Clare, one to Belinda, two to Sam and
the last to Sophie. I smile at the excitement I can hear in their
voices as they congratulate their friends on what they just
achieved with their horses. Of course. They'll have been every bit
as affected by what they saw as Cliff was when he watched us
yesterday.

As I walk with Zeal to the water trough, a thought strikes me. I
stop in my tracks and look over at Tania, who is shutting the gate,
then at Will, who is removing the bar from across the barn
doorway so that the horses within can come out if they want to.
They knew. They knew that some of those coming for their lesson
this morning would bring friends who are looking for horses, and
they knew how those friends would be affected by our
connections with our horses, and what would happen as a result.

Will grins at me as five of the horses exit the barn at a trot,
leaving Heart and the other three calmly munching inside. 'It's a
good job some of the new horses arrived with their own tack, isn't
it?' he says. 'You'd be running really short otherwise, in fact, it
would be a good idea to buy a load more later when we've

finished with this lot. I can adjust them as necessary so that they're comfortable.'

I turn to watch the five who are now standing back at the fence, watching the horses cavorting around in the heat, and then look back at Will, my right eyebrow raised.

He grins and nods towards where Zeal is drinking from the trough. 'Come and give me a hand with five saddles and bridles when you've washed him down?'

I shake my head with a smile as I walk towards my horse.

When the trailers and lorries vacate the car park only an hour later, Sam's lorry carries two horses in addition to Hector, Clare's trailer carries the grey mare next to a flat-eared Maple, Belinda's Clicka is happily sharing her trailer with the bay gelding, and Sophie is also towing two horses instead of one. All of those who stayed when Phil, Jimmy and Chloe left with their horses, will be late for work. None of them care.

After having briefly ridden each of the five horses who burst out of the barn, Tania instructed the five slightly bewildered looking friends of my friends to each approach the horse to whom they felt drawn. I thought that was going a bit far even for Tania – I really thought all five would want the appaloosa – but each of the five walked alone to the horse of their choice.

Will quickly tacked the horses up and between him, Tania and me, we soon had all five astride their new horses. I've never been party to a viewing like it. Tania proceeded to give them all a lesson as if that was what they had come for, and they all went along with it with exactly the same attitude.

'Why are you so surprised?' Will asked me as we stood

watching them. 'You saw the effect the eight of you riding your horses together had on Cliff yesterday, is this so different?'

'I guess not, but Cliff is one man. There are five of them all behaving like... like... that.'

'They want for themselves what they saw, and what they felt when they were seeing it, it's as simple as that.'

'They're doing really well, but there's something missing, isn't there? It's not the same as when the eight of us ride together.'

Will grinned. 'When they come back for their lesson tomorrow, they'll be joined by the three who are coming to view the other three horses this evening. Then it will be.'

I could hardly believe it when all five riders offered me the full asking price for the horses they had just ridden. I can hardly believe it now, and keep looking down at the bank balance I've left showing on my wrist, hoping that at some point it will sink in that Tania has just sold five horses in less than an hour.

'I didn't sell them,' Tania says as we walk back to the barn. 'I just helped their people to recognise them.'

'You find the thought of selling horses distasteful.'

'Not distasteful so much as... untrue. You think you're selling horses when in fact, they choose who they go with, as Photon demonstrated yesterday. Your transfer of numbers on a screen is irrelevant to the process.'

I nod slowly. 'I see that, I think, but the transfer of numbers is hardly irrelevant, we all need to make a living.'

Tania nods. 'Money has a use until it doesn't.'

'You don't have money in your time?'

'No. We have something else. Soon, you will too and then you'll be happy to let those numbers on your wrist safe go to good use.'

'What is it that you have? That we'll have?'

'You won't believe it until you have it,' Tania says. 'For now, just focus on figuring out how you're going to keep a straight face when Cliff realises five of his horses are missing.'

I look over to the house to see Cliff hurrying out of the door, his shirt untucked and his hair standing on end. 'Cliff! We forgot to wake Cliff!'

Tania chuckles. 'I think he'll forgive us, in fact he'll be so happy, he'll forget how much he hates Shield for a few hours.'

The rest of the day passes by in a blur. When the celebrations about Tania having sold so many horses at once are over, Cliff and I set to scouring the internet for the next eight that Tania demands we find. When friends of the friends who bought the five horses earlier in the day arrive to view the remaining three, Cliff and I are content to view the goings on in the paddock from the house, only venturing outside when Will brings our new clients to transfer the money they are more than happy to pay.

By the early evening, we've arranged for six horses to be delivered the following day, however the remaining two need to be collected before the sun goes down in order for the deal Cliff has negotiated to stand. Cliff is adamant that he won't leave until he's had his evening session riding Heart, so we eat a light meal and then he heads out to the paddock with Will. He comes in an hour later, sweaty and smiling, downs a pint of water and then heads straight back out having barely noticed Shield curled up asleep around the fruit bowl on the kitchen worktop. He doesn't even comment about the large grey cat sharing my pillow when he crawls into bed in the middle of the night. He kisses my forehead, murmurs, 'Night, love,' and almost immediately begins to snore. I smile, feeling more content than I can ever remember having felt before.

The days that follow settle into a pattern. I take to rising with the dawn alongside Will and Tania, early though that is in the middle of summer. We head straight out to the horses – Zeal, Heart and however many horses we have in for sale – and I sort the hay racks and water trough while Will and Tania make dung and soiled straw fly through the air. I learn to scan my surroundings thoroughly before moving so I don't walk into a trail of dung on its way to the muck heap, and constantly marvel at the speed I have accepted it as a necessary thing to have to do.

My friends always arrive with plenty of time to get themselves and their horses ready for our riding session at six, during which our connections with our horses and one another steadily strengthen and solidify. Belinda, Phil, Clare and I always gravitate towards one another, as do the other four to each other, but when we ride together as a group of eight, there is a sense of completeness that none of us can explain.

By the time we've finished our session, the next eight to have bought horses from Cliff and me are in the car park, preparing their horses for their lesson together. Tania insisted from day one that I stand with her as she teaches the group, and as the days go by, she involves me more and more until I am teaching them, and the groups who follow as more and more friends of friends come to watch the lessons and either buy the horses we have for sale and agree to return for lessons, or arrange to bring those they already have.

Within ten days, I am out in the paddock all day teaching one group of eight horses and riders after another, happy to have my time paid for by the donations of those I am helping. The horses we can find to buy within a comfortable driving distance have reduced to a trickle, for which I'm relieved, as I've run out of hours in the day and space in the paddock to accommodate viewings.

'You're exactly where you need to be,' Will says over dinner one evening. 'You've got a decent pot of money behind you from all of the horses who've passed through here during the last few weeks, so you can just relax, teach and encourage those who come here to strengthen their connections with their horses, and improve their abilities to support their horses when they ride them. You've got a centre where people and their horses can come and have a great experience together, where friendships and connections have formed that will see all of you through anything life can throw at you.'

I find myself nodding along with everything he says.

Cliff leans back against his chair and rests the top of his beer bottle against his chin thoughtfully. 'I've watched it all go on around me,' he says. 'To start with, I didn't question anything because I was so happy to finally be making money, and because out of nowhere, I found myself happily married and riding again. Then, I didn't question anything because I was scared the bubble would burst, even though that bubble now contains a large and very obnoxious cat.' He squints at Will. 'I told you I'd ask you every day who you are, until you gave me a straight answer, but I haven't. You're talking as if you knew what you wanted to achieve here, and as if your job is done, so I'm asking you now. Who are you and your daughter? And while we're here, where are you from?'

Will grins. 'Like I told you when you asked me before, we're a father and daughter who've come from the distant future to help those who'll ensure the future exists.'

Cliff stares at him for some time. Eventually, he says, 'And you think those people are us?'

'We know you are,' Tania says.

Cliff is silent again. His voice is hoarse when he finally says, 'It's really that bad?'

'It's not really a case of being bad, more that things have become very unbalanced,' Will says. 'And everything is always trying to rebalance, whether that's bodies, populations, ecosystems or the world as a whole. Sometimes that rebalancing process is very uncomfortable, but it can be eased by those who see it for what it is and help others to move through it.'

My friends' faces flash through my mind. Phil's, Belinda's and Clare's appear first, smiling and strong, determination shining from their eyes. Their faces are joined by Jimmy's, Chloe's, Sam's and Sophie's, whose eyes are, without exception, soft, knowing and wise. I see them all with the horses from whom they've gained their sense of who they are and I know that Will is right. We have everything we need to see us through life and anything it can throw at us.

My eyes flick to Tania's. She smiles at me, knowing that I've just realised what it is that she and the people of the future use in place of money. Trust and cooperation are fickle in this messed up time of ours, but the horses have shown us that both can exist in a form that none of us could have fathomed without them. I trust my friends because we share a connection; to hurt one of them would be like hurting myself. I think of all of the groups I teach and know that the same connection exists within them, and because it does, it can exist between all of the groups of eight.

'You came here to build an army,' Cliff says.

'More of a resistance,' Will replies. 'For the human race to survive, there have to be some among you willing to resist the lies you're all being told about who you are, and hold on to the truth. Your horses have helped you to see that truth, and they'll give you the strength to hold on to it and to each other.'

I nod. I understand, I think. But I'm uneasy; when I pictured those who I knew would be at my side in the months and years to come, Cliff wasn't among them. I remember Will telling me that

Cliff will be instrumental to the process, but ultimately, he won't be involved.

Tania leans across me on the pretext of reaching for the salt. 'When your mind wants to worry, reach for the truth instead,' she whispers. 'You have everything you need.'

Cliff slams his beer bottle down on the table. 'Resistance, I like it, I'm in. We both are, aren't we, Pam?' I nod and try to smile.

'So is Shield,' Tania says. 'Cats can hold anything that isn't true away from you.'

'You're kidding, right?' Cliff says.

'Nope, he protects you while you sleep.' Tania selects a piece of carrot from her plate, puts it in her mouth and then gazes evenly at Cliff as if she's just confirmed that grass is green.

Cliff glances at Shield, who is lying upside down on the windowsill, snoring softly, then looks back at Tania as if willing her to laugh and admit her joke.

'That's the thing that trips you up?' she says. 'You've allowed two complete strangers to turn your business and your private life upside down, you have a horse you adore and will never sell however much you're offered for her, you've been told that we're from the future to incite you, your wife and all your newfound friends into rebellion, but it's the fact that cats can protect you that you can't accept?'

Cliff shakes his head and starts to laugh. We all join in, and by the time I've laughed until I've cried, I'm feeling better.

THIRTEEN

Tania

_I_ sit on the paddock fence and watch the original eight as they ride. Sometimes they ride alone as they work with their horses, sometimes they ride in pairs or small groups, and sometimes, without speaking, their horses feel their need and gravitate towards one another to form a large circle. The connections that flared into life between them all as a result of them connecting with their horses, are strong now. It's time for them to start helping Pamela to teach the students who bring their horses for lessons. Everything is in place for the members of the resistance to gain their strength and recognise one another as who they are.

None of the eight have any traces of grey in their energy now. That of Belinda, Clare, Phil and Pamela is nearly all red and orange with flares of blue, although Pamela's flares of indigo and violet are increasing in number and size.

The energy radiating from Jimmy, Chloe, Sam and Sophie is principally indigo and violet with flares of blue, green and pink.

When the eight take it in turns to teach the other seven groups of riders whose energy is likewise tending to either strong, determined red-orange or peaceful, intuitive indigo-violet, they will sense which of the riders have the same tendencies as themselves and which are like the other half of their own group, while the infinite energy of each group of eight powers those energies to gradually strengthen. When the time comes, all of them will have the strength of their horses and friends to sustain them and the energy to do what they will need to do.

Zeal heads in my direction and stops in front of me.

'You're leaving soon, aren't you?' Pamela says softly.

I smile at her even as her flares of violet energy condense into tendrils that probe at me; had she the time to achieve perfect balance with Zeal, her Awareness would be great. 'I'm afraid so.'

Pamela nods. She's trying not to cry. 'Will you... will you ever come back?'

'Absolutely. You won't need us for a while, but when you do, we'll be here. In the meantime, keep doing what you're doing. You're the glue that holds all of this together.'

'What about Cliff?'

I follow her gaze to where Cliff blazes with red energy streaked with orange as he watches the other seven riders. 'He needs you to be everything you are, just like everyone else does. You need him to be the force of nature he's capable of being. You're a perfect team.' I know that wasn't what she was asking, but she can't bring herself to ask the question whose answer she already knows but isn't ready to acknowledge.

'I'm going to miss you both. We both will,' Pamela says. 'Oh, and Shield will too.' The grey cat who checks on her constantly throughout the day walks along the fence rail until he's as close to her as he can get, then sits down. He stares at her, his green eyes perceiving both the energy she radiates and that which swirls around her. Satisfied that her connection with Zeal has strengthened the positive energy exuding from her and is keeping at bay the negative energy that constantly tries to pull her down, he sidles up to me and rubs his cheek up and down my arm.

'You'll be busy having the time of your life,' I tell her. 'By the time we come back, you'll be yearning for these days, so enjoy them.'

'You'll stay for dinner tonight?'

'Of course. We'll go tomorrow.'

I tiptoe along the landing to Dad's bedroom. He's awake and Aware of my approach, and opens the door so that I can step straight over the creaky floorboard.

They won't like this, he tells me.

It's after midnight. I told Pamela we'd be going today, and that's what we're doing. Tearful goodbyes won't help anyone. You're sure about going home? We could just hop to the time they need us next.

I'm completely sure about going home. Your mum hasn't seen us for weeks and she'll appreciate a little time with us to help her adjust to the direction your life has taken, and re-centre herself before we disappear again.

She can do all of that without us, she's already strong enough and it'll help her to be even stronger.

She can, but she doesn't have to because we can make it easier for her.

I sigh. *We're back to compassion over dispassion again. We've spent the last few weeks being completely objective, and look what we've achieved. Hurl a bit of emotion into the mix and we lose momentum.*

But gain in humanity, which is, after all, what this is all about,

Dad tells me. *Remember to reform in your bedroom so you can get dressed, you don't want to frighten the neighbours.*

Fine, see you there.

It's even easier than it was the last time. I focus on the part of myself that vibrates at the highest frequency, and speed up the energy that has been my body and clothes for the past few weeks, until it matches the rest of me. I sense Mum reaching out to me as part of her energy constantly has since I was born, and as more of her energy is now that she senses my intention to return.

I could reform shortly after I left, but that won't help her. She needs to experience her side of the events that are playing out as much as Dad and I, and everyone in the past, all do. I have a net of calming energy around her and all three dogs as I materialise in my bedroom where they are waiting for me, to help them cope with the sight of my slowly reforming body and prevent them from being moved to interfere with it before I'm ready.

The second I lift the net, all four of them are upon me. Mum reaches me first and manages to wrap a bath towel around me from my shoulders to my knees, but it isn't enough; the dogs' claws scratch my legs and neck as they knock me to the floor, even as their tongues lick the blood they liberate.

'It would have been easier to shut them out on the landing until I was dressed, wouldn't it?' I say, laughing as I stroke and cuddle the three dogs currently on top of me.

'And have them break the door down?' Mum says, grabbing one of my hands and trying to haul me to my feet. 'They knew you were coming as soon as you decided you were, just like I did. Thanks for waiting until I was awake.' When she finally manages to pull me upright, she rewraps me in the towel like she used to when I was little, then holds me at arm's length. *I've missed you so much.* She pulls me to her and hugs me tightly as if she never wants to let me go, which I'm Aware part of her doesn't.

Um, I'm back too, you know. Dad's thought has barely registered when the dogs stop jumping up at me and turn towards his bedroom, their noses twitching. All three bark with excitement and hurl themselves out of the door and along the landing.

You'll need a towel, I tell him, but his yells confirm that I'm too late. I heal his scratches as they form, while at the same time healing those the dogs inflicted on me.

I take it all in; Dad's laughter as he greets the dogs, and the love that bursts out of him, surrounding the dogs and drawing Mum to release me and go to him; the dogs' utter delight that the two missing members of their pack have returned, and confusion over which one of us to shower with their affections; Mum's relief at our return and the sense of completeness she feels; Delta's hurry to get dressed and race over here so she can see for herself that which she already knows; the remainder of my family's anticipation of seeing Dad and me at some point during the day once they sense Mum is ready to share us; the rest of Rockwood waking up and registering all of the thoughts hurtling around regarding Dad's and my return; the horses' Awareness that the two with whom they are most familiar are back when in truth, we never really left.

That which strikes me the most and holds my fascination above all else though, is my Awareness of the energy of The New. It eases its way through and among us all like the gentlest of breezes, caressing minds and easing away sorrows. I breathe in deeply and then breathe out all the way, feeling an unexpected relief at the respite from the waves of distress and aggression that have lashed at me constantly over the past few weeks.

There is a crash downstairs as the front door is hurled open with such force, it slams against the wall. Rebel barks and launches herself down the stairs.

'Rebelllllllllllllllll,' Delta shouts and welcomes her favourite of our dogs as Rebel jumps into her arms.

I pull on some clothes and hurry out onto the landing, closing the door to my parent's room so they can carry on their conversation in peace, before going downstairs. 'You nearly slammed the door off its hinges,' I say to Delta. 'Just because you have your dad's strength, doesn't mean you have to use it.'

My cousin's mouth drops open. *You're actually having a go at me after what you did? Disappearing into the night without so much as a goodbye? I'm your cousin and your closest friend, and you didn't tell me what you were going to do, where you were going, NOTHING!*

You're just annoyed you didn't figure it out. I reach the bottom of the stairs and turn towards the kitchen. *Come on, let's have breakfast.*

'That's it?' Delta says, lowering Rebel to the floor. 'That's all you have to say?'

'How about, if you hadn't already told me you have no intention of dropping your boundaries, I'd have taken you with me?'

'You'd have lost me. You nearly lost yourself. I may not have been able to take my Awareness to the past, but I was Aware of you and what you were up to the whole time, just like your mum was, and it was excruciating for both of us.'

'Well, you should both have more trust in me, and if you can't do that, then have more trust in the perfection of everything. I was nearly back to being physical by myself, and Dad arrived to help me with the last little bit.'

Delta grabs my arm and turns me to her. 'We aren't Aware of the future like you are now, Tan, how were we to know that the "perfection of everything" didn't entail you never coming back?'

'Trusting in the perfection of everything means that if I hadn't come back, it would have been perfect for me and everyone in my life, whether it felt like it or not,' I reply.

'That doesn't mean it wouldn't have hurt, why can't you understand that?' Delta says.

'I do understand that and I'd have reached out to you and helped you over the worst of your grief.'

Delta stamps her foot as if she's a child, and shouts, 'IF YOU'D LOST YOURSELF, AS YOU VERY NEARLY DID, YOU WOULDN'T HAVE BEEN ABLE TO!' Tears leak from her eyes and she wipes them away angrily as Rebel squeaks and runs back up the stairs.

'But I didn't, because of...'

'The perfection of it all, I KNOW! Just like I know that the fact I'm furious with you means every parent in Rockwood is currently scrambling to strengthen the shields they have around their children so that my temper doesn't floor them all, which is good practice for them, but it doesn't mean I'm happy to be causing them to have to do it!'

'You forgot to mention Rebel and how your shouting caused her to go upstairs and scratch at my parent's door so that they let Ash and Chase out, which is perfect because as it happens, Chase needs to pee,' I say, trying not to smile as Chase comes tearing down the stairs with the other two dogs close behind, and all three tear out of the open front door.

Delta bends down, hurls herself at my waist and throws me over her shoulder. She marches to the front door, her dad's strength allowing her to carry me easily whilst also restraining me so I don't wriggle out of her grip – not that I try very hard. By the time she dumps me in the middle of the street, I can't stop laughing.

For those who were planning to give Tania and her family space until later, Delta broadcasts to all in Rockwood, *don't worry about it, she's right outside her house and she'd love to see you all now, because it's the PERFECT time, isn't it, Tan?*

Faces appear at windows and a few doors open, but everyone is well Aware what is happening and no one comes outside. Light bursts from every cottage and settles around Delta. I add my own flow to those of the rest of the village, and Delta's fury visibly lessens. Her mouth twitches as I continue to laugh, but she wrestles with herself and straightens her face again. When it twitches again, she says, 'You're flaming impossible,' and starts to laugh with me.

'Can we have breakfast now?' I say.

She pulls me to her and hugs me. 'You can, I'm going home. Your mum needs time with you, I know that, I just needed to see with my own eyes that you're really here and you're really okay.' She releases me. 'Let me know when we can catch up properly. I got the gist of what you and your dad got up to, but there's so much I want to ask you.'

'Absolutely.' Delta turns to go but I catch hold of her hand. 'I missed you too, Del.'

She smiles and continues on her way.

Mum and Dad are waiting for me when I reach the front door. Dad grins and says, 'Of all my sisters, Prime had to fall for Ivy. With her dad's strength and her mum's temper, Delta could have hurled you as far as the paddocks.'

I chuckle. 'She's brilliant, isn't she? I wish she'd come with us, she could have taught Cliff to wrestle, he'd have loved that.'

'Happily for Ivy, Delta's intelligence tempers her Awareness and physical strength,' Mum says pointedly as she wraps an arm around me and draws me inside.

'Oh, Mum, not you too. I'm sorry you've had a hard time, but it wouldn't have been any easier had you known in advance I was going. I knew what I needed to do and I did it, just like you when you disobeyed your parents when they told you to keep barriers up against your Awareness.'

'That was very different, Tania, as you well know. I didn't risk my life.'

'Just your sense of smell,' I retort. 'How long was it you and the others went without washing again?'

She chuckles. 'I like to forget those details.' She guides me down the hallway to the kitchen and sits me down at the table as if I'm a frail old lady.

'You sit down too, love, I'll get breakfast,' Dad says.

Mum takes the chair next to mine. She takes both of my hands in hers and immediately picks up in her Awareness all of the details from the last few weeks of my life that she couldn't quite pick up while they were happening. She smiles at me. 'I'm more proud of you than I can say.' She glances at Dad. 'That goes for both of you.' Then she says to me. 'So, how long are you here for?'

Dad's thought is the merest hint, so thin, so refined, there are no words to it and even Mum doesn't pick it up, but I do and I understand. 'We'll stay as long as you'd like us to,' I say.

'And when you leave, what point in the past will you aim for?'

'We'll arrive at the point when they think everything's lost and they can't go on.'

I hold the details in my Awareness for Mum to pick up, and she shakes her head and sighs. 'I wish you could stop all of that from happening.'

'It needs to happen for everyone involved, you know that. Just like me and Dad going to help them move forward needs to happen.'

'Well, thank you for at least not telling me how perfect it is,' she says. 'If you had, I might have been tempted to ask Delta back here.'

I grin. 'I could have stopped her assaulting me any time I wanted, and you know it.'

She turns to Dad. 'How do we talk to our daughter now that she's even more infuriating than you are?'

He chuckles. 'When you figure it out, let me know.'

Once we've breakfasted, the three of us head out towards the pasture with our three dogs bouncing happily around us. A five-minute walk takes us nearly an hour as we're frequently stopped by our family and friends wanting to welcome Dad and me home. We both hold all of the details of our journey to the past at the very front of our Awareness, so that all those who haven't had the time or inclination to pick it up so far can do so within seconds. Those who don't tend to use their Awareness further than enjoying a sense of connection to All That Is or picking up where a delayed family member is and when they might be home, ask us questions which we answer in brief before continuing on our way.

When we catch our first glimpse of Ember's herd, Dad and I each let out a breath. We've had access to the horses the whole time we've been away, but as always, the physical sight and feel of a herd with perfect balance reminds us that we have it too. Any tiny irritations within us are drawn to the surface, where we release them and immediately feel better for it.

I sense Mum doing the same thing; now that Dad and I are back with her, she releases all of the concern to which she has been holding, even the tiny bit lodged deep within her that has steadfastly refused to budge when the rest was released on her twice daily visit to the herd.

Ember stands tall, watching our approach. I sense the love that swells within Dad for the horse who was Grandfather Jack's

Bond-Partner in his previous incarnation, and is one of Dad's most treasured companions in this. I also sense the moment when Ember is satisfied that we are all back in balance and need no further assistance beyond that which he and his herd have already provided. Dad's gratitude, and Mum's, radiate from them for the role the horses have adopted in the process, but the horses are just doing what they were born to do, like I am.

'Oh, to be young and so sure you know better than your parents,' a familiar voice says from behind me.

I turn around with a grin. 'Aunt Em, it's so good to see you.'

She smiles the smile that still looks slightly uncomfortable on her, and holds her arms out to me. I hug her as I've been moved to whenever I've been near her since I was a little girl, trying as always to draw the bits of herself to which she yet holds, to the surface, so that she can let them go. She is still a little rigid, but nowhere near as much as she used to be. The horses, and the rest of us who love her, will help her to forgive herself eventually.

'It's good to see you too,' she says in my ear. 'It would be even better were you to accept that your superior Awareness may be as much of a hindrance to you as a help, as your parents have repeatedly tried to tell you. It would also be a blessing to us all were you to admit that although you're Aware of your own future, you choose to focus on the bits that interest you, and ignore the bits that don't. In that respect, you're exactly the same as every other young adult who has ever lived.'

I pull back from her and laugh. 'I love you, Aunt Em.'

She tries to look as stern and formidable as she did when she led the Elite of Supreme City, but the wrinkles at the corners of her purple eyes deepen and she smiles. *I love you too, little one.*

Mum hugs her and then Dad holds his arms out to her. 'It's great to see you, Eminent, it's been too long.'

'Is it my fault you decided to leave us all at The Gathering and move back here as soon as Tania hit double figures, then hardly ever visit?' she replies as she hugs him. 'Some of us don't have horses who show up whenever we need a lift somewhere, you know. If only you'd consider building a few roads and transport vehicles.' She winks at him in imitation of the mannerism that irritated her so much when he was her prisoner, and we all laugh.

She winks again, this time at me. 'I'm still better at it than you.'

'So, you're a poor old lady who still can't accept that walking is good for the body and soul, but you can wink – sort of. Congratulations,' I retort with a grin. 'And don't pretend you're here just to see us when we're all well Aware you knew Ember was here, and decided to sow two seeds with one shake of the hand.'

She laughs. 'I'm glad to see you're every bit as worthy a sparring partner for me as you've always been. Everyone else at The Gathering has gone soft.'

'Even Sovereign?' Mum says.

Aunt Em brings the latest goings on at The Gathering to the forefront of her mind so that Mum can catch up with that which Dad and I already know.

'He's taken in a litter of wild cats?' Mum says.

Aunt Em nods. 'He was forced to kill their mother when she attacked him. He sensed her triplets were nearby so he gathered them up and brought them home. He's going to release them when he's confident they can fend for themselves, but I know him, he'll be living out on the plains for months so as to be close by if they need him. Look how he was with Guide's litter of pups, it was hellish getting him to let them go after he hand-reared them when Guide was so poorly.'

The soft thud of hooves causes Aunt Em to turn at Ember's approach. Her eyes light up and her body visibly softens. 'Hello, beautiful,' she says and reaches a hand out to him. 'You're looking as old as I feel. What are you still doing running around with all the youngsters?' She senses the nerve of Dad's that she's just hit at the same time as does Ember.

They both stare at Dad, Ember's orange eyes every bit as intense as Aunt Em's purple ones. Ember blinks and Dad releases his momentary hurt.

Aunt Em takes hold of one of Dad's hands. 'I'm sorry.' A glint appears in her eyes. 'You know, if I'd had any inkling how much of a weak spot this horse is for you, I'd have had you grovelling in the dirt at my feet when we first met.'

Dad grins. 'Keep telling yourself that. You'll stay with us?'

'No, I'll stay with Amarilla and Justin. You three need time alone together, and I need the discomfort of having Infinity glaring at me; I'm worried I might be going as soft as Sovereign.'

If the lie would serve her, I'd keep quiet, but it won't. 'You're worried you'll never be as soft as Sovereign, and you want Infinity to tell you how to let go of the bits you can't admit are still there, while Ember's here to help you cope with the fallout,' I say. 'Well I can tell you all that, I'm every bit as blunt as Infinity.'

Mum and Dad both chuckle. 'It's true, they're pretty evenly matched,' Mum says.

Aunt Em nods. 'Absolutely, but if I'm going to open myself up to hearing things I really don't want to hear, it'll be easier to do with a discarnate horse than with a young woman who also doesn't hear things she doesn't want to hear.'

'Ouch.' I start laughing. 'I've missed you.'

She chuckles. 'I've missed you too, but I'm still not staying with you.'

Chase, Ash and Rebel choose that moment to return from the circuits they've been running around the horses, and launch themselves at Aunt Em.

'Oh, for goodness' sake,' she says, fending them off, 'I see you still don't hold with teaching your dogs to have any sense of decorum.'

'Where would be the fun in that?' Dad says, and pats his leg. 'Here.' All three dogs leave Aunt Em and sit at his feet. He jumps up and lands with his hands on his knees. 'That's my pups!' They all leap on him and he and they go down in a heap of arms, legs and fur.

I link my arm through Aunt Em's. 'We'll just leave them there, come on, let's get you to Am's.' I turn my head and call over my shoulder, 'I'll be back in a bit.' I sense Mum instinctively reaching after me but I carry on my way, knowing that she's centred and will be fine without me for a bit.

'So, what's news at The Gathering?' I ask Aunt Em.

'As if you aren't already fully Aware that we're full to the rafters. I really thought it would just end up being the final few of us who were the top Elite when so many of the others came to terms with themselves and left to build homes of their own in the surrounding villages, but then those who stayed got married and had families, others came and we now have a thriving community, if one that is a little sad to be growing crops in paddocks where horses used to be. Your parents knew that would happen, we know that now, that was why they moved back here despite our pleading with them to stay. We'll always be grateful to them for everything they did to help us get on our feet. And to you, for teaching some of us that children can be bearable, even if you've grown out of it.'

'Eminent! Hey, Eminent!' We turn to see Ace hurrying to catch up with us, dragging Victor with her. 'We didn't sense your approach.'

'You didn't sense my approach because I hid it from you,' Aunt Em says haughtily, 'to prevent just such a scene as is about to ensue.' Ace ignores her and hugs her while Aunt Em holds her arms stiffly at her sides.

Victor hugs me and then says to Ace, 'I told you, if either Tania or Eminent wanted our company right now, they'd have let us know.'

'We could have been waiting for days,' Ace says, releasing Aunt Em while telling her, 'I've been telling you for months, you're too bony. Now you're here, you need to stay with Will's gran, she'll sort you out.'

I try to keep a straight face as Aunt Em sucks in her cheeks, her eyes flashing.

'It's no good looking at me like that,' Ace says, 'it's been more than twenty years since I was scared of you. She's too thin, isn't she, Vic? Tan?'

'You truly are the bane of my life,' Aunt Em tells her. 'Not content to boss me around at home, you presume to do it here. Victor, take your wife away from me before I throttle her. Tania, please accompany me to your great-aunt's house, where I'll be for the duration of my stay.'

Victor mouths, 'Sorry,' at me and Aunt Em, then says to Ace, 'Come on, we said we'd help Prime and Ivy.'

'No we didn't.'

'Well, I did.'

'Then you can go and help them while I accompany Tania and Eminent. Tan, what were you thinking, by the way, disappearing in the middle of the night when Vic and I had only just got here?' She puts her arm through mine and starts walking. 'Never mind, we forgive you, especially after everything you pulled off, you and your dad.' I sense her fondness for Dad when she thinks of him, and Victor's that flares to life a second later.

'Delta wasn't quite so forgiving, was she?' Victor says with a chuckle as he trails the two of us and Aunt Em. 'You and she are your fathers' daughters, Tania.'

I grin. 'Delta's fine. Here we are at Am and Justin's, so we'll see you both later.'

'Yes, you will,' Victor says firmly. 'Come on, Ace, we've gatecrashed long enough.'

'Dismissed by someone we've known since she was in nappies,' Ace says, but allows herself to be led away, calling, 'I'll let Mailen know you're here, Eminent, she'll be round before the day is out with those cakes you like.'

Aunt Em rolls her eyes and tuts.

'Why do you pretend you don't like her fussing over you when we're all Aware you do?' I say. 'And yes, it's a rhetorical question. I'll leave it to Infinity to sort out.'

Amarilla opens her front door before we've reached it and looks from one of us to the other with her and Infinity's eyes. She hugs me first and then releases me with a smile. 'Off you go.' I turn to obey her as she hugs Aunt Em, saying, 'Come on in, I've got the kettle on.'

I practically skip back down her front path. As Am was Aware, the horses are waiting.

FOURTEEN

Will

———

*L*ia and I sit on the same grassy slope upon which we sat with Tania when she was a toddler, watching the teenagers of Supreme City ride their horses before Victor returned there to let Eminent and the rest of the Elite know it was safe for them to come above ground. Now, we watch Ember and his herd grazing peacefully as we wait for Tania to return.

'It seems like a lifetime ago,' Lia says, picking up on my thoughts. 'Even knowing Tania would be capable of so much, I never dreamt for a moment that she'd be capable of doing what she's done. Or that you would. I really thought you'd pushed the limits of what humans can do as far as they could go.'

'So did I until I picked up what she and I would do.'

Lia sighs as Tania appears and approaches the herd. 'I have to stop seeing her as a child, I know it, I have to trust her like the horses do.'

We both smile as we sense our daughter's joy at being with horses of The New, all perfectly balanced and as unencumbered by life as she is. They would tolerate no one else skipping among them as she is now, arms outstretched and twirling around as she soaks up everything they are and welcomes their energy as her own. They tolerate her because she is one of them. Because in her previous incarnation, she truly was one of them.

I knew it as soon as she was born. I've never shared the information with anyone, not even Lia, because if anyone should, it should be Tania herself. She's known from the moment I stopped shielding her from the past. She's also known that her challenge in this incarnation is to bring everything of the horses to the human experience, to lead us all forward by breaking down the limitations we still put upon ourselves – whilst being human. She's never needed any help with the first part of her challenge, but she isn't quite there with the second.

She chose Lia and me as her parents before she incarnated, in part because it would mean that Amarilla and Infinity would be part of her life and when she needed extra help, it would always be there, and it has been; it was the main reason I wanted to move back to Rockwood when Tania was ten and really challenging the shields that Lia and I had in place around her Awareness.

Infinity has given my daughter the support of the horses and Amarilla the support of one who knows what it's like to be different. Between the two of them, they've helped to soothe Tania's soul when she's been thrashing around within the human constraints she chose for herself this time around, reminding her by their very existence that a horse can learn to look out of the eyes of a human, and easing her into her role as a young woman.

One moment, Tania is on her own two feet, the next she's on the back of one of Ember's daughters; she senses the restlessness of the youngsters of the herd after weeks of relative inactivity, and their need to run is now hers. There is no one Ember trusts more than one who was a lead mare in her previous incarnation, to take his offspring in the opposite direction from where the chestnut stallion who covets his herd grazes just out of eyesight. Ember and the older mares of the herd watch passively as the rest tear off behind Tania and the black filly who carries her.

Their pounding of hooves is heard by many in the village, the pounding of their hearts is felt by the rest. Heads poke out of windows and doors fly open as villagers run to watch the horses and Tania gallop by. When they are almost out of sight, the horses turn a large circle and head back towards all of us who are watching and feeling their power and delight. When they reach the pasture, the horses slow as one to a trot. They separate and spread out around the grassland before slowing further and dropping their heads to graze.

It isn't just Lia and I who let out long, relaxed breaths; the whole of Rockwood does too, any small concerns or niggles having been drawn away from us all and blown into the ether by the horses' might.

Tania slides down from the black filly's back and rubs the horse's fur where she was sitting. Then she slowly wanders among the rest of the herd, enjoying the physical proximity of those with whom she has such an affinity. Eventually, she wanders up to where Lia and I are sitting, and squashes herself in between us as she used to do when she was little.

None of us speak, all of us content to watch the horses, to feel their power and peace, to enjoy the feeling with which the antics of Tania and the younger horses have left us. By the time we get to our feet several hours later, our growling stomachs having reminded us that it is lunchtime, everything feels easy again.

Tania and I stay in Rockwood for five days. We both feel the past pulling at us to return as the imbalance that we can help to correct

calls to us with an ever increasing urgency, but we also feel the
influence of Ember's herd as the horses' energy constantly
reminds us to not leave imbalance behind us when we leave. Lia
needs a little more time with us, as do the rest of our family, Delta
in particular.

We spend time with all of them, most of it sitting in various
spots on the slope Lia and I have always favoured, looking down
on the horses who occasionally work their way up to us and graze
all around us.

'Will you both be coming back?' my mother asks me as I sit
with her, my father, Amarilla, Prime and Victor one afternoon,
watching Ember and two of his mares grazing around our feet. I'm
at the end of the line in which we're sitting, and all five heads tilt
forward and sideways so that they can see me as I answer the
question everyone has been wondering, but so far, no one has
dared to ask either me or Tania.

'We'll be returning to the past at a volatile time, but it's
nothing we can't handle,' I reply.

'That wasn't what your mother asked, son,' my father says.
His hair may be completely white now, but his eyes are as bright
and as piercing a blue as ever.

Infinity comes to my rescue. *Whichever answer he gives will
act as a distraction from the present. He is wise to give neither.*

*My son and granddaughter being surrounded by the violence
of the past will be a distraction from the present anyway, how can
it not be?* my mother fires back. No one speaks. Eventually, my
mother says, 'Sorry, it's just that when you went off to deal with
the people of Supreme City, Will, we all knew exactly what was
happening, we could follow it in our Awareness, and we were able
to help you when it became necessary. I can't be Aware of the
past, only of you and Tania. When you both went back before, I
could only follow what most of your attention was on at any given

time, I couldn't sense what was happening around you, I couldn't
step in to help if either of you needed it... I felt helpless, and I'm
going to feel helpless when you go back again. At least if I know
you're both coming back, I won't worry so much, and neither will
Lia.'

Or you could choose to not worry regardless, Infinity persists.
*You could choose to trust Will, Tania and me that everything will
happen as it should.*

Ember nuzzles my mother's foot, drawing to the surface the
concern she has felt and released over and over. She releases it
again and sighs. She puts her arm around me and pulls me to her.
'I'm sorry, it's just tough being a mother sometimes.'

'It's not always easy being a father either,' Prime says ruefully.
'Delta's not going to be easy to live with when Tania goes off
without her again.'

Victor chuckles. 'Don't worry, Ivy's already asked me and Ace
to stick around a bit longer for moral support, but I really don't
think it's Delta you need to worry about, she'll be a breeze
compared to Mailen.'

Prime groans. 'I'm going to get it from both sides.'

Victor grins at me. 'I would never have dreamt that the lad
who tried to kill you, Will, would be so scared of his daughter and
second mother.'

'It's interesting, isn't it,' Amarilla says while feeding a handful
of grass to one of the mares, 'that a family whose members have
played such a major part in helping everyone else to be centred, is
having such trouble managing it now that a new dimension has
been added to our lives.'

Everyone falls silent.

Eventually, my mother says, 'That's all it is, isn't it? Change.
We've all become comfortable with how we are, and now we're
uncomfortable because we're being moved on again.' She slaps

my father's knee. 'Jack, we have work to do. We need to refocus ourselves and when Will and Tania go back, we'll shake Levitsson loose from his armchair, and all of us will work to help people bring their Awareness of Will and Tania into their daily lives instead of allowing what they can't be Aware of to distract them. Lia can help us, and so, Prime and Victor, can you, Ivy and Ace, and come to that, Delta can roll her sleeves up too.' *Lia, are you in?*

I sense my wife pause her conversation with Tania over what to have for dinner, and catch up with the conversation into which my mother has just brought her. She is as quick as was my mother to understand the situation once it is pointed out to her, and just as quick to make her decision. *Absolutely. Thanks, Kat. You too, Am.*

When the evening comes, and Tania and the young horses of the herd once again shake loose any lingering concerns held by the villagers for the two of their members who will once again disappear into the past, it is for the last time.

All of our family come to the pasture to see us off.

'You don't want a quick shower before you go? You're all sweaty from riding,' Lia says to Tania, picking our daughter's hair away from her sweaty forehead.

Tania rolls her eyes. 'I can leave the dirt and sweat here, Mum.'

'Nice,' Delta says. 'Come here, I want a hug, sweat and all.'

Tania and I hug our way through all of her cousins, my sisters and their partners, my parents, Am and Justin, my grandparents – with whom we pause so that Gran can make her customary scene – Eminent, who is considered family, and lastly, Lia.

'Go with our daughter, and know that I and the rest of your family will be fine,' Lia says. 'I love you, Will.' She pushes me. 'Go.'

'I love you too,' I tell her with a grin. 'Consider me going.'

I step back and hold Tania's outstretched hand. We both wave to our family and then as I sense my daughter willing the energy that comprises her body to speed up, Maverick's echo darts between Lia's and my mother's legs and then comes to sit in front of me, panting. We will protect our pack. I speed up my body's energy until it vibrates at the same speed as that of my soul.

There is a gasp as my and Tania's bodies become indistinct and then disappear.

FIFTEEN

Pamela

I lean back against the tree upon whose roots I'm sitting, and sip my tea. The steam coming off it makes it look hotter than it is; the cold, spring air of dawn has cooled it rapidly. I pull the zip of my coat right up to my chin and wiggle my fingers until they have fully retreated up the sleeves of my coat and I have to clasp my mug between my fists.

I love to be out here at this time of day; I love to watch the horses grazing or pulling hay from the racks attached to the fence at intervals. I love to hear them snort and whicker to one another. I love to see those who have taken shelter in the barn emerge, blinking, with straw in their manes and tails, and kick up their heels before joining the horses who are eating or at rest. I've loved to do it ever since Will and Tania showed me that dawn is the best time to rise and greet each new day.

If only they could see us now. I look past the horses who now fill not only our original paddock but the huge adjoining field we hired and then bought, to the high rise apartment blocks that now surround us on all sides. Our fields are the only green space left around here now. The only space, period. So far, we have been allowed to keep our land because we have provided boarding for the horses of our students whose homes, land or yards were seized so that the high rises, food factories, and the road network that serves them all with automated passenger vehicles, could be built. I wonder though, as I do every morning, how long we can hold out before they close us down, take our land, and force us into the same sterile, heavily regulated lifestyles as everyone else now living in the high rises.

Safety and comfort. It's all we hear from the newscasters on every radio station and on every screen in every home and now on the outside of many buildings. We're constantly assured that the twenty-foot wall being built around what we're told is our "super city", will ensure our safety once it is finished, as it almost is, but I don't think it has anything to do with keeping unspecified dangers out, it's more to do with keeping us in; if we can't escape, we can be more easily controlled.

It's not enough that our movements are constantly tracked by our wrist safes, there are now eye scanners in every passenger vehicle and at the entrance to every building. Cliff envisages a time in the future when the governors will have everyone so assimilated into the regime that money will no longer be deemed necessary, and they won't bother enforcing the implantation of wrist safes to track everyone's locations at every minute of every day; the buildings and vehicles of the city will do it for them.

I pour my remaining half mug of tea onto the ground. It isn't even tea. It tastes a bit like the tea I used to love, and the caffeine hit is the same, but it comes in granules, not leaves, from one of the city's food factories. I try not to think what I put in my mouth these days, like I try not to think what will happen to the horses we've all tried so hard to keep safe, if we lose our land. Even if we don't, the last of the hay we managed to get hold of before the winter will run out in a few weeks' time.

I've sat here, morning after morning for weeks, willing the grass to grow so that the horses will have enough to eat, and judging by the fact that so many horses are grazing instead of eating hay this morning, I think we might just have made it far enough into spring to be okay. I can't think any further forward than that; I can't think about what will happen if we have another drought this summer, or even if we don't, how we will get more than sixty horses through next winter with no hay coming in from outside of the wall and no land available on which to grow our own.

Zeal wanders in my direction and as always, my heart lifts at the sight of him, at the feel of him close by. He has to be affected by the huge buildings looming over him, by the smells and sounds of so many human beings living on top of one another as well as on top of him; if I, as a human, am, he just has to be. But he never shows it. His eyes are as full of vitality, of fervour as ever. He stops in front of me and turns to the side. He wants me to ride him.

I get to my feet and glance around at the apartment blocks again, feeling hundreds of eyes on me. I nod to myself. Clare was telling me only the other day how the wallscreen in her bedroom has begun waking her with a shrill trilling sound through which it is impossible to sleep, then announcing in a robotic voice that it is time for her to get up. The horses and I must be a strange contrast to everything else that those around us see and experience during their day. How long before someone informs on us? Accuses us of resistance or rebellion for the simple act of being with our horses? Zeal stamps a foot.

I stroke his neck. 'Sorry. Okay, I'm with you.' I vault onto his back and immediately, all of my thoughts and worries are forgotten. I focus on his body and what it needs from mine, and on staying with him as he weaves between the other horses at increasing speed. When we pass Heart, she falls in behind us. Others join her and soon we have half of the herd following in our wake as we canter around the field. The remainder of the horses raise their heads, ears pricked, and begin to move.

Exhilaration. Strength. Focus. We feel all of those things, the horses and I. The dark powerhouse that is Photon tears past us and takes the lead. He was an impressive looking horse when he arrived at our yard four years ago, but he's magnificent now. Jimmy still rides him every day as well as teaching any of the other riders who ask for his help, and the other six who found their horses on the day I found Zeal do the same. We, and all of those whose horses reside with ours, are firm in our belief that we are the only ones in the city who are still sane, and we know it is our horses whom we have to thank for it.

As the other horses fall away from us, their excitement satisfied, I smile, knowing – feeling – that I've come back to the version of myself who is focused on fulfilling my mission, and knowing that everything will be alright because Zeal thinks it will be. I know it in the same way that I've known so much else about him in the past, but have never been able to explain to myself. I also know, in exactly the same way, that it isn't just me who has been affected by the horses; those watching our spin around the field from their apartments also feel a sense of strength where before they felt only weakness and exhaustion.

Zeal comes to a halt and I lean forward along his neck and hug him, thanking him for all he is to me. He takes me back to the tree – one of only around twenty left in the whole city – from which he took me, and against which Cliff is now leaning, grinning at me.

'Showing off to the neighbours so early in the day?' he says.

I return his grin and dismount. 'Don't blame me, it was Zeal's idea.'

Cliff kisses me on the cheek. 'No one's blaming anyone, that was a sight to behold and a sound to revere, sixty-five sets of hooves pounding life into the ground of this miserable place. It'll have reverberated off those high rises and have those idiot police cowering in doorways.'

My heart plummets. 'You don't think it'll bring any of them here?'

Cliff chuckles. 'They aren't bright enough to figure out what caused it, they're probably scanning their radar screens for UFOs. Hello, that looks like Phil heading our way, it's early for him.'

Melody lifts her head and whinnies, confirming that the figure in the distance is indeed Phil.

I don't know what we'd have done without him during the past few years. He's continued to work for his family, who still all but own the government, while insinuating those few who are loyal to him into key positions and feeding information and warnings to all of us who form the resistance-in-waiting, as Cliff likes to call all who keep our horses – and our sanity – here.

He warned Sam that his family had been reported for holding back some of their food rations in order to help a friend on restricted rations following an "infraction". By the time police raided Sam's home, there was no trace of any surplus food. It didn't stop the family being "rehomed to more suitable accommodation" in an apartment block, their home being razed to the ground and its plot added to those dotted around whose owners had suffered a similar fate, but it did prevent any beatings, imprisonments or worse.

When Sophie's dad was arrested for complaining at his car being taken once the automated passenger vehicles were in use, it was Phil's people who somehow managed to engineer his early release.

It was only because Melody was here that we avoided being shut down once the land grabbing intensified, and because those who have moved their horses here since were all warned to do so before their horses' former residences were seized. Phil has repeatedly argued – and on many occasions threatened – on our behalf, and as a result, our horses have helped us to grow steadily stronger.

Cliff is right though, it's early for Phil to be here. He's usually here after work on weekdays, and late in the morning at weekends. It's Saturday today. Something is wrong.

I gasp as a weight lands on my shoulder. 'Shield, how long have you been up there?' I look up into the branches of the tree in case any more of our half dozen cats are also planning to try to scare the life out of me. The large, grey cat is alone. I rub his head. 'I should've known you wouldn't be far away.'

His warmth comforts me as much as his soft fur against my cheek. He purrs in my ear as Cliff says, 'The others are arriving too. Phil's obviously got word to them to come here where they can't be overheard. Come on, we'd better go and meet them.'

I pick up my mug, wincing as Shield's claws pierce my shirt and coat as he attempts to keep his balance, and hurry after my husband.

Phil raises both hands and pushes them at us. I stop in my tracks, feeling as if ice cold water has been poured over me. 'He wants us to stay here.'

'So, we've been bugged too now,' Cliff says. 'Bastards, how the hell did they pull that off? It must have been one of our students.'

I shake my head emphatically. 'No. None of them would do

that to the rest of us, let alone risk the only place all of our horses are safe. Absolutely not.'

'So then, they must have sneaked around while we were asleep,' Cliff says.

My heart turns over at the thought of black-clothed and helmeted police creeping around us, our horses and our cats while Cliff and I were in bed.

'If we're bugged, then we're in trouble,' I say, my legs feeling as if they're made of jelly. I grab hold of Cliff's arm and he puts his hand on mine. Shield purrs in my ear again and rubs his cheek against mine. I take a breath and turn around to see Zeal watching me, and remember how I felt only minutes ago. Everything will be okay. I bite my lip and lift my chin.

Cliff and I watch as Phil stops off at the barn and then re-emerges a few minutes later carrying Melody's tack and grooming kit. He lifts his saddle up slightly until Chloe lifts a hand in acknowledgement of his silent instruction for the rest of them to also get their horses' gear, then continues on towards us.

'So, there are cameras here too,' Cliff breathes.

Immediately, I remember the uncomfortable, prickly feeling down the back of my neck that started when I walked into the kitchen to make my tea this morning, and remained until I was well past the barn. 'There's one on the corner of the barn,' I say. 'We're out of view here.'

Cliff frowns. 'How do you know?'

I rub my neck. 'I can feel it. They aren't watching us here, but there's definitely a camera in the kitchen and another on the barn that covers where Phil is now. There were loads of people watching me and the horses from the apartment blocks this morning, but I felt okay with it. When I was in view of the cameras, I felt far from okay. Whoever's watching us is evil, Cliff.'

He shudders and it isn't from fear. I recognise the red spreading up his neck to his face only too well.

'Calm down, love,' I tell him. 'We'll need clear heads to deal with whatever it is that Phil's here to tell us.' I squeeze his arm. 'Please, calm down.'

He clenches his jaw and nods curtly. 'Let's see what the lad has to say.'

Phil smiles a forced smile as he reaches us. 'We'll talk while we groom the horses,' he says between his teeth, 'then if anyone's watching us from the high rises, we're just doing what we normally do when we're out here.'

'Whoever might see us from over there is nothing compared to the ones watching us through the cameras,' I say, turning to walk at his side.

'It will only take one informer to fast track the wheels that are already in motion, and that can't happen before we've had a chance to talk, so humour me, okay?' Phil says. His smile is genuine when Melody trots over to him, tossing her head. 'I know, you're beautiful,' he tells her, laying his bridle over his saddle so he has a spare hand with which to stroke her.

He reaches the fence and dumps his tack atop it, then puts a headcollar on Melody and loops it over his arm as he begins to brush her.

'Can I borrow one of your brushes for Zeal?' I say, and he hands one to me. I wander over to where Zeal is grazing and put my hand under his chin. He obliges my request to lift his head and walk at my side, and by the time we reach Phil and Melody, the rest of our group are converging on the same spot with their horses, having also left their tack on the fence nearby.

'You have bad news for us,' Clare says. 'Are they coming to give notice that they're taking the land? Are we going to have to beg places for the horses elsewhere?'

'Are we going to have to split up our group and move the horses to different yards miles away?' Sam says.

'I'm afraid it's worse than that,' Phil says. 'They're coming for the horses.'

It has been minutes and still no one has been able to speak; I imagine everyone else's throats have all suddenly gone as dry as mine, and their brains to mush, as we all fail to allow ourselves to fully comprehend what Phil has just said.

I can hardly hear for the blood pounding around in my head, and I have to steady myself against Zeal so I don't collapse. Shield rubs his cheek against mine and Zeal turns around to look at me, his pale brown eyes boring through me as if willing the person he has been cultivating to come out and meet him head on. I can't let him down now.

'Why are they...' My voice falters. I swallow and try again. 'Why are they coming for the horses? What do they want them for?'

'They don't want them for anything, that's the point,' Phil says as he continues to brush Melody's coat. 'They see them as dangerous animals who've served a purpose in keeping a small proportion of the population occupied and out of trouble, but whose presence in the city is now no longer needed or wanted. The last block was put into place in the wall last night, so they're coming to drive the horses outside the city walls, where they'll be left to fend for themselves.' He pauses, then clears his throat and continues, 'Once they've dealt with the horses, they'll start rounding up all of the other animals they're calling "dangerous and unpredictable drains on resources". All pets will be outside the city gates by the end of the week.

'I'm here to tell you to ride your horses for the last time and then to let them take them when they get here later this morning. If you don't, they won't just arrest or beat you, they'll shoot you dead and then they'll take the horses anyway. They'll make an example of anyone who protests, even me, so that those with dogs, cats, birds, reptiles, whatever, will let them be taken without a fuss.'

'They'll take the horses over my dead body,' Cliff says.

'And mine,' Belinda says, her arm around Clicka's neck.

'That goes for me too,' Clare says, setting her mouth in a firm line.

'I can't deal with this,' Sam says, his voice trembling.

Chloe lets out a sob from where she's buried her face in Minerva's mane.

'Chloe, you have to behave normally in case there are watchers in the apartments,' Phil says. 'No one can know we're having this conversation, these plans have been kept even from me. It's only because I have an informant in the right place that I found out in time to warn you all to listen to me, believe me, and then ride your horses until you're calm enough to accept it.'

'No one's watching us at the moment,' Chloe says with a sniffle. 'I'd feel it, I always know when I'm being watched.'

'She's right,' Sam says. 'I know when I'm being watched too, and we're okay for now.' He clears his throat to hide his own sob, and is suddenly very busy brushing Hector.

'We can't let them be taken, they'll die,' Sophie says, combing Pebble's mane with a shaking hand.

Jimmy stops brushing Photon and covers his face with his hands.

'No one is taking anyone,' Cliff says firmly.

'Yes they are, we can't stop them,' Phil says. 'We'll find a way to fight this, just not today. Today, we spend as much time as we can with our horses, we let them help us to feel as strong as they always do, and then we let them go.'

Cliff's shoulders shudder and he sounds as if he's choking. He turns and heads for where Heart is grazing nearby.

'Do you have any idea how we could begin to fight this, Phil?' I say. 'Maybe if we could form a plan to hold on to, if we could create some hope that we might get them back, we'll be able to get through this?'

'We're not going to be able to fight it,' Jimmy says from behind his hands. Photon nuzzles his knuckles until he lets them fall away from his face to reveal bloodshot, tear-filled eyes. 'Not and win, anyway. When has anyone ever managed to do that?'

Zeal puts his nose into my hand and wiggles his upper lip on my palm. A warm, steady feeling of resolve slowly spreads through my body.

'We aren't anyone,' I say. 'We've all been chosen by horses who know we can resist the craziness that surrounds us, and who have worked hard to ensure it. They've prepared us for this and we won't let them down. Phil's right, we'll fight this, just not today.'

'But how will the horses survive? What will they eat, how will they find water?' Sophie says.

'They'll eat grass, leaves, herbs, just like they always have,' I say, knowing deep down that I'm speaking the truth. 'They'll scent water and they'll find it. It's spring, the grass is starting to grow and it's getting warmer. The horses will have what they need.'

'Except us,' Chloe sobs, 'they won't have us and we won't have them.'

'Until we find a way to make that happen,' I say firmly. 'And we will. For now though, we need to do as Phil says. Our only hope of helping our horses and one another is to stay alive.'

I look around at my friends. They all stare unblinkingly, unseeingly, back at me.

The eight of us and Cliff spread out when we ride, all of us wanting our own space to be with our horses. Zeal is as strong and forward going as always as he weaves his way between the rest of the herd at speed, forcing me to concentrate on him to the exclusion of all else. The sense of purpose that has always been magnified in his presence swells within me. This is it. It's time for me to be as strong and determined as he's shown me I can be.

I won't let you down, Zeal, I think to him, *and I'll make sure the others hold to everything their horses have shown them.* I think I feel a sense of satisfaction from him, or maybe it was just my imagination.

I don't want my last ride on Zeal to ever end. My body matches his effortlessly when he's choosing where we go, and his matches mine in return when I take over the decisions from time to time. It's as if we were born to be together, as if we were always going to find one another and experience this connection, this blending of souls.

It is only due to the depth of that connection that, when I see others beginning to arrive, I find the strength to ask Zeal to stop and allow me to dismount so that I can join Phil, Belinda, Clare and Cliff in greeting the newcomers as if we haven't a care in the world… and then watch the blood drain from their faces as we give them the news.

Jimmy, Sophie, Chloe and Sam need longer with their horses, the rest of us know that. Where we're all far more sensitive than we were to our horses and everything going on around us, those four have taken it to a much higher level, as have the students they tend to teach. When I begin to have a sense of something, Jimmy's lot already know it for sure. Where I have a deep connection with my horse and often know what he's feeling, Jimmy's lot know that constantly. But their level of sensitivity is all of them; they don't seem to have room for the resourcefulness and determination that those of us who are less sensitive have. So, we've learnt to look out for them and their horses.

We've schemed and fought for supplies so that the horses have had everything they've needed, and they've shared with us when their horses have brought up something new from which we can all learn. It has worked, and it has to carry on working, this love we all have for one another and the cooperation between the two distinct bands that have formed within our number, because one thing is for sure – we have been cultivated to be this way by the horses, and that means we are all necessary to one another if we are to survive.

I smile at each and every one of our students as they arrive anxious to learn why the message they received was necessary. Phil set the message system up several years ago once most of our number were living in the high rises and more closely watched, but we've never had to use it until now. On his way here, he delivered a typed invitation to come to the yard by midmorning, to the first person on the list below the message, and that person passed it to the next as they also made their way here. It has meant that everyone will arrive in a slow, surreptitious stream rather than all at once, and it gives us a chance to blend them in with everyone else while we explain what is happening.

By the time the last person has arrived, had a meltdown, been consoled and is astride their horse, the initial group of us are exhausted.

But we can't be. My insides clench together and exude a surge of strength. I hurry to the barn and make nine mugs of tea, which I carry back out to the field on a tray. I catch Cliff's eye and then those of the other seven, and tilt my head back imperceptibly, drawing them to me.

'This is the nightmare none of us have allowed ourselves to dream, I'm not going to pretend it isn't,' I say as I hand their mugs to them. 'But we're prepared. We all have our strengths and weaknesses, which is the sign of an amazing team. Those of us who are more sensitive can provide an extra level of information to the rest of us if necessary, but will need to take our strength in order to get through this. To that end, we're going to need to pair up.'

I look at Chloe, who is so pale, her skin is almost grey. 'I'll be right beside you at all times, Chloe.' I nod to Jimmy. 'Phil will be with you. Listen to him, lean on him, take his strength.' I glance at Phil, who nods. 'Sophie, Clare will take care of you, and Belinda will be with Sam.' Clare and Belinda both nod their agreement. 'I'm guessing we don't have long, so quickly then, there are seven other groups of eight, and the four of us,' I glance at Clare, Belinda and Phil, 'need to each take our partner and work our way around the other groups so that their members are paired up in the same way we are before the police get here. Then each pair needs to take up a place around the outside of the field, so that none of us can be tempted to obstruct either the police or the, um, the horses as they, um…' I gulp and blink away the tears that are trying to form. 'Or the horses as they leave,' I finally manage to say. I clap my hands before anyone can react or respond. 'Go now. Quickly.'

We all drain our mugs and then eight of us hurry off to arrange everyone into pairs while Cliff carries the tray of mugs back to the barn. I breathe a sigh of relief that he has made no more mention of resisting.

All sixty-five of us spend time stroking our horses, walking with them, standing with hands on withers as they graze, talking to them, trying to find the words to tell them how much they mean to us, how grateful we are for the time we've had with them, and how sorry we are that we'll be letting them down.

When I hear sirens in the distance, I allow my tears to flow, and wrap a handful of Zeal's mane around my hand and hold on tightly as if that will be enough to stop him being torn away from me. As the sirens get closer, I drop all but a few hairs, which I gently pull free from my horse, and wrap back around my hand.

'I have to leave you now, my beautiful boy,' I whisper to him through my tears. 'I'm sorry, so, so sorry for what's about to happen. You stay alive out there, you hear me, because I'll find a way to get to you, I promise.' He nuzzles my back as I hug his neck, unable to let go.

'Pam, they're nearly here,' Cliff says in my ear. 'You have to get yourself and Chloe to the fence, out of harm's way. Come on now, let go of him.'

I feel a traitor for allowing myself to be gently pulled away from my horse. I want to stand in front of him so he can't leave, but Cliff turns me towards Chloe, who has all but collapsed against Minerva. Her breathing is erratic and she's trembling so violently, it's a wonder she's still standing. I run to her and pull her off Minerva and into my arms, and hold her tightly.

'Chloe, we have to move, come on, I've got you.' I look back at Cliff, who nods and tries to smile. He flicks his fingers, shooing me towards the fence, and I go, taking Chloe with me.

By the time the police vans – the only vehicles now not restricted to rails and still driven by people – screech into the car park, we have all somehow managed to find the strength to tear ourselves away from our horses, and are arranged in pairs around the perimeter of the field. Many of the sensitive members of each pair are sitting with their foreheads resting on their knees or against their partners' chests, backs or shoulders, others have their hands over their eyes so that they don't have to watch the nightmare that is about to play out in front of them. The rest of us stand strong.

I count everyone in order to check that none have sneaked down to the barn with the intention of hindering the police in any way. Sixty-four including Chloe and me. My heart lurches. Where's Cliff? He was right behind me only a few minutes ago. I scan the fence line again for his tall frame. He's definitely not here.

Movement catches my eye as Cliff walks into the gap between the barn and the fence that separates our original paddock from the field in which we and the horses are all standing, watching as the first black-clothed police come into sight. My husband turns to face the police, and lifts something to his shoulder.

My blood turns cold in my veins. He has a gun.

'Where the hell has he been hiding that?' Phil hisses from where he is standing with Jimmy a little further along the fence.

I shake my head. 'I don't know. I thought we'd surrendered all the guns we had, he must have got hold of that one since.'

'The idiot! Pamela, don't you go to him, you can't, we need you. Chloe needs you.'

I stop and retrace the step I have just taken. Chloe is sitting in the grass, rocking backward and forward and whimpering. I drop into a crouch, put my arms around her and cover her ears. 'We can't just leave him there, we have to talk him down or he'll die,' I say over her head. 'Phil, do something.'

Phil shoots a glance at his hand resting on Jimmy's shoulder. Our friend is staring unseeingly into the distance while tears pour down his face. 'I can't,' he says in a firm, low voice.

I nod; of course he can't. I look back to Cliff just as a shot rings out across the fields. My husband crumples to the ground.

The sound of the shot reverberates off the surrounding high rises, and the horses gather into a single mass and gallop around, unsure where to go as the sound pounds at them from all sides.

I watch them as if I'm removed from the situation, as if I'm half watching them on the television whilst doing something else. All I can hear are the words my husband spoke only a few hours ago. 'They'll take the horses over my dead body.' He wasn't just reacting to Phil's news, he was stating a fact, and I should have known. I should have known that he would have been terrified of reverting to the man he was without Heart. I should have known that he would never have been able to live with himself if he hadn't at least tried to protect us all and the horses. I should have known he would do this. I made sure that everyone was paired up with someone who could protect them, except for my own husband.

I fall to my knees next to Chloe as the police stream into fields on quad bikes they no doubt liberated from the thousands of farms they ruined, still watching it as if it isn't happening for real.

The bikes tear around the outside of the field up to us at the far end, and get behind the herd. Then they race back and forth behind the horses, herding them towards the barn. Melody and Pebble break away with a few others and gallop back towards us. Out of the corner of my eye, I see Phil stiffen and take a step forward. Jimmy groans and Phil stands still, looking down at Jimmy and then back at his horse.

Three quad bikes cut the escapees off and herd them back to the others.

'NOOOOOOOOOOOOOO!' Phil's yell carries everything within it that we all feel but are too numb to express. He turns and punches the fence post, then kicks it repeatedly.

I reach behind me for a fence rail and pull myself to my feet on shaking legs. I can see Zeal. He's galloping next to Heart, with

Minerva on his other side. I feel his strength as if he is beneath me, carrying me as he so often has. As he still is, I realise as I begin to fight my way through my shock and come back to myself. I only have to think of him and I feel everything he has instilled in me.

None of us move as the horses disappear from sight. We all stare at the spot where we last saw them as we listen to the clatter of their hooves on the road, heading towards the city gates. Eventually, there is silence.

SIXTEEN

Tania

I am ready for the energy of The Old this time, and as I materialise in the barn, I hold firmly to my idea of myself as an individual, to my memories of my parents, our dogs, the horses, my life. I push light out and around myself until I am solid and not so susceptible to the negative energy that tries to insinuate itself into mine, then maintain a shield of it just under my skin. I roll my eyes at Dad as he holds on to Maverick while reaching protectively out to me until he is also solid.

You don't need me and Maverick to be able to keep a hold of yourself, you just think you do, I told you before, I tell him.

Yes, you did, he replies. He watches Maverick's echo fade and then as grief and fury continue to assail us both, he too pulls his light back to just underneath his skin so that it is invisible to all but me. He glances at me. *Perfect timing.*

Of course.

We wait until the sound of machines chasing horses down the road has faded to nothing, then walk out of the barn. As soon as we turn for the fields from which much of the pain we can sense is emanating, we come across Cliff's body lying in the grass. It's too late for us to do anything for him. As Dad said, perfect timing.

You'll look after them? Cliff's thought is as faint as the echo of him standing next to his body, watching Pamela and the others race towards his body.

They'll be fine, Dad tells him.

After everything I've put Pam through, I didn't want to cause her any more pain, Cliff says, *but I've gone and done it anyway. Them taking our horses was the last straw and I couldn't just stand there and let them do it with no resistance whatsoever, but now I've left my wife on her own to deal with everything.*

She isn't on her own, she has everyone here and she has the two of us, Dad replies. *You've played the part you were meant to, Cliff, you've shown Pamela what she needed to see. You can check in on them all whenever you want to, but you need to let go and move on now; the Sensitives among them will pick up on your presence and so will Pamela, and that will distract them all from what they need to do.*

We both resonate our energy with his and give him our love. He fades away and is gone.

'Where the hell have you two been?' Pamela cries as she bears down on us. 'You could have helped, you could have stopped it, you could have... done... something.' She pounds on Dad's chest with her last few words, and he lets her. Then he supports her as her legs give way and she lands in the grass beside her husband. 'No, no, no, no, no,' she wails, stroking his forehead. 'This should never have happened, you should still be here with us. With me.' Shield appears and pushes his head under her arm.

I sense the herd energy, which the horses shifted towards their people to give them the strength to stay out of the way as they were being taken, shifting back to the horses themselves as they are chased out of the city gates. All of the Sensitives slump, their indigo and violet energy pulsing as they sense the same thing I do, without knowing exactly what it is they sense.

'Your horses have left the city,' I say loudly. 'There's grass out there, loads of it, actually, it's growing throughout the area that was cleared to allow the necessary vehicles and machinery to the wall while it was being built. Heart has already scented water. They'll be alright, they just need to focus on themselves for a little while as they come to terms with their new surroundings.'

I look around at them all. Many of those whose energy is now predominantly red and orange are propping up the indigo-violets.

'How do you know they've left?' one of the red-oranges says, glaring at me.

'She knows it because it's true,' an indigo-violet replies miserably. 'I didn't know what it was that I was sensing, but now Tania's said it out loud, I know it was that.'

'Like Pamela said,' Belinda says, glaring at Dad and me, 'where the hell have you been, you two who know everything? You turned all of us into different people like it's something you do every day, and you could have done the same to those police, you could have made them different so they just went away and left our horses alone, but you didn't. You turn up now Cliff's... Cliff's dead and the horses have gone, and calmly announce that the horses are fine and we just need to get a grip and let them get on with it?' She's practically spitting at me. 'What if any of them get injured? What then?'

All eyes flick between Dad and me. Those of the red-oranges challenge us to answer Belinda's questions while those of the indigo-violets are haunted, beaten.

'If any of the horses get ill or injured, I'll heal them,' I say calmly.

Clare lifts her hands and slaps them down hard against her thighs as she leans towards me. 'How the hell are you going to do that? In case you haven't noticed, there's a huge frigging wall around the city. We're trapped inside it and the horses are now trapped outside it.'

'Dad and I aren't trapped,' I say, 'and we'll find a way for you all to get out to see your horses.'

Sophie's eyes brighten a little. 'You're telling the truth, I can feel it, but I don't understand.'

'You'll never be able to get out, let alone help us to do it,' Phil says. 'I know how the wall has been built, it's unscalable and impenetrable.'

Dad grins. 'The engineers who designed the wall made it impregnable according to the laws they believe are true. Tania and I operate according to different laws.'

Pamela's head shoots up, her eyes full of hope. 'So then, you can bring Cliff back?'

Dad crouches down beside her and takes her hand, giving her a burst of light. 'He's already moved on, Pamela. He's let go of his life here. It's up to you now.'

She straightens her back and stares at Dad and then at me, all the while trying to gather her strength. She shifts her focus to Zeal and immediately burns red and orange. 'What do we need to do?' she says, her lips trembling.

'You can't be serious, Pamela,' a red-orange says. 'You're asking them for advice after they disappear for, what's it been? Four years? Then turn up out of nowhere within minutes of everything they started having gone to crap?'

'Has it though?' I say.

Tania, what you're about to say may be what they need to hear in the long run but it isn't what they need right now.

They'll process it later even if they can't hear it now, I tell Dad, at the same time continuing out loud, 'Your belief in good and bad, right and wrong, is limiting the abilities your horses have instilled in you. They've spent the past four years showing you who you are and what you're capable of. The time has come to put everything you've learnt to use.'

'In case you haven't noticed,' another red-orange says, 'Cliff was a big part of everything we've achieved here – everything you started. He and Pamela gave us all a place to come and be with our horses, a place where we could store our sanity and keep it safe so that when the rest of our friends and family were behaving like lunatics, we had somewhere to come and remind ourselves that we don't have to be like them. The man we all love is lying dead at your feet and you haven't even looked at him.' His voice breaks. 'You tell us there's no such thing as good and bad, right and wrong? What the hell do you know?'

'What does it matter?' an indigo-violet says miserably, looking up at the corner of the barn. 'There's a camera up there. With all this talk of rebellion, they'll be coming for us all now. By this evening, we won't be in a position to worry about anything anymore.'

'The cameras aren't working, Dad and I disabled them,' I say. 'They'll be here very soon to fix them though, in the hope of recording exactly the sort of conversation we're having, so we need to be quick.'

Tan... Dad warns again.

We don't have time for compassion, Dad, you know that as well as I do.

We don't have time to be without it. They're grieving for their horses and for the father figure they've just lost.

They took their horses' guidance without ever being indulged in unhelpful emotion.

But we're human and we need to be relatable as such, otherwise they won't let us help them.

No time. 'You all need to go home now,' I say to everyone. 'We'll be in touch very soon, but for now you need to go.'

'We can't leave Pamela and Cliff here alone,' Clare says.

'You can and you must,' I reply. 'Dad and I will help Pamela.'

'By acting as if her husband hasn't just been murdered in front of her?' Belinda spits. 'Come on, Phil, Sam, Jimmy, you too, Lloyd, we'll carry Cliff to the house.'

Before I can reply, Dad says, 'Cliff was a very brave man. He resisted the current regime here as much as he could without putting all of you and your horses at risk. He fought for you to be able to spend as much time as possible with your horses because he knew this day would come. He and Pamela gave your horses the time to make sure you all have the abilities necessary to continue resisting the regime, to keep the best aspects of human nature safe until the regime eventually falls. His loss has hit all of you very hard and I'm so sorry that you're all in so much pain at the moment, but please, go home before the authorities get here. Don't let everything Cliff fought so hard for go to waste.'

Pamela stands up unsteadily, takes the arm Dad offers her, and looks around. 'Please, do as Will says. He and Tania will stay here and help me, but what will help me more is knowing you're all safe. We'll be in touch very soon. Keep a low profile, don't contact one another unless you absolutely have to, and know that I'll be thinking of each and every one of you. Go now, hurry.'

Phil glares at Dad and me, then bends down and puts his hand over Cliff's heart. He hugs Pamela and then turns to the others. 'Do as she says, everyone, come on, quickly.'

One by one, the others follow his example and then hurry away, many of the indigo-violets supported by red-oranges. I send subtle, almost invisible flows of light to settle over them from behind, until the Sensitives can walk by themselves. Some of them sense the light and turn to look at me in consternation before hastening onward. Most are too grief-stricken to be aware of anything besides the memories they are playing over and over in their minds of Cliff being shot and the horses disappearing. When the red-oranges turn to check that Pamela is really okay with them leaving, they all scowl at me before hurrying on their way.

I have created anger and mistrust, as Dad warned me I would. In coming here to help correct a large imbalance, I have created many smaller ones. It's frustrating. Humans are frustrating. Yet they're also perfect, as is this whole situation. I will be more compassionate. I will say what those around me need to hear in order to accept my help.

'Pamela, I'm sorry for your loss,' I say to her as she sways on her feet, clutching Dad's arm in order to remain on them. 'Cliff was a strong partner for you and I know you'll miss him greatly.' She is stiff in my arms as I hug her. When I step back, she stares at me.

She knows you don't feel for her. Dad tells me as if I don't know. *You accept her husband's passing as being the perfect part of the process it is and your focus is on helping her to use the situation to continue moving forward towards balance. But she won't accept your help unless she knows you feel sorrow that she's in pain.*

But I'm not sorry. Cliff's soul left how and when it did for a very good reason and one day very soon, she'll see it that way too.

Not if we can't reach her right now, she won't. You already know what you need to do to fix this.

He's right. It doesn't mean I like the fact. I incarnated as a human in order to bring more of my previous incarnations' ways of being into the human experience – in order to sweep aside even more of the limitations in which humans believe than Dad and Am have already done. But I have resisted certain aspects of being human, preferring to focus on those with which I am familiar. It hasn't mattered up until now; the people of The New accept me as I am. But in The Old, my resistance is creating resistance in return, as is always the way. There is an imbalance calling for immediate correction, and that imbalance is within me.

I focus on my body in all of its complexity, all the way down to my DNA. I sense which genes are being blocked by my refusal to fully embrace my human personality, and I withdraw the blocks. I am here as a human. Attempting to navigate this incarnation without living it through the lens of humanity is missing the point of my current incarnation, and will cause me to forsake my purpose.

I look at Pamela who is crying silently as she stares down at her husband's body. While her soul is as focused and determined as always, her personality is in a great deal of pain. Instead of immediately placing her grief into the perspective of the bigger picture, I stay with it until I understand. My face takes on an expression that is new to me.

Pamela has only blinked twice since my failed attempt at compassion. She blinks again when I put my hand on her arm and say, in a much softer voice than usual, 'Cliff loved you very much and I know how much you loved him in return. I'm so very sorry he's gone. Dad and I will do our best to help you through this.'

Pamela attempts to smile. 'Thank you, Tania.'

Way to go, Tan, Dad tells me. *Look after her now, I'll do what I can to make this next bit a little less upsetting for her.*

I sense his intention and gently take Pamela's arm. 'Kneel down with me,' I say to her as Dad hurries towards the car park. When Pamela does so, I continue, 'Now that the police have secured the gates behind the horses, some of them are coming back for Cliff. Say everything you need to say to him before they get here, okay?' Pamela nods miserably. I know she has things to say that are private, so I add, 'I'll wait just over there. I'll know when you need me and then I'll be right back here, okay?'

Pamela blows her nose and nods again. She takes one of Cliff's hands in hers and kisses it. Her whispers follow me as I walk away, watching the two black vans that have just pulled into the car park.

Dad strides over to the nearest van, his hand outstretched as the driver gets out. I sense the light he sends the man as he introduces himself and requests that Pamela is given a few minutes before Cliff is taken away. I feel the man's need to demonstrate his command of the situation receding from Dad's light, and his slight confusion and consternation as he finds himself nodding along with Dad's request.

I pick a few spring flowers, chuckling to myself as Dad goes on to show enthusiastic interest in the man's vehicle, to which the man responds with a loud explanation about how it's one of only a few now remaining, and launches into a detailed explanation of its features.

I feel the pain of Pamela's final goodbye as if it were my own and am back at her side within seconds. I gently lay the flowers I've picked on Cliff's chest and then help Pamela to her feet. Shield rubs his face up and down one of her legs, purring loudly. I pick him up and hand him to her. 'Come on, let's get the two of you inside.'

She looks back at Cliff. 'I can't believe this is happening. They'll cremate him and chuck his ashes out with the rubbish because he died resisting them.' She stands up straighter. 'I won't let them take him. This is still our land.' Her voice breaks and she whispers, 'My land.'

I want to tell her that they won't be taking Cliff for he's already left of his own accord – that they'll just be taking his body. I feel slightly strange that I don't, even as I say instead, 'I understand how you feel, I really do, but if you resist they'll kill you too. Cliff would have wanted you to live on, to continue what you both started here, you know he would.'

Pamela looks over at the men now all chatting animatedly to Dad in the car park. She clenches her jaw and narrows her eyes as fury courses through her.

I pull her closer to me so that she can't race over and scream at them as she wants to. 'Don't focus on how much you hate them,' I tell her. 'Focus on how much you loved Cliff and how much you love your friends and the horses. Find your strength.'

'Zeal,' she whispers, vitality surging through her again as she pictures her horse in her mind's eye. Her eyes take on the passion, the focus of the skewbald gelding's. She clenches her jaw again and then breathes out a long breath. 'Okay, let's go to the house.' She walks at my side without looking back.

Pamela and I are sitting, sipping tea at the kitchen table when Dad comes in holding two sheets of paper. He puts them down on the side and joins us at the table.

'They've taken him?' Pamela whispers, clutching her mug so hard, her fingers are white.

Dad nods and flicks a glance up to the camera I've already confirmed to Pamela is there. 'They have. I know it won't help much, but they were respectful.'

Pamela stares at him and we both sense the questions she wants to ask.

'You need to eat,' Dad tells her. 'We all do. Then we'll go for a walk around the fields, shall we?'

Pamela twists in her chair, ready to get up, but I hold a hand out to her as I get to my feet. 'We'll do it. Sit there, and we'll have a nice bowl of steaming soup in front of you in no time.'

She slumps back in her chair but I feel the anger that arises in her at the thought of being monitored in her own house. She remains silent as Dad and I prepare soup and slice a loaf of bread into big chunks, Aware that two engineers are currently scratching their heads outside as to why the camera on the corner of the barn is now working perfectly.

We eat in silence and then I clear away and wash up our bowls, plates and mugs. The men have gone by the time we wander outside into the sunny but chilly spring afternoon. Pamela chokes as she takes in the sight of the empty paddock, barn and fields beyond.

I put my arm around her and whisper, 'All of the horses are okay. You'll be able to see them soon. Keep walking.'

We continue to the spot where Cliff fell and where Dad has placed the flowers I picked. I sense Pamela's grief swell within her and it is some time before she takes the first step towards the field.

When we're clear of the barn, Dad says, 'You want to ask why I let them take him when I could have stopped them, and you want to know why Tania and I arrived back here at the exact moment we did. You already know the answers to both questions, Pamela.'

She walks between us in silence, every pile of dung over which she is forced to step evoking more grief within her, distracting her until she thinks of Zeal and refocuses herself.

Eventually, she says, 'You let them take him because if I'd buried him here, he would just have been dug up when they take the land off me, which judging by the paperwork you brought into the kitchen with you, will be soon.'

She is quiet again for a time and then says, 'The last time you came, you brought change with you. You've come to do it again.

You started us all off on the path that's led us here, and now you're back to show us where we need to go next.'

Dad nods. 'Exactly. You're the glue that holds your friends together. You're strong and determined enough to lead those with the same energy as you, and you're gentle and intuitive enough to lead those who are more sensitive.'

'Those with the same energy as me?' Pamela says, then realises she knows exactly what Dad means. 'Phil, Belinda, Clare… all of the others – lead them? You can't be serious, I'm no leader, it should be Cliff sitting here, not me.'

'Zeal chose you, not Cliff,' I say quietly.

Pamela's love for her horse swells and recedes continually as her grief for his and Cliff's losses battles for predominance. Eventually, all of her emotions combine. 'When can I see my horse? How can I see him? How will it even be possible?'

'When you can see him really depends on how soon you can organise your kindred spirits to cheat the system,' I reply. 'And it's possible because like I said before, Dad and I don't hold with all of the physical laws that most believe in.' Aware that no one in the surrounding buildings is watching, I speed up the vibration of my body's energy and say, 'I'll see you later, I'm off to visit the Sensitives.'

You could have warned her, Tan. Dad tells me as I disappear. His reprimand is rendered pointless by the amusement with which it is accompanied.

You know as well as I do that she wouldn't have believed it until she saw it. She has hope now she's seen for herself what we can do.

Take care.

You too.

I sense when Jimmy is in his apartment alone, and reform in his grey-tiled bathroom, knowing he's watching his wallscreen in the living room. It's a two-way screen that watches and listens as well as broadcasts, but it can only do that if it's operational. I disable it and walk into the living room.

The grey-carpeted floor is littered with a multitude of rugs of all different colours and the white walls are covered in pictures and family photos dating back many generations; Jimmy's parents have tried to inject personality and soul into an apartment designed to be devoid of both.

Jimmy's pale face manages to lose what little colour it had when he sees me. 'Tania! What are you doing here?' He glances back to the now blank screen, his eyes full of terror. His grief has opened him back up to the fear and anxiety that his connection with Photon allowed him to hold at a distance, and the energy of The Old is revelling in having reclaimed one who was lost to it.

'Don't worry, they can't see or hear us,' I tell him, 'the screen's temporarily out of order in both directions. I'll fix it before I go and no one will be any the wiser. I'm here to help you.'

'It's been two days,' he whispers. 'Two days since they took Photon. Since Cliff died. You said you'd be in touch with us all soon, but it's been two whole days. I can't eat, I can't sleep, I can't go to work – they'll be coming for me soon, I'll be arrested for passive resistance, I know that but I still can't do anything or go anywhere, I'm a mess.'

'I couldn't come until you were alone,' I say. 'Now that the weekend's over and your parents are back at work, we can talk.'

'How did you even get in here?' Jimmy says. 'You're not a resident of this apartment block, you shouldn't have got past the eye scanner at the entrance, let alone the one by our front door.'

I smile at him. 'I didn't use any doors. I'll show you how I got in here when I leave, but for now, we need to focus on you. You're feeling the way you are because you've lost your connection with Photon. I'm here to help you get it back.'

Jimmy's eyes fill with hope. 'You'll take me to him?' Hope is once again clouded by terror. 'No, I can't leave here, I can't. I can't face everything that's out there. I felt so well, so strong when I had Photon, but my strength has gone.'

'No it hasn't,' I say. 'It's still there, you just have to find it.'

His eyes flick between mine. Where before he would have known I was telling him the truth, now he feels nothing except the fear that roils around the apartment, the whole block of apartments and all of those that surround it.

'I know that at the moment, you can't feel everything you used to feel, but you know me,' I say. 'You know I care about you and you know I care about Photon. Let me help you find your connection with him, let me help you find the person he made you into.' I sit on the low table in front of him and hold my hands out to him. 'You can do this, Jimmy.'

He takes my hands in his trembling ones. I send him a burst of light through our physical connection, and then expand it so that it surrounds him. He tightens his hold on me as he stares around himself, then his grasp gradually loosens until it is more comfortable.

'That's good, now close your eyes just like you did when you first rode Photon,' I say. 'Brilliant, now take yourself back to when you last rode him. Feel him moving beneath you. Take your time... that's good. Now feel the connection you had with him. Feel him right there with you in every moment. Now reach out to him through that connection until you know he's with you as surely as you know I am.'

Colour fills Jimmy's face as a broad smile spreads across it. 'Photon?' he whispers. 'Is that really you?'

You have found me where I will always be.

Jimmy's eyes fly open. He sits motionless, barely breathing as he wonders if what just happened can possibly have done, and scared that even if it did, he won't be able to make it happen again.

I grin. 'You just heard Photon in your mind for the first time, Jimmy, it really happened. All you need to do is maintain your connection with him and you'll be able to communicate with him whenever you want to.'

Immediately, Jimmy focuses on his horse. *Photon, how are you? Where are you?*

I am as I always am. I remain nearby. I will always be nearby.

Jimmy puts his face in his hands and cries so hard, he nearly passes out. When he has released all that he needs to, he looks up at me with bloodshot eyes. 'Sorry.'

I smile. 'Don't be. I need to leave now so that I can re-enable your wallscreen without it having been out of operation for too long. You'll be okay?'

Jimmy stands up, pulls me to my feet and hugs me. 'Now I know Photon's still with me, I'll be fine. Thanks, Tania.'

'Don't mention it. Just stay open to Photon, okay? When I can get you out to see him, he'll let you know where to go.'

Jimmy nods. 'Before you go, how's Pamela?'

'She's doing fine. She and Phil are busy organising their kindred spirits into a formal resistance.'

Jimmy looks evenly at me as his intuition and intelligence make sense of what I've just told him. 'And the rest of us?' he says.

'You all have a part to play too, but for now, you need to focus on your horses, get your strength back and wait. I'm off to see Chloe now.'

Jimmy nods slowly. 'I'll get myself back to work. I'll leave after you do, which is how, exactly?'

I grin as I disappear.

Like all of the others who had horses until a few days ago, except Pamela, Chloe is unusual in that she is in her twenties and not yet married, and still living with her parents. None of the singletons would consider marrying anyone outside of their band of equestrians and up until now, Phil has advised them against drawing attention to the group by pairing off within it, but that will soon change. It has to.

Chloe is standing by one of the floor-to-ceiling windows of her parents' top floor apartment, looking out over all of the other grey buildings that look like giant tombstones crammed in against one another, almost as far as the eye can see. Her apartment is in one of the newest and tallest buildings, and as a result, she can see the monstrous, grey wall. I sense her hatred for it.

Unlike Jimmy's parents, Chloe's have kept the minimalist style of the apartment and put up only a few pictures on the glaring white walls. The grey floors seem to meet the windows and carry on outside them into the equally grey buildings all around, resulting in a gloomy room despite the amount of light that the windows let in. It's a room, an apartment, designed to suck the life out of its occupants, and it's doing a good job.

I disable the wallscreen and say, 'Hi, Chloe.'

She bangs her head on the window and then spins around with wide, terrified eyes.

I smile. 'Don't worry, the wallscreen isn't working, they can't see or hear us.'

Chloe races over to me, throws her arms around me and holds on tightly, desperate to prove to herself that I'm really there.

I hug her back and tell her, 'It's okay, everything is going to be okay.'

She begins to sob. 'How can you say that when they've taken the horses from us? I can't live here without Minerva, I'm not strong enough and there's no point anyway; without her, it's just one horrific grey day after another.'

'You don't need to live here without Minerva, she's not going anywhere,' I say.

Chloe pulls back from me and looks around her apartment. 'Well, I don't see her?' She flings an arm in the direction of the window. 'She's out there somewhere, probably miles and miles away by now, and I don't blame her. People are horrid, if I were her, I'd get as far away from here as possible.'

'But she won't. She'll stay close in order to be near you, in order to remind you who you are and what you can do.'

Chloe is breathing so fast she's almost panting as she searches my eyes for the lie that a few days ago, she would have known isn't there. Then she looks past me to the hallway. 'How did you get in here? I put the chain across after my parents left for work. How did you even get into the building?'

I grin. 'As I've just explained to Jimmy, I don't need to use doors.'

She sinks onto the sofa. 'Jimmy? You've seen Jimmy? How is he?'

'A lot better now he can communicate with Photon.'

Chloe frowns as she once again searches my eyes for a lie. Then she whispers, 'He can what?'

'He can communicate with Photon. Would you like to reach Minerva?'

Chloe nods frantically. 'How? Tell me how.'

I sit down beside her. 'Close your eyes. Go back in your mind to the last time you rode Minerva. Remember her moving beneath you, how you felt. Good, now feel the connection you had with her. There's no rush, take your time.'

Chloe is bright red and on the brink of tears when she finally opens her eyes and says, 'I can't. I feel myself riding her and then I remember it was the last time, and all I can see is them chasing her away from me.'

I put a hand on her shoulder and send her some light. 'Chloe, it's okay. You have binoculars. Would you fetch them please?'

She's off the sofa and by a large sideboard in a single breath. She rushes back to me and thrusts the binoculars into my lap. 'Here. How will they help?'

I walk over to the far side of the room and beckon her to stand beside me. I point into the distance. 'Look over there, beyond the wall, to where there's a stand of trees. Minerva's waiting there for you.'

I see the dainty, dapple-grey mare through Chloe's eyes as she spots her mare in the distance. Minerva is standing, resting a hind leg, her eyes soft even though her ears are pricked in our direction.

Chloe's breath catches in her throat. 'I see her! It's like she knows I can see her too… she does, I can feel her, it's like she's right beside me!'

I put a hand atop the binoculars. 'Put them down now, and close your eyes.'

She shakes her head frantically. 'No, I need to see her, I might never see her again, I might never feel this connection again.'

'The connection isn't between your eyes and hers, it's between your soul and her soul.' I put a little pressure on the top of the binoculars. 'She's helping you this time by standing in plain sight, but you need to be able to reach her when you can't see her. Keep the vision of her in your mind, keep the feel of her in your mind, and close your eyes.'

Chloe swallows hard, then does as I ask. I take the binoculars from her. 'Now reach for her. Not out there where she's standing, but inside yourself, where the connection is that you have with her.'

Minerva's thought is as delicate and gentle as the mare herself. *We are part of one another. It bodes well that you have discovered such.*

I chuckle as Chloe's eyes spring open and she looks at me, her mouth closing and opening without sound.

'Way to go, Chloe. Do you not have anything to say to her in return?'

She turns her head so fast to look out of the window, she cricks her neck. She barely notices the pain as she asks Minerva, *How are you?*

You need not ask that which you can know for yourself. You have suffered as a result of our physical separation but your strength is returning. You can know whatever you need to about me.

'I do,' Chloe whispers. She turns to me. 'I do know how she is! I do! She's fine, she has plenty of grass and water, and the other horses are all with her, they've stayed together as a herd, so she feels safe and she's been sleeping well, oh this is amazing.'

I grin. 'Keep practising finding your connection with her, okay? It'll be harder to do when things are difficult, so practise reaching for her inside of yourself until you know exactly where she is, until you can find her without even thinking about it, then she'll be able to help you. She'll let you know when we've created a way for you to get out and see her, and she'll tell you where to go.'

Chloe nods, her face bright with delight. 'And Jimmy'll be there too? He'll get out to see Photon?'

'You can count on it. I need to get going now, I disabled the wallscreen but I need to get it going again before they send someone out to look at it. You need to get back to work, okay? If you don't want to today, then definitely tomorrow. When the wallscreen comes back on, act as exhausted and upset as you were when I got here.'

'Okay, yes, sure. You're going however it was that you arrived?'

'Yep, see you on the other side of the wall. Any questions, ask Minerva.' I step back from her and disappear.

Sophie's and Sam's families live in the same apartment block, two floors apart. When I appear in Sam's white and grey bathroom, Sophie's voice wafts in through the open doorway. She is dictating a recipe for some sort of stew to him, but I'm Aware that isn't what he's writing down.

I disable the wallscreen in the living room, then walk into the kitchen and tell them both, 'It's okay, you can talk out loud now, they can't hear you.'

Sophie squeaks and jumps on Sam, who flushes red as he catches her.

I smile at them both. 'Sorry.'

'No you're not,' Sam says.

'No, I'm not,' I agree with a chuckle, and nod at the paper on the table. 'Nice ruse you have going there.'

Sam glances at the wall on the other side of which is the wallscreen, and then back at me. 'Lovely to see you. Sophie was just telling me what went into a casserole she made for my family, so I can try to replicate it.' He writes ARE YOU CRAZY? on his piece of paper.

'No, just good at disabling wallscreens,' I say with a grin. 'We have about fifteen minutes before I'll need to get it going again. Like I said though, nice ruse, finding reasons to write things down for one another so you can discuss things without being overheard.'

Sam wanders into the living room and peers at the wallscreen. 'You literally just walked in. How did you disable it? Come to that, how did you even get in here? You shouldn't have been able to get into the building, let alone this apartment.'

'You're not the first to tell me that, and I'm pretty sure you won't be the last,' I reply, 'but as I said, we don't have long.'

'We've been going nuts, worrying about the horses, wondering what's going on and when someone is going to contact us, it's been three days,' Sam says. 'We've both taken time off work as holiday, there's no way we can go in when we're freaking out. Have you come to get us, to take us to the horses like you said you would?'

'No, Pamela, Phil and Dad are still working on a way for you to get out. I've come to help you stay calm while they're doing it.'

'I don't think I'll ever be calm again, you know what I was like before I had Pebble,' Sophie says.

'You still have Pebble, you just need to trust that you can feel him in your mind when you aren't with him as well as when you are.' I look at Sam. 'The same goes for you.' I nod in the direction of the sofa. 'Have a seat, both of you, and close your eyes.'

Within minutes, Sophie is laughing and crying at the same time as she converses with Pebble. Her success causes Sam to tense up and try too hard to reach Hector. I send a flow of light to settle around him and he relaxes. Then he smiles as Hector welcomes him to where their minds meet. He opens his eyes and accepts Hector's explanation about the cloud of white light that remains in place around him. Then he beams at me.

'Have you always been able to do this?' Sophie asks me.

'Yes, although the horses don't find it necessary to communicate with me as such; it would be a bit like one of your toes telling its neighbour what to do.'

Both of them frown and Sam says, 'Who are you? Where are you from and where have you and your dad been for the last four years? Come to that, why don't either of you look any older than when we last saw you?'

I grin. 'I'll leave your horses to explain that. I need to get your wallscreen working again and then help the rest who are sensitive enough to communicate with their horses. Get back to your daily lives and practise checking in with Pebble and Hector while you're doing a variety of different tasks. The more you do it, the easier it will be, and the easier it will be for the horses to let you know when you can get out to see them and where you need to go. It shouldn't be long now, okay?'

'Why are you risking yourself for us and our horses?' Sophie says.

'I'm not risking anything,' I reply, 'but if I were, it would be because you're what the human race needs. To that end, do us all a favour and have the relationship you both want, will you?'

Both of them flush red and look everywhere but at one another.

My attempt at a wink diffuses their embarrassment somewhat. My disappearance from in front of them dispels it completely.

SEVENTEEN

Will

---

*P*amela gasps as Tania disappears. 'How did... how did she do that? Where's she gone? Oh no, don't tell me you're both ghosts? Or holograms? No, you can't be, I've touched both of you, you're solid and warm. What the hell? Will? Talk to me. Hang on, is this how you get back here from your time? Is it like in all the sci-fi movies?'

I wait for her to exhaust herself of questions and then say, 'Everything is made up of energy vibrating at a certain frequency. Energy that vibrates slowly enough appears to be solid matter but its vibration can be speeded up until it is no longer so. Tania can influence her energy to be either solid or not, that's all. She's with Jimmy, helping him to communicate with Photon, and she'll visit all of the other Sensitives in turn until they can all communicate with their horses too.'

Pamela stares at me, then up at the sky, and finally back at me. 'I feel just like I did when I first met the two of you, like I have to be dreaming. I mean, seriously? You're actually serious?'

'I've never lied to you about anything.'

She takes in a deep breath and blows it back out. 'So you can make yourselves, what, pure energy? Then you just materialise wherever and whenever you want?'

I nod. 'Exactly. Tania finds it easier than I do so she's better off flitting around between the Sensitives while I stay here with the rest of you.'

'And she's teaching them to communicate with their horses? Can you teach the rest of us to do it too?'

'A few of the others may get a sense now and then of how their horses are and when they're close, but none of them except you are sensitive enough to be able to communicate with their horses. They won't have such a great need; they're strong and determined and once we have a way for you all to get out of the city, they'll use it to go and see their horses pretty much whenever they want to. The Sensitives will find it much harder to be brave as things get more difficult.'

'But you can teach me to do it?'

'Yes, but we need to carry on walking, we have fifty-three watchers dotted around in the high rises.'

Pamela starts to move. 'The Sensitives always know when we have watchers, and I usually do too, but not exactly how many. You know that because…'

'Because I'm Aware of everything and everyone, all the time.'

'I have no idea how that's possible, yet I find myself having no doubt it's true.'

'Once you can communicate with Zeal it will become a little clearer. I'm going to put my arm around you as if I'm having to support you because you're upset. Close your eyes, I won't let you fall. Now go back in your mind to when you last rode Zeal.'

I describe the process through which I know Tania has now led Jimmy and is currently leading Chloe – though she is with them two days from today, all time is now.

The fortitude Pamela's horse awakened in her enables her to reach her destination much quicker than either of her friends. Her legs almost give way with the relief of hearing her horse in her mind as he tells her, *You have accomplished much. The time has come to establish the foundations on which the future will rest. I will be your strength when you feel you have none of your own. You will never be alone.*

Pamela stifles a sob.

'Don't hold it in,' I say. 'Zeal and I have got you. Cry as much as you need to, and then when you're ready, we'll form a plan.'

When we arrive back in the kitchen an hour later, Pamela is feeling strong enough to read the two forms I was given when the police took Cliff's body. I've told her their contents, but she wants to read the evidence for herself. One of them is an official warning that if she demonstrates the slightest tendency to resist as her husband did, she will meet the same end as did he. The other informs her that her house and land are being requisitioned so that another high rise can be built, further ensuring the safety and comfort of all. She has one week to vacate the premises, and may enlist the help of friends and family to move her possessions to the apartment to which she has been assigned in a high rise nearby.

When she's finished reading, Pamela bites her lip until it bleeds, then nods at me, managing not to glance at the camera that she knows is recording her words and movements. 'I'll get on with organising the help I'm going to need. I'll get some of my former students to come and help me pack and move out, and the rest can help you clear the paddocks of dung as we've been ordered to. Can you go out and start clearing out the barn while you're waiting for them? They want all animal waste left in one place. I'm sorry you'll be out of a job after this, I feel awful for having already had to let Tania go.'

I grin at her, reassuring her that she's performed her lines to perfection despite her grief and stress. My lowly, short-term role here needs to be clear in order to avoid any of our observers attempting to cross-reference what they are seeing with wrist safe records for me that don't exist. 'Not to worry, it can't be helped. I'll get on outside.'

I have the barn cleared of dung and bedding by the time Phil and Clare arrive. Out of sight of the camera on the outside corner of the barn, but within hearing of it, our greetings to one another are brief even as Phil and Clare glare at me. We speak no further until we are out in the field, each armed with a wheelbarrow and shovel.

'Still here then?' Phil says. 'Should we be grateful?'

'Yes, and no, not at all,' I reply, 'especially as it was my idea for you two and Belinda to be the first Pamela asked to come and help me spend the afternoon shovelling dung.'

'Where's Tania?' Clare says.

'She's busy visiting all of the Sensitives the rest of you kindly saw home.'

Phil laughs. 'No she isn't.'

'I can assure you she is.'

'And how is she doing that, exactly, when she can't possibly know where they all live, let alone get into a building she doesn't live in?'

'I think that in the interests of saving a lot of time and hostility, I'm going to need to show you,' I say. 'We'll need to work in a line, Phil, you to my left, Clare to my right, so we don't miss any dung piles. Ah, perfect, here's Belinda. She can join the line on your other side, Clare.' I nod and grin at a very hostile Belinda, then continue, 'When I tell you it's safe to, look quickly at me. Then carry on working as if nothing has happened.'

'Well, that won't be hard, because nothing will have happened. You're full of it, Will, do you know that?' Belinda says.

'Let's just get shovelling,' Clare says. 'And while we're about it, we can start figuring out who we're going to make pay for taking our horses.'

'We'd be much better talking about which of your number Pamela has suggested you insinuate into the security services, Phil, so that you all have a means of getting out to see your horses,' I say, upturning my shovel so that dung lands in my wheelbarrow with a thud, 'and which should be advised to apply for positions from which they can work their way into key roles within the health, food production and social services systems. Keep shovelling, we're being observed.'

'We're always being observed,' Phil growls, picking up his wheelbarrow and moving on to the next dung pile. 'Belinda's right, you're full of it, just stop talking, Will.'

Our last watcher turns away from her bedroom window. 'Look at me now,' I say. It's much easier and quicker the third time. I disappear and reappear in little more than a second. 'That's how Tania is getting around undetected,' I tell the three stunned faces. 'She's nearly halfway through visiting the Sensitives. When she's finished, they'll all be ready and waiting for their horses to let them know where to go to breach the wall, and when, so I really think we should get on and discuss how we're going to make that happen.'

You could have warned them, Dad, Tania tells me. I sense her attempt at a wink.

I did.

Saying "look at me now" hardly counts.

It's still more warning than you gave Pamela, I was accused of being both a ghost and a hologram.

'Who are you? I mean really?' Phil says.

'I'm going to let Pamela fill you in on that, you'll believe her more readily than you will me and it will save a lot of time. We need to plan now; the sooner we get organised, the sooner you can see your horses.'

Belinda dumps her wheelbarrow next to mine with a grunt. 'So, tell me this. How are more than sixty of us going to walk through a solid wall? It doesn't matter if any of us manage to get transferred to the security services, no one is allowed out of the gates for any reason, let alone back in.'

'Leave that to me and Tania, we'll create a way.'

'Why should we trust you?' Clare says. 'We trusted you before, we did everything you told us to do with the horses, but then you left without so much as a goodbye and you didn't come back until it was too late.'

We are once again without observers, so I lean on my shovel. 'Everything that's happened was always going to happen, Tania and I just ensured that you were all together by the time it did. Now that you need help to find a way forward, we're back to give you that help. Don't trust me if you don't feel you can, but trust Pamela, always. Trust her, follow her and support her, because she's the key to everything and she's going to need you.'

'Why do I find myself believing everything you say, just like the last time you were here?' Belinda says, her voice full of challenge.

'Because Clicka has shown you how sensitive you are, and you trust yourself to know when someone is telling you the truth,' I reply.

I sense anger draining from all three of them as I resume my shovelling.

'One more thing,' Clare says. 'You said the Sensitives will be ready for their horses to let them know where and when to go to breach the wall. I get who you mean by the Sensitives, but you mean Tania's helping them to communicate with their horses? Like, telepathically?'

'Yes. The Sensitives will panic about using the system too much that you have in place to reach one another. Communicating via their horses will get them around that.'

'I'd love to be able to do that,' Clare says wistfully. 'I guess I'm not sensitive enough.'

I smile as I sense the horses beginning to move. 'You're sensitive enough to feel what's about to happen. Hold on to your shovels and use them to stay on your feet if you need to.'

The horses have been grazing peacefully for most of the day, but they sense that their energy is needed. Heart begins to trot alongside the wall. Zeal falls in just behind her, followed by Maple, Hector and Photon. Pebble and Minerva canter over to join them, as do Melody and Clicka. The nine of them speed up, and the rest of the horses gallop to join them, only slowing once all sixty-five horses are moving as one big mass of thundering hooves.

I am Aware that the Sensitives whom Tania has already visited are smiling as their horses take them with them on a huge circle around the city wall. I am equally Aware of those she has yet to visit sensing something other than the misery that has plagued them since their horses were taken from them. They'll be in touch with their horses as soon as Tania shows them how.

Phil is the first to use his shovel to steady himself. 'Woah, do you guys feel that?'

Clare is next. 'Maple?' She looks at me. 'What's happening? It's like the horses are here with us.'

Belinda gasps. 'The air feels lighter. Everything feels lighter, as if there's nothing to worry about. It feels just like when...'

'We used to ride in a circle,' the three of them say together.

'Your horses are circling the city,' I say. 'It's a long way, but they're doing it because they know you can feel the energy it creates; they know it'll give you the courage and strength you need, and it'll magnify the Sensitives' abilities. They'll do it whenever they sense you need them to. The horses may be outside the gates, but they haven't left you. They'll never leave you. They're everything you need.'

'Okay, so let's discuss the plan,' Phil says.

By the time more helpers come to join us, we're ready to split up and fill them in on Pamela's proposal as we work.

By the time the sun is beginning to disappear behind the high rises to the west, the fields, paddock and barn are all completely clear of dung, and the fifteen of us, who have achieved by hand what I could have done in seconds with my mind, are all energised by the horses' circuit of the city and completely clear on what we need to do.

The other fourteen all stop off at Pamela's house and collect a box of her possessions each, which they'll drop off at her new apartment on their way home. I'm Aware that each of them hugs her and whispers that they'll be back the following day to collect more boxes. I know they'll suggest nostalgic walks in the field with her so they can fill her in on their news and thoughts, and get her instructions and news passed to her by Zeal from the other Sensitives. We've achieved a lot.

'You're exhausted,' I say to Pamela once we're alone in the kitchen. 'You've done amazingly today after everything that's happened.'

'I'm not nearly as exhausted as I would have been without all the help,' she says, holding my eye to make sure I know she's as energised as the rest of us as a result of the horses' efforts.

'Your friends are all here for you. I'll cook you some dinner and then I'll get off home.'

Pamela frowns and I sense her confusion and worry; we haven't discussed where Tania and I will go now that the camera in her kitchen means staying with her isn't an option.

'There's no place like home at the end of a long day, is there?' I say. 'It's where your heart is, where you can whistle your own melody with zeal, and where you can rest like a pebble on a maple leaf.'

Pamela frowns at me in confusion for a second. Then a smile spreads across her face. 'I'll have a new home like that soon, I'm looking forward to settling into it. I won't hear of you cooking for me after all your hard work today, you get off home.'

'You'll be okay here by yourself?'

Pamela glances at Shield sitting on the kitchen table and looking between the two of us as if he's part of the conversation, which of course he is. 'I'm not by myself, I'll be fine.'

Even if I weren't Aware of her grief, she would have given herself away by biting her lip so that it bleeds again, and reaching a shaking hand towards her cat. He is acutely Aware of the energy Pamela will need to get through her first night without her husband, as well as the energy from which she needs protecting. He stalks along the table, rubs his face against her fingers and then jumps onto her shoulder. She's in safe paws.

She holds her hand out to me. 'Take care, I'll see you around.'

I shake her hand. 'You take care too.'

I leave the house and head for the road. When I am Aware that I am unobserved, I spin my energy out of the physical, returning to it in woodland on the other side of the wall.

Tania is standing between Minerva and Photon, a hand on each of their necks as she eases the various strains and areas of tension in their muscles caused by their long canter around the city wall, while doing the same for all of the other sixty-three horses at the same time.

The horses all stand with their heads hanging low, eyes half closed, and resting a hind leg. They are like exquisite, breathing statues dotted amongst the trees, all dappled by the early evening sun that stretches past the recently emerged leaves above. The peace emanating from them highlights where in my being I hold that which isn't quite peace. I release the small amount of grief that belongs to Pamela and the others but which, in recognising it, in remembering having felt it myself, I assimilated as my own.

I breathe deeply, easily, relieved that the constant battering of the negativity of The Old is weaker here. I gather my energy and shift it towards the herd with the intention of invigorating them, revitalising them, loving them for who they are and for expending so much of themselves in order to strengthen their humans.

Tania finishes healing them all and joins her energy with mine. The horses begin to lift their heads and stretch their necks. Some stretch their hind legs out behind them in turn, others shake their bodies, grunting and shuddering as they come back to themselves.

I am Aware of the Sensitives' concern reducing as they sense their horses recovering from their efforts. Amarilla joins me in my amusement as the horses calmly refuse their humans' requests to never tire themselves like that again, to never again draw attention to the fact that they have remained so close to the city wall, to never risk themselves. My aunt remembers only too well that there was a time when she too believed that horses need protecting.

It feels strange that they have come to the trees to rest, when woodland was the last choice of resting place for our bonded horses, Am observes.

The Enforcers don't exist yet, let alone their descendants, I observe in return. *I hadn't thought of these horses as being bonded, but I suppose they are. Do I break it to Jonus that he isn't the first Horse-Bonded after all?*

I sense Am's amusement. *Leave him be, he was still the first to respond to being tugged. You're going to tell him you've met his – what are Sophie and Sam, his great-great-great-great-great-great-great-great-grandparents? – though. That's nice, he'll be glad to know about them. And you're about to start work on the tunnel. You know Lia has a full roast on the go for you both, don't you?*

We can be back the moment it's ready, no matter how much time we spend preparing things here, Tania points out.

You're both more than hungry now, Am replies.

And Mum knows it, Tania observes. *She wants us home to look after us. I understand.* We are all Aware of her surprise at her realisation. *Um, we'll just prepare the undergrowth and then we'll be back.*

I smile at Lia's relief. Am turns her attention to a conversation with Justin.

'It'll feel strange for a while, change always does, no matter who you are, what you know and how Aware you are,' I say to Tania. 'It's part of being human.'

She nods. 'Come on, there are brambles waiting to have their growth accelerated.' She takes my hand as she hasn't since she was a little girl, and squeezes it as we wend our way through the trees until we're in sight of the wall.

Tania points across the grassy area the horses have been grazing, to where we both sense a lone bramble poking up out of the soil. 'There. Where there's one bramble above soil, there'll be the seeds of loads more beneath. A tunnel there will bring everyone out where they have the shortest distance to get to the cover of the trees, and the horses can move their grazing to the far side of the forest and then come into the trees to meet them. It's perfect.'

'If we build a longer tunnel, they can exit it in the trees with no risk of being seen,' I reply.

'That too,' Tania replies, having already focused her attention on the seeds she wants on the far side of the wall. She resonates with them and despite them having been buried deeper underground by the wall excavation than is optimal for their germination, she has young shoots growing out of them and towards the surface by the time I find the wherewithal to add my strength and intention to hers.

Within minutes, there is a mass of freshly emerging brambles on the city side of the wall. We'll check in with them and fuel their growth further every day, so that by the time the first of our tunnels is finished, its entrance will be well hidden.

We move our attention to the ancestry of the seeds we have germinated, and sense the position of all of the other related seeds that have been dispersed by animals eating blackberries or by the machinery that excavated the foundations for the wall. They respond immediately to our energy and encouragement, their outer surfaces splitting to allow their rapidly growing shoots to emerge and reach the light. There. The clumps we need will be among many dotted along the base of the wall. By the time the governors decide that plant life needs to be limited in the vicinity of the wall, the resistance will have people in place to ensure that they are only ever cut back to a degree conducive with concealing the entrances to the tunnels that will be in place.

'It's definitely time for dinner,' I say as Tania fades away leaving an echo of a grin behind. I look down at where my favourite echo bounds around my legs, and say, 'Come on then, let's get after her, shall we?'

Lia is just putting plates of steaming vegetables on the table when we both appear in the kitchen, Tania sitting on one of the chairs with a cheeky grin on her face, and me at my wife's side.

Tania picks up her knife and fork and pretends to dig into her food, then chuckles at Lia's indignation and jumps out of her chair and kisses and hugs her mother. 'Sorry for being a pain my whole life, I get it now.'

Lia blows a kiss at me while hugging her daughter and telling her, 'You've never been that, Tania. I'm blown away by what you did to get past your resistance, we all are except Delta; I'm sure you're Aware she's furious you didn't do it before.'

Tania chuckles as the door crashes open and all three dogs burst into the kitchen. I sit down on the floor and welcome their exuberant pouncing and licks, and the energy it gives me.

Lia holds out her hand and pulls me to my feet. 'You're tired. I know you need to be with Ember, but eat first, while it's hot?'

I smile gratefully and tuck into the meal she's prepared, enjoying listening to her and Tania discussing our day. As soon as I've finished, Lia flicks her eyes to the door, giving me her blessing to go and see my old friend. I know he's fine and has no need to see me, it's just habit, really; whenever I've been subjected to the energy of The Old – whether from Jonus's time or when Eminent's people were at their most aggressive – I've sought out his company. I've already rebalanced myself by spending time with the horses of The Old, but I still feel a need to be with him, as if only then can I be sure that I'm completely myself.

There would have been a time when Tania would have had something to say about my feelings and actions, but I sense her understanding and only then realise, through her, that my feelings and actions once again arise from the knowledge that he won't always be there, not physically anyway.

He's lying down when I reach the pasture. Rebel, Ash and Chase tear off in search of rabbits, leaving me to wander over to him and sit by his head, which he lowers into my lap. 'You're tired too, aren't you, old boy?' I say as I stroke his muzzle and rest my forehead against his. It's all I need.

When he lifts his head from my lap twenty minutes later, I get to my feet and move away, knowing he wants to rise and eat. I stroke his flank as I leave him. 'Thanks, mate.'

We arrive back in The Old just as the huge city gates are closing. Dogs of all ages and sizes mill around looking every bit as confused and frightened as they feel. Some are injured due to being roughly handled or attacked by other dogs; I've only just registered the fact by the time Tania has them all healed.

I'm in my element as I merge with the collective consciousness of all of the dogs who have ever lived, drawing all of those who are lost into it with me, pulling them away from their fear, their grief at having been parted from their families. They all fall silent as they remember what it is to live as part of a pack, what it is to roam together, hunt together, sleep together and protect one another.

Tania is with us all too. She is the dogs, all of them. She knows which will do well together and which will clash. She gathers them into packs which she sends off in different directions to live out their lives far away from humans. When all that remain of them are the distant barks that reach our ears, she turns to me and reassures herself as much as me, 'They'll be fine. We need to get further back into the trees, they're bringing out the cats.'

The gates begin to slowly open again. Once there is a large enough gap, trucks drive out onto the grass. Their drivers and passengers jump down from the cabs and begin loosening straps that hold cage upon cage of terrified cats crammed in with one another. Machines appear with long, metal arms that slide under rows of cages and lower them to the ground. When the trucks are empty of cages, they and the machines disappear back through the gates, which close behind them.

The cages are all opened, and in many cases shaken so that their occupants spill outside. The empty cages are thrown to land near the gates, and when all of the cats have been released, a small door, just large enough to admit one person at a time, opens in one of the gates. The cages are passed through and then the remaining people disappear through the door, the last of them closing it firmly behind them.

I leave Tania to heal all of the cats, knowing how much quicker she is than I. Then we both surround each and every one of them in a calming, soothing net of energy that will remain as long as they need it. The first few of them stalk towards the trees, eyeing the small birds that flit around in the branches. Others follow, their ears soon picking up the scurrying of mice and rabbits through the forest's undergrowth. More of the cats stream towards the woodland, needing little help from us to leave their domesticated lives behind. Before long, only a few cats remain sitting where they were dumped. A large, grey male looks back to the gates and mewls. He isn't at all sorry for himself, he's just determined.

I grin. Shield intends to slink back through the gate the second it opens; as Cliff said, the cat is as relentless as the tide coming in. Pamela may have been forced to hand him over, but he has a job to do and he won't be prevented from doing it for long. I show him a better way to reach Pamela, and immediately, his head swivels around towards me. He's too far away for me to see them, but I'm Aware that his green eyes are focused on me and on everything he can see within me. His tail shoots vertically up in the air as he gets to his feet and races over to me. He sits at my feet, stares up at me and opens his mouth, emitting that which if he were human would be a shout. Hurry up.

I sense Zeal communicating with Pamela, and show him images of Shield with me. Her relief reassures Shield, so I pick him up and stroke him. 'You'll be with her again soon.'

Tania and I spend the best part of a week returning to The Old each morning after a good night's sleep and a hearty breakfast provided by Lia, working on the tunnel all day and then returning home for dinner and a hot bath in the evening.

We salvage materials from nearby abandoned farms, and use a combination of what used to be earth-singing, rock-singing and metal-singing before Adam and Amarilla discovered how to dispense with the need to sing, to excavate a tunnel far beneath the wall and reinforce it using a combination of rocks and metal manipulated into our desired structures and positions.

'They really are very wasteful here in The Old,' Tania says as she arrives back at the clearing in the forest that we are using as our base, with five metal gates and hundreds of rocks floating along behind her. 'All of those farms are just littered with materials they could have used in constructing the high rises. Still, all the easier for us, these should be the last we need for this tunnel.'

Melody whickers to her as Tania allows her findings to gently come to rest on the ground. The horses often come to spend time with us as we work, mostly the original eight and Heart, but all of them at one time or another. The Sensitives are fully aware of our progress as a result, and have passed everything they learn from their horses on to the others. Everything is almost in place.

The sixty-four will be coming to visit their horses tonight. The Sensitives are, without exception, terrified. The rest are determined but nervous that something will go wrong, that the plan they have put in place will be discovered or one of the Sensitives will give them all away. The horses sense the moment that the plan is about to go into freefall, and there is a crashing and pounding of hooves all around us as the herd barges through the forest to the clearing around the wall. Infinity is with them as they gather themselves together for another canter around the city wall, and fuels their energy and purpose with her own.

'Well, that will cheer everyone up,' Tania says. 'And we'll have the tunnel finished by the time the horses get back. We can heal any of them who need it, get back home for some dinner and then get back here by the time everyone arrives.'

EIGHTEEN

Pamela

I t has been ten days since Cliff died, yet it seems like just a few hours and more than a year at the same time; so much has changed that my perception of time has become completely distorted.

The police came for Shield and the other cats the day before I left my old home for good. The barn cats led them a merry dance before finally being funnelled into a cage by beams of sound beyond the hearing range of humans but which were clearly intolerable to the cats. Shield was a different matter. He watched the black-clothed, hooded and helmeted police barge into my kitchen, now empty apart from the kitchen table upon which he sat cleaning his whiskers. When one of them reached out to grab him, he looked at the black-gloved hands as if they were beneath his contempt. When he was lifted and carried away from me, he merely fixed his green eyes on mine as if it were exactly what he wanted to happen. All I could do was clamp my hands over my mouth to stop myself from screaming. First Cliff, then Zeal, and finally Shield.

I managed to sleep the whole night through after losing my husband and horse, and every night afterward until the first night without Shield. I haven't slept much since. It's as if the madness of the world around me waits until I close my eyes, then creeps around me as I lie in bed, poking me, prodding me, sniggering at my loneliness, my heartbreak, my grief. If it weren't for Zeal, I truly believe I would have given up on life that first night by myself, the last in the house I shared with Cliff. As it is, my horse has continued to give me the strength to keep going.

When I left my house for the last time, feeling overwrought and exhausted, it was Zeal who filled my mind so that the grief that wanted me to refuse to leave, that wanted the waiting police to shoot me, couldn't fully take a hold. He drew me to him, away from the house in which I had come to be happy, and towards the apartment to which my friends and I had moved my possessions, near the outskirts of this ugly, horrific city of ours. By the time I reached it, I was almost smiling; I was closer to my horse, so it wasn't all bad.

Your current thought pattern is one you would be wise to cultivate, Zeal informed me.

Looking on the bright side? I asked.

It is not so much a case of viewing your surroundings and situation in terms of being positive or negative but in terms of that which will assist you in your purpose and that which will not.

The steely determination that accompanied his thought sparked my own, and after negotiating the eye scanner at the entrance to my apartment block, I resolved to take the stairs in preference to the lift up to my twenty-ninth-floor apartment – I would retain my fitness for when I needed it. When the eye scanner outside my apartment flashed green and the door clicked open to admit me, I felt energised and ready to begin the task of unpacking. This was my new home. This was the place from which I would continue to co-ordinate my friends and their future recruits into a well organised network that would resist the insanity into which everyone else was sinking.

But nighttime came around all too quickly, bringing the demons that have continued to plague me every night.

You're not clever enough, they always tell me, *and you're nowhere near strong enough. Who do you think you are to even be thinking of trying to lead all of your friends in some sort of clandestine resistance against the might and power of the governors, when you can barely hold yourself together without your horse reaching into your mind every few minutes to reassure you? You'll get yourself killed, and everyone else alongside you. You'll let Cliff down, you'll let Zeal down, you'll let everyone down. Just admit defeat. Live the safe, comfortable life the governors have promised you.*

It's always so tempting to give in, and often the only way to get even a few hours' sleep is to fold; to agree with everything my demons tell me so that they give me some peace. But then I wake and instinctively reach out to Zeal. He's always comfortable within himself, as if he'll be that way whatever happens, as if his very makeup renders him immune to the worries about survival that plague me. I question the decision I made before I went to sleep, and that brings my demons flooding back to convince me all over again that I'm weak, stupid, and have no chance whatsoever of resisting the regime in any meaningful way.

Once I'm up and about, it's a little easier. I focus my mind on the tasks of the day – to date, which boxes I will unpack next – and block the demons out. As soon as I do, I sense Zeal at the edge of my mind, ready as ever to reassure me of his continued presence, to advise me when I can't see the way forward, just as he is this morning.

I have only a few boxes left to unpack, and one more day to

myself before I am due to start the job into which Phil has managed to manoeuvre me, as the administrator of the brand new city hospital. I know he has argued that having run my own business for years, I have all of the skills necessary for the job and will learn quickly from those around me. It's a perfect position from which to have access to the records of the city's inhabitants as well as to medical supplies, and the exact position for which I asked when detailing the positions in which I wished him to insinuate members of our fledgling resistance.

While he has made sure that I and those we need in the security service immediately are in place straight away, he will ensure the others get the positions for which they will apply in the security, social and food production services over a period of time, so as to not attract unwanted attention to our infiltration.

When we are all in place, we will have eyes, ears and influence in all of the departments and will do our best to disrupt violence, greed and unfairness, and protect ourselves, the Sensitives and anyone else we feel we can. This, all thirty-two of us with the strength to fight agreed during our walks in the fields and while lugging my possessions between my old house and my new apartment. And when each and every one of the others asked for my promise that I would continue to be their leader, I gave that promise which has weighed so heavily on me ever since and which tomorrow I will need to begin to fulfil. As a result, my demons were particularly vociferous during the night, and even though my hands cease their trembling as I slice the packing tape from the penultimate box to be unpacked, my heart thumps and a cold sweat breaks out over my body.

Zeal increases his presence in my mind as I hoped he would, and I latch onto him, desperate for a way out of my fear.

Those of us who live apart from humans tend to form family groups led by a female, Zeal tells me. *She decides when it is time for the herd to move away from impending danger or find water or a different food source but she does not do it alone. She senses everything that is felt and sensed by her herd members. She responds to their feedback by either remaining in place or moving on. When she moves on they follow her whilst continuing to provide her with information so that the way forward remains clear to her. She leads but she does so in response to those who follow her. She isn't necessarily the cleverest or the strongest or the fastest female in the herd. She is the wisest.*

I'm fascinated; that which he is telling me is completely the opposite of how our leaders have always gained power. *Leading isn't so much about having all of the answers, but about listening for them? But there'll still be situations where I'll have to decide what to do with the information I'm given, won't there? I mean, your lead females have to decide where to go to flee danger or to look for water. What if I get it wrong, what if I get someone killed?*

The lead female trusts her herd to give her the information she needs and she trusts her instincts to tell her how to use that information. The humans of your herd have spent enough time with the members of mine to be able to recognise their lead female. Trust them and trust yourself. Nothing else is required.

Except for you. I need you every bit as much as the others need their horses. I can't do this without you, Zeal.

Nor will you have to. Yet future generations of your resistance will not have us to advise them. You must ensure that both your purpose and ideology grow strong enough to endure after you and we have all moved on.

I feel exhausted all over again. *There's so much to do and so few of us to do it.*

Then find more. Reach out to everyone you meet in the same way you reach for me. You will resonate with those who are like you without yet knowing it and you will know what to say to let them know that they can trust you. Grow your network until it is self-perpetuating and able to survive without you. And remember that you are never alone.

I feel stronger. Actually, it's more than that, I feel a little excited; Zeal's suggestions for the future have made our idea of resistance more real, something that will actually happen and be effective rather than just a notion to which to cling in the absence of hope for any kind of a fulfilling life.

Your fellow humans approach, Zeal informs me. *Your means of bypassing the wall is almost complete. We will await you all in the darkness of this day. Those among you who can hear us will require the strength of those of you who cannot.*

Tonight? Wow, that's brilliant! Okay, so I'll need to give the message to whoever's coming – Clare and Belinda at a guess – to pass around our network, and the Sensitives will all know from their own horses?

Zeal doesn't reply; I sense that he doesn't feel it necessary and has already moved his attention to following Heart towards water, along with the rest of the herd. Heart is the lead mare of the herd. Of course she is. Tears fill my eyes at the thought of how proud of her Cliff would be if he knew, but I blink them away hurriedly at the knock on my door. By the time I open it to Belinda and Clare, I am managing to smile, albeit it weakly.

'It's lovely to see you both as always, but you don't need to check up on me every day, I'm okay, really I am,' I say for the benefit of the wallscreen in the living room.

'You still have a few boxes to unpack and all of your pictures to hang, so we're here to help,' Belinda says and blows me a silent kiss before striding into the living room.

'We have an hour before work, so we'll get cracking, shall we?' Clare says as she follows Belinda. 'If there's anything you need, write me a list and I'll drop it off on my way home later, that way you can just relax on your last day of being a lady of leisure.'

'There are a few things I need, actually,' I say, 'thanks, I'll get a list together.'

I go into the kitchen, leaving my friends unpacking and unwrapping in full sight of the wallscreen. I grab a pen and write a short list of food items on one side of a piece of paper, then write on the back in pencil so that the message can be erased once it has been read.

W & T have finished the first tunnel and the horses will be waiting for us on the other side of the wall after dark this evening. Pass the message along to the others that they'll each need to collect the Sensitive they've been paired with, as Zeal tells me they'll need our strength. They'll know from their horses which section of the wall to head for, and we'll know exactly what time we'll be able to safely reach it once Phil has confirmed the guard patrol rota.

'Here you go,' I say to Clare, holding out the note. She puts it straight into her pocket. 'There are a few odds and ends on there that will take a little longer to fetch, and I don't want to make your day any longer than it needs to be, so why don't you go now, then all you'll have to do later is drop everything off?' I hold her gaze for just long enough to warn her not to argue.

'Sure, yes, sure, okay then,' she says. 'I'll head off now.'

'You too, Belinda,' I say. 'I'm grateful for you coming to see me, but Clare could do with your help picking up some of the things I need.'

Belinda puts down the ornament she's just unwrapped, and

smiles. 'I understand. Clare and I will make sure we get everything on the list. I hope picture hooks are on it, you can't possibly have enough to hang all of that lot.' She nods to where my pictures are stacked against the wall.

I smile. 'You've got me, they're on the list.'

I walk them to the door and hug them both. 'Tonight's the night,' I breathe into Belinda's ear. 'Take care.' She hugs me more tightly, then lets me go and walks out of the door without another word. 'Take care,' I repeat to Clare. She gives the barest of nods and hurries towards the lifts after Belinda.

I am just about to close the door when movement catches my eye. I look towards the stairwell where the door to our floor – whose hinge causes it to close slowly and silently so as to be conducive to the safety and comfort that we're repeatedly told is so desirable to us all – is still closing behind whoever last came through it. It wasn't that which caught my eye though, it was something moving much more quickly.

My eyes are drawn to the shadows along the opposite side of the corridor, below the small, opaque windows which, according to the Resident's Pack that awaited me on my arrival, allow enough light into the corridors to ensure our mental health without allowing too much heat to escape – as if windows in corridors can ever make up for having had my husband, my horse and my cat taken from me.

I blink, truly believing for a moment that my eyes are deceiving me. It can't be. A grey streak leaves the shadows and passes between my legs, into my apartment before I have a chance to say his name. I open my mouth and then bite my lip as I realise the error I almost made. *Shield?*

I spin around to find him sitting in my hallway, front feet together, tail curled around him, green eyes calmly looking up at me as if he hasn't just put both of us in mortal danger. I look back out into the hallway which, thankfully, is empty, then close the door quickly behind me. I run past Shield to the living room door and close it; he cannot be picked up by the wallscreen. He stalks over to me and weaves in between and around my legs, purring loudly. I pick him up, hold him close to where my heart is pounding in my chest, and take him into the bedroom, shutting the door firmly behind me.

I go to put him down on the bed but then realise I don't want to. I don't want to let go of the warmth that doesn't just seem to be confined to him, but now surrounds me, making my white and grey bedroom seem less stark, a little more welcoming somehow. I sit down on the bed.

'How on earth did you know where I was, let alone get back to me?' I whisper to him. 'I'm going to have to sneak you back out to the other side of the wall with me later, you can't stay here.'

He will always know where you are in the same way you will always know where I am, Zeal informs me. *Should you return him to whence he came he will find his way back to you. You will not stop him.*

But he's putting us both in danger. If they find out he's here, they'll shoot us both. I'll have failed before I've even started.

You may learn much from he who would shield you.

I look down to where Shield has nestled into my lap. His breaths are deep and even as he sleeps peacefully. My eyelids feel heavy. I feel as if sleep is close by and beckoning to me as it hasn't since my cat was taken from me. I curl up around him and close my eyes. When they open again, I feel disorientated. Why am I lying across the end of my bed, fully clothed? I glance at the clock on my bedside table. Twenty minutes past three? I sit up and my stomach gurgles. I've had a full night's sleep during the day?

Shield sits up and stretches, then yawns, revealing his long, white fangs momentarily before closing his mouth and looking unblinkingly up at me. He helped me to sleep, just as he did every night after taking up residence in my house. A pang of grief causes me to catch my breath, but I catch sight of the clock and remember the time – it's the middle of the afternoon!

I leap to my feet and hold a finger up in front of Shield's face. He sniffs it and then looks back up at me. *Stay there,* I think to him, hoping he'll understand me as Zeal does. He blinks and remains where he is.

I go out into the hall, then silently open the living room door, pushing it to behind me. I cross in front of the wallscreen to the kitchen, yawning and scraping my hair back away from my face with my fingers so that it's obvious I've been asleep. I select a large box of cereal which I'm hoping will be a perfect candidate for use as cat litter, a cup – in which I place some raw meat – and saucer, a bottle of milk and a glass of water. I rummage around in a cupboard and find a tray with raised edges that will be perfect as a litter tray. I place everything else on top of it and head back to the bedroom, hoping I appear keen to have a very late breakfast in bed.

I freeze when I spot Shield stalking along the wall beneath the wallscreen, holding his tail vertically with its tip wafting in concert with his stride as he so often does. Immediately, I look up at the wallscreen as if that were the original object of my focus. 'Wallscreen on,' I say, and stand looking unseeingly at it while watching Shield in my peripheral vision. He stays close to the wall so that he is invisible to the wallscreen, then slinks into the kitchen. He flipping well knows to stay out of sight! How the hell does he know where our watchers are?

Consider how he reached you unseen and you will deem it less of an impossibility, Zeal advises me. *My previous counsel extends to all aspects of his life and actions. You will be less reliant on knowing in advance the movements of those who watch from the wall when you realise that you can sense their location as well as their attention or lack of it.*

I almost nod but catch myself. It seems that Shield is my teacher as well as the guardian of my sleep. I look down at the tray and sigh as if I've forgotten something, then return to the kitchen to find Shield sitting on the worktop, looking at me expectantly. I put the cup of meat on the floor by the bin, and pour water from the glass into the saucer for him. He lands on the floor with a thump and pounces on his meal as if it were alive.

I pour the whole box of cereal into the tray and spread it out, then put it next to the bin, hoping he'll find it an acceptable place to toilet, then I smile to myself. If he doesn't, he'll no doubt just take himself back outside in the same way he got in, slinking through doorways behind people who are oblivious to his presence. I admire his single-mindedness, his wiliness and his resilience and then realise that Zeal is right; I need to do far more than admire him, I need to learn from him.

If I enter and leave the building behind someone else, I won't need to present my eye to the scanner by the door in order to open it, and my movements won't be logged – which means that when a member of our resistance activates the virus this evening which will scramble the location data provided by our wrist safes, I'll be completely invisible. I'll take a book to my bedroom so it appears to my wallscreen as if I'm planning to read before having an early night, then leave exactly as Shield would. I just have to work on becoming as sensitive as he is to potential watchers.

I make myself a huge bowl of porridge and a pile of toast, and take it back to the living room. I sit down in front of the wallscreen and reach for it in the same way I reach for Zeal and as he told me to reach out to people to see if they might be open to joining us. The hairs stand up on the back of my neck and my heart pounds. Dammit, there are three of them scrutinising me,

I'm sure of it; I can actually feel their eyes boring into me. My absence for the best part of the day, and my behaviour since, must have piqued their interest. I need to get them off my back so that I'm not being watched as closely by this evening. I move my wrist safe close to my mouth and say, 'Call Jimmy.'

His wrist safe buzzes twice before he takes my call. 'Hi, Pamela, how are you doing?' His voice is more high-pitched than usual. He's stressed.

'Hi, Jimmy, I'm doing a lot better, thank you. It's my last day before starting my new job, so I decided to go back to bed this morning and see if I could catch up on some sleep. I slept for more than seven hours straight and I feel like a whole new woman. How are you?'

'Oh, you know, okay I guess, just trying to get to grips with my new job, I mean I love it and I'm glad to have it, but there's so much to learn and I sometimes worry I'm not up to it.' There's a slight tremble to his voice now. This is about more than his job; he knows, Photon has already told him.

'You're up to it, Jimmy, you're up to anything and everything that comes your way,' I say firmly. 'I won't get you into trouble by keeping you from your work, it's just been a while since I've seen you so I wanted to say hi, and I'll see you very soon, okay?'

'Thanks, Pamela, it's good to hear your voice. Yes, I'll definitely see you soon. Bye.'

He is the Sensitive assigned to me. I know he will have picked up the meaning behind my words, and hope he'll feel a little reassured that I've confirmed I'll be collecting him later, but I'm not convinced; I think he's losing it.

They all are, Zeal confirms. *Worry not. We will give them our strength.*

I don't know what he means, but his reassurance works. I focus my attention back on the wallscreen and immediately feel calmer; there's now only one of them watching me, they must have bought my explanation for my behaviour. Then I feel something else. It's as if a maelstrom of energy has been whipped up around the city, and I try very hard not to smile as I realise it has; the horses are cantering a circle around the city again.

I stare at the wallscreen as I put one spoonful of porridge into my mouth after another, and even manage to smile when the news anchor makes jokes, but most of my attention is with Zeal, with all of our amazing, beautiful horses who are putting all of their energy and strength into those of us lucky enough to know them. My worries about the coming evening fade away as I gradually begin to feel stronger and full of self-belief, as if I can do absolutely anything.

When I've finished my porridge and toast, I hurry to the bedroom and get dressed in black jeans and a navy t-shirt and hoodie, then set about hanging pictures on the walls. I see Zeal in all of them, regardless of their content. He's blowing hard as he pushes onward, his mane and tail lifted away from his sweating body by the air through which he and the rest of the herd are forcing themselves. I hear shouting through his ears and then gunfire – the herd has been spotted by some of the guards on top of the wall! It's all I can do not to scream out loud, but I keep my back to the wallscreen and grind my teeth together.

I will Zeal to be okay. I know he is unaffected by either the noise or the bullets, as are the rest of the horses. How do I know that? I immediately know the answer. Because he does. He senses their wellbeing as easily as he does his own, for they are linked somehow. The herd is one giant beast with all of its component parts contributing to its movement, its energy, its flow. And all of us who are sensitive enough to know it are linked by association.

Jimmy is the next to realise it. *Pamela? Is that you?*

Yes, it's me. Go to the toilet, Jimmy, and shut yourself into a cubicle or you'll attract attention. Chloe, you too. CHLOE!

Yes, sorry, I'm, err, I'm going. How is this happening?

Chloe? Pamela? The horses! They're shooting at the horses. That's Sophie. I have no idea how I know, but I do.

Sophie, go and make yourself a cup of tea and calm down, I tell her. *They're okay, you can feel they are. Keep yourself moving or you'll freeze in place and people will want to know what's wrong.*

I suddenly realise that I need to follow my own advice. I bend down to pick up the next picture, and hold it against the wall as if deciding whether it's right there, all the while being aware of Sophie telling Sam to get a hold of himself and get out of sight of anyone.

Your horses are safe. Dad's had a lot of practice at destroying bullets and I'm not bad at it either.

TANIA? I sense all of the other Sensitives asking the same question in the same instant that I do, and know that none of us need an answer for we know it's Tania as surely as if she were standing in front of each of us. More gunfire erupts and we sense Tania's amusement.

It'll take a while before they realise they're always going to miss. Your horses have put themselves in this position for good reason. Take strength from them and from one another. We'll see you later.

This is amazing, Sam announces, *I can feel all of you, who you are, what you think... oh!*

Yup, we can feel you too, Chloe tells him. *Don't worry, we all knew about you and Sophie anyway.*

We all fall silent as we realise that nothing is private between any of us any longer. We feel Chloe's mortification as Jimmy senses how she feels about him, and then her relief when she discovers that the feeling is mutual. I begin to pull myself back from the others, feeling uncomfortable about knowing what I know, but then sense the others recoiling back to themselves too.

No, don't, come back, all of you, I plead, *this is important, it has to be, Tania's right, the horses wouldn't be allowing us to experience this through them if it wasn't. Feel the energy they're giving us and use it to be brave, to stay in this group mind of ours.* I sense them all hesitating. They reach for their horses and feel the confirmation of my thought.

It's kind of cool, I guess, Sophie observes. *Weird, but cool, as if we're all fragments that have broken away from each other but now we're back together, we're whole and strong again.*

Her thoughts resonate so completely with the rest of us that none of us feel the need to answer. None of us feel the need to volunteer anything else. We all slowly continue with the tasks that keep us appearing to be normal, while basking in the togetherness our horses have afforded us with them and one another.

When we sense that the horses are close to completing their circuit of the city, we all think the same thought at the same time, for any idea of separateness isn't possible. *Thank you.*

I bite my lip at the sense of loss I feel as I find myself alone in my own head, then smile as I remember I am never alone. Zeal is tired, I can feel it, and a little sore… and then he isn't. I recognise the touch of Tania's energy on my horse's as she relieves him of his strains and gives his body a gentle boost.

Thank you, Zeal, for everything. You and the other horses are just amazing, I tell him.

We are as we are. As are you.

I jump at a knock on the door, and glance at the clock. It's half past five! It'll be getting dark soon. I hurry to answer the door, noticing on my way past the bedroom that Shield is fast asleep in the middle of the bed.

Clare smiles at me. 'You look better. Here, take these and I'll bring the rest.' She hands me two bags of shopping and then carries the remainder past me. 'Wow, you've been busy!' She nods at the pictures that now cover the living room walls, most of which I have no recollection of hanging. 'Just the last few to put up, I see. You'll be glad to know I managed to get more nails and hooks.' She puts her bags down on the living room floor and passes me a tatty piece of paper from her pocket. 'Here's your list, I've ticked everything I managed to get in the quantities you asked for, and I've marked those I could only get in a smaller quantity.'

'You're a star, thanks very much.' I take the piece of paper and head for the kitchen. 'I managed to catch up on a load of sleep which is a great relief.'

'Oh, it is, that's brilliant.' Clare sounds a little too relieved, as if she were more worried about me than I realised. 'I'll just unpack the bits for out here onto the coffee table, shall I, then I'll be there with the food.'

As soon as I'm out of sight of the wallscreen, I look at the back of the list where my message has been erased and another written in its place.

Guards change at 7.35pm tonight. We'll have 15 mins to reach the tunnel while debriefing occurs. Next guard change is at midnight. 15 mins for our return. Virus to scramble wrist safe location data will be released at 6.30pm. See you later, Phil

---

Zeal, please let Photon know I'll collect Jimmy at seven tonight.

You may confer with him yourself. I sense Zeal becoming Photon and Zeal, and immediately sense Jimmy.

Pamela? They're doing it again? Awesome!

Yes, it feels as if they know we can handle this now. It's easier, isn't it? Anyway, I'm just letting you know that Clare's just given me the timings for tonight, and I'll be with you at seven.

I'll be outside as seven strikes. Thanks, Pamela, are you sure you don't mind? I feel as if I should be able to go by myself now, I can feel where Photon is.

There's strength in numbers, remember?

I sense his smile. *I don't think any of us will ever be able to forget.*

Can you ask Photon to link you with all the others, and tell them to exit their buildings behind someone else so they don't register on the scanners, and that we have between seven thirty-five and seven fifty to get to the tunnel; it'll give them an idea what time their partners will be there to collect them. They might feel strong enough to go to their horses alone now, but their partners still need their guidance to get to the tunnel, they can't feel where their horses are like we can.

Sure. See you later.

'Your sleep really has done you the world of good, hasn't it?' Clare says, putting a bag on the worktop. She glances at the note in my hand and mouths, 'Okay?'

I nod and mouth back, 'You?'

She nods and mouths, 'The horses helped'.

I smile and say loudly, 'It really has, such good timing, what with starting work tomorrow.' I draw her into a hug and whisper, 'The Sensitives are feeling much stronger too, they'll be ready and waiting for the rest of us to collect them.' I push her gently away and say, 'This is fantastic, you and Belinda got everything, honestly, I can't thank you enough.'

She lifts a hand and waves to me as she says, 'Don't mention it. Have a good day tomorrow, I'll be thinking of you. I'd better be getting home, so I'll see myself out. See you around, okay?'

I blow her a kiss. 'See you around.'

I'm not really hungry, having had such a late breakfast, but I make myself a spaghetti bolognese and eat it in the living room in front of the wallscreen. I have no idea what I'm watching; all of my attention is turned to thinking through my plan for this evening and on periodically reaching through the screen to check whether I'm being watched and by how many. I'm pleased that there are periods when I'm not being observed at all, and when I am, it's by a single observer whose interest in me is fleeting.

I finish eating and take my time washing up and cleaning the kitchen. Then I make a big show of looking through the books in my bookcase. I choose one, then make my way to my bedroom where I turn on the sound system and select a compilation of easy listening music. Shield's ear flickers but he doesn't wake up. I check my watch. Half past six. Jimmy's apartment block is just around the corner from mine so I have plenty of time, but I want to exit my building without putting my eyes to the scanner in order to open the main door, so I'll need a bit of time to ensure I can coincide with someone else's entrance or exit. My heart starts to beat more quickly and I begin to feel a little nauseous.

I hurry across the hall to the bathroom and empty my bladder, then splash cold water on my face. I can do this. I go back to my bedroom and select a black scarf and a black, padded jacket from my wardrobe. It may be spring, but the nights are cold. I put a lipstick in my pocket, then lean into the middle of the bed and stroke the top of Shield's head with the back of my finger, whispering, 'See you later I hope, little man.'

I go out into the hallway and silently open my front door. I put my lipstick on the floor against the doorframe, then allow the door's slow-closing hinge to bring the door to rest against it so that there is a small gap. If I make it home, I'll be able to enter without using the eye scanner, and if I don't, Shield will have a way of getting out. When I get to the lift, I look back at my door. The shadow of the door frame is hiding the fact that it isn't quite closed. Perfect.

I say, 'Ground,' and the lift begins to descend. I watch the numbers above the door light up red in turn as I pass each floor, willing the numbers of the floors I have yet to pass to turn green, indicating that someone is waiting to join me in the lift. I feel as if my heart is thumping in my throat by the time the number six flashes green. I let out a long, deep breath and wipe the sweat from my forehead.

The lift comes to a stop and I smile as the door slides open and a young woman steps in, pushing a pram. She smiles nervously and turns her back to me. My heart sinks as she says, 'Second,' and I begin to sweat again, but when she exits at the second floor and a man enters the lift in her place, I can't believe my luck. I hold my breath until he says, 'Ground,' then let it out silently.

He turns around to me. 'Evening. I haven't seen you before, you must be new to the block.' His eyes are cold and hard.

I remind myself, as I have so many times over the past week, that his harsh, suspicious air is normal for people who aren't in regular contact with horses, but each and every hair on my body stands on end nevertheless. 'Um, yes, I'm on the twenty-ninth floor.'

He nods as if he doesn't believe me. 'And your name is?'

'Pamela.' I hold out my hand, which I'm sure is clammy.

He takes it in his leather-gloved one. 'David.'

Thankfully, the lift comes to a stop and the door slides open. David stands to the side and holds out his arm towards the foyer. 'After you.'

'Er, thank you.' Dammit, I need him to go before me so that it will be his eye scan that opens the door. I walk slowly, hoping he'll overtake me but his heels click steadily on the tiled floor behind me. When I'm almost at the scanner, I begin to panic. They must be on to me, they must know I've sneaked out of my apartment and David must have been sent to find out what I'm doing. I'll have to go back and when they question me, make some excuse about wanting to know exactly how long it takes for the lift to reach the ground floor in preparation for my first morning at my new job. But then I won't see Zeal. My horse's face floods my mind and I reach out to him, finding him as calm and determined as always. My panic subsides. I need to calm down and stay focused.

I stop suddenly and rub my eye, then stagger forward slightly as David brushes my arm on his way past. 'Sorry,' I say, 'I've got something in my eye.'

'It's called an eyeball,' he mutters and continues on his way.

I rub my eye for a second longer and then walk after him. He pauses to look into the scanner and when the door opens, I hurry through behind him and immediately turn in the opposite direction to that which he has taken, sighing with relief as his heels click steadily away from me.

I let out the breath I've been holding, and check my watch. Twenty to seven. I have time to walk on past Jimmy's block and then double back to check I'm not being followed. I don't think David was on to me, but I need to be sure.

I arrive at Jimmy's block bang on time, just as he is exiting the building behind an elderly woman. His face lights up when he sees me, his eyes full of relief. I hold out my arms and he doesn't hesitate to join me in a hug.

'I nearly turned around and ran back up the stairs,' Jimmy whispers. 'I need to see Photon but I'm scared. Are you sure about this? You think we can actually do this?'

I knew he'd be scared despite the horses' efforts earlier, and I worried that his fear would fuel my own, but it has the opposite effect. I find that I am more determined than ever to get us both out of the city to our horses, and more than that, I want to defy those who want to take our choices, our happiness, our very souls from us. They may think they have succeeded in disguising their malignant desperation for power and control with their apparently benign provision of safety and comfort, but they haven't, and I will ensure that an ever increasing number of people see that.

'I know we can do it,' I whisper to Jimmy. 'More to the point, our horses know we can do it, you can feel that as well as I can. They're waiting for us, so let's go, we have half an hour to get into position to cross the open space between the outermost building and the wall when the guards are changing. You can feel where Photon is, right?'

'Yes, absolutely.'

'Come on then, let's go.' I take hold of his arm as if we're just friends huddling together in order to keep warm whilst out for a walk.

None of the police patrolling the streets give us a second glance, but I feel Jimmy tense each time one of them passes us. We don't speak much as we weave our way between everyone else hurrying along the brightly lit pavement, at this time presumably on their way out for the evening to spend time with friends and family. I find myself wondering how much longer that will be allowed; whether our social plans will gradually become as controlled and limited as our other choices. I promise myself that whatever measures are introduced, we'll find ways around them. We are the resistance. We are family.

I squeeze Jimmy's arm and murmur, 'Okay?'

'Just about,' he murmurs back. 'Thanks, Pamela. I couldn't be doing this without you.'

The crowds gradually lessen as we approach the outskirts of the city. By the time we're almost at Chloe's block, we are alone. We turn a corner and see Belinda leaning against a wall in the distance. She straightens as Chloe emerges from her building having caught the door from someone who has just entered it. The two embrace and hurry away from us. I check my watch. Half past seven. We're bang on time.

I glance behind us. There are only a few people around and they all have their heads down as they hurry to their destinations. 'So far so good,' I say to Jimmy. 'For once, I'm actually relieved that we're all spread out across the city and approaching from different directions. Hopefully we'll all get beyond the reach of the lighting before we've amassed in any kind of number.'

Belinda and Chloe turn the corner ahead of us, towards where Jimmy, Chloe and I know the horses are waiting on the other side of Will and Tania's tunnel. Then they stop in their tracks as two black-clothed figures step out of the darkness, in front of them. Police.

'Oh no, oh no, Chloe,' Jimmy whispers. 'What do we do?'

I pull him around to face me. 'They haven't seen us yet. Pretend we've just met on the street and are talking, and I'll watch them over your shoulder.'

'They'll be arrested,' Jimmy says, his eyes darting around. 'We will be too, none of us have a good reason to be at the city limits and heading out there. What's happening, Pamela? Tell me, what's happening to Chloe?'

'She's okay at the moment, Belinda's talking to the police.

You know what she's like, she's capable, she'll take care of Chloe. I need you to look at me. Jimmy. Look at me.' Jimmy's eyes settle on mine. 'Keep looking at me. Look right into my eyes. See me, Jimmy.'

'I s...see y...you,' he says. Then he gulps and repeats, 'I see you.'

I nod. 'Good. Now reach for Photon and when you find him, hang on to him, okay? Have you got him?'

Jimmy's eyes slacken and his shoulders relax a little. 'I've got him.'

'Okay, now ask him to link with Minerva. When he does, you're going to need to reach Chloe through the horses and keep her calm while I watch what's going on, okay?' He nods.

I glance over his shoulder at where Belinda is shaking her head at the police. One of them laughs and pushes her. The other catches her and pushes her back to his friend. Chloe puts her hands to her head and shakes it.

'Jimmy, keep talking to Chloe, I'll sort this, I just need you both to stay with your horses and one another, and stay calm,' I say.

He nods and then his eyes widen as he looks over my shoulder. I turn to see Phil approaching with Sam, whose face is shaped by horror as he watches Belinda and Chloe.

'We outnumber them,' Phil says in a low voice. 'Come on, let's get going. You, me and Belinda against the two of them. We'll take them down and deal with them when we get back later. We haven't got time to hang around.'

He walks past me, but Sam stops and looks as if he's about to turn and run. One of the police is now holding Belinda's arms behind her back while the other slowly runs his tongue up the side of her face. Chloe is leaning against the wall, her hands now over her face.

Time slows right down. My inward breath is like a silent breeze that builds up to a gale before ever so slowly blowing itself back out. I remember Cliff stepping out, gun raised, in front of the police who came to take our horses. I flinch as I hear the shot and watch him crumple. I don't feel grief. I feel gratitude to my husband for showing us so clearly what will happen if we try to fight like with like. We will lose.

I sense Zeal's approval of my thoughts and as time continues to move at a hundredth of its usual pace, I remember the advice he gave me earlier. *You must ensure that your purpose and ideology grow strong enough to endure after you and we have all moved on.* I understand. We will never get our resistance off the ground if we do it according to the ways of humans. If we are to survive long enough to create a resistance that will survive into the future, we must adopt the ways of the horses. But what to do now? More of Zeal's advice swirls around in my mind. *The lead female trusts her herd to give her the information she needs and she trusts her instincts to tell her how to use that information.*

I turn to Jimmy and Sam. 'Do you trust me?'

They look at one another and Sam says, 'Yes.' Jimmy nods, his eyes flicking between me and Chloe. 'Then wait here. Don't run, okay? I know how to sort this out. When the police leave, come and join the rest of us.'

'Okay,' Sam says. He nods sideways at Jimmy. 'I'll look after him. Good luck.'

I run after Phil, who is striding towards the police. I have to act according to the ways of the horses, and that means filling myself up with Zeal. I allow my sense of him to fill my mind and I know what to do.

I catch up with Phil and fall into place beside him. 'Let me handle this, okay? I know what I'm doing.'

'So do I,' he says. 'I'm going to beat those two senseless and then I'm going to get everyone out of here.'

'And then you, Belinda and Chloe – and probably I – will never be able to return. Sure, we could run, but even if we survived out there on our own, what then? We need to be here, Phil. Our horses have prepared us to create a resistance, not to run at the first sign of trouble. The others need us. I've got this. Okay?'

He growls as one of the men slowly unzips Belinda's coat.

I move across in front of him to stop him running to help Belinda. He glares at me and I stare back up at him. 'We can't let them see you here, you're too valuable to us. Put your hood up and go back to Sam and Jimmy. Belinda can handle herself and so can I. Let. Me. Sort. It.'

He glares at me for a second longer and then turns and heads back towards Jimmy and Sam.

I hurry over to the police who are assaulting Belinda, and say, 'Evening, nice evening for a stroll, isn't it?'

Belinda, bright red with fury, glares at me as if I've gone insane. The man holding her scowls at me. The other turns around, his eyes bright with the thrill of violence and lust, and looks me slowly up and down. 'Get on your way or you'll be next,' he says.

'I'll be gone just as soon as you release my friends and agree that you never saw them or me,' I say. I hold out my wrist. 'Will a grand for each of you do it? The money's just sitting in my account, waiting to be transferred to yours.'

The man looks at my wrist safe and I see the violence in his eyes fading away and being replaced by avarice. 'Two grand each.'

'Two grand each,' I agree. 'Done.'

The man moves his wrist close to mine and I say, 'Transfer two thousand.' When my wrist safe flashes, I hold out my wrist to his partner, who can't let go of Belinda quickly enough. He thrusts his arm towards me and I transfer the money to his account.

'Remember, you never saw us here,' I tell the men. 'If you ever feel yourself beginning to forget that, please be very sure that if you try to take me down, I'll take you down with me.' I hold my wrist up to them. 'My account will show the amount I just transferred to each of you. There's more where that came from if you look after us in the future when I call on you to, there's jail and probably the firing squad if you betray us. Have a lovely evening, gentlemen. Come on, you two, we have a stroll to finish.'

Belinda is already helping Chloe to her feet.

'I want four grand,' one of the men says.

'I imagine you do, but you already have the two we agreed.' I hold my wrist up to my mouth and say, 'Wrist safe instruction. At seven fifty pm, transfer account records to the police station, marked for the attention of the duty sergeant.' I glare at the men. 'You have five minutes to get out of my sight. If you manage it, I'll cancel my request. If you harm any of us or even speak to any of us again, the request will go through.'

Both men look at me with hate-filled eyes. The man who restrained Belinda spits at my feet and walks away. His partner glowers at me for a few seconds longer, then follows him.

Belinda is holding a sobbing Chloe to her. I put my arms around both of them. 'You're okay now, they're leaving.'

Belinda hugs me back tightly. 'Thank you,' she whispers.

I murmur, 'Wrist safe instruction. Cancel previous instruction.' Then I say to Chloe and Belinda, 'We're all in this together, the three of us, the others and all of our horses.'

'Four grand though?' Belinda says.

I chuckle. 'Cliff and I lived off the money you all gave us for lessons and livery. We never spent a penny of the money we got for selling you all your horses, it didn't seem right somehow. I can't think of any better way to spend it than bribing our way further into the system, can you?'

'So that's how you did it,' Phil says as Jimmy runs to Chloe and takes her in his arms. 'Good thinking, that money will go a long way; we'll only have to bribe someone once and we can blackmail them into helping us forever after that.'

Belinda chuckles. 'Pamela's all over that already.' She looks at her watch. 'Look at that, seven fifty and they're out of sight.'

'And we've missed our window to reach the tunnel,' Phil says. 'The new shift of guards will be patrolling the wall.'

'So this was all for nothing?' Chloe says with a sniff.

'No,' I say firmly. 'We can make it past the guards.'

'How?' Sam says. 'They'll have night vision goggles as well as guns, they'll shoot us down easily, one by one.'

'You, Chloe, Jimmy and I have an exact sense of where the tunnel is, thanks to our horses waiting for us on the other side,' I reply, 'and we know when we're being watched. We'll find something to hide behind at the edge of the darkness until we sense eyes focusing in our direction. Then when we can't sense them anymore, we'll know they've moved on and we'll have a gap to make a run for the tunnel.'

'Lead the way,' Belinda says to me, and Phil steps into place beside her. Chloe, Jimmy and Sam hang back. 'Sorry,' Belinda adds, and moves back to Chloe's side. 'Come on, Minerva's waiting for you. I won't let anything happen to you, Chloe, I promise, none of us will.'

'Jimmy?' I say, holding out my hand. 'You can close your eyes if it helps, I won't let you fall. Fill yourself up with Photon, he'll carry you to him.'

Phil moves back to Sam's side. 'I don't know where the tunnel is. You lead me and I'll have your back, I promise. You can do this, you can make it out to Hector.'

At his horse's name, Sam stands a little straighter. 'He says everyone is there except for the six of us. They're waiting for us.'

Phil holds up his hand and Sam high fives it, albeit weakly. Jimmy takes my hand. Chloe links her arm through Belinda's and points with a shaking finger. 'That way.'

We walk along the back of the building, the last before the wasteland that separates the city from its surrounding wall. Lights shine from most of its windows, highlighting mounds of rubble and remnants of building materials, and the odd bush, for some distance. No one else is around. No one else would risk being caught where they have no reason to be.

Chloe, Jimmy, Sam and I all stop at the same time and look out into the darkness. I point past the nearest pile of rubble. 'The tunnel is in a dead straight line that way. Come on, let's leave the light behind.'

I hurry away from the building pulling Jimmy behind me, and looking slightly away from my direction of travel so that my peripheral night vision kicks in as I move into the darkness. I head for a pile of what looks like wooden pallets and stop behind it, invisible now to the buildings as well as the wall.

Jimmy murmurs, 'Someone's looking in our direction.'

'I know,' I whisper. 'We'll wait here until the guard has moved on. At least we have a bit of light from the moon so that when it's time to move, we should be able to do it quickly and quietly.' I turn to the others. 'Everyone okay?'

'Yep, happy to wait,' Phil says. I could hug him for managing to sound so relaxed.

It is more than ten minutes before I feel as if the space in which we're standing belongs to us alone. Jimmy and I move at the same time and I sense, rather than hear, the others following behind. Interesting; I can sense the proximity of others as well as when I'm being watched, just like Zeal told me. If I can sense it, the three Sensitives with me will be able to as well. I hope they know it because I don't want to risk telling them this close to the wall.

The huge barricade that has kept us from our horses looms out of the darkness – we're nearly at the tunnel! I hurry past the last pile of rubbish… and immediately realise my mistake. This close to the wall and with nothing else behind which to hide, I should have waited behind the rubbish pile to make sure I couldn't sense anyone but the six of us in the vicinity. I sense the guard now. I stop suddenly, as does Jimmy. Chloe grunts as she walks into me, then whispers, 'Oh no!'

'What is it?' Belinda whispers urgently.

'There's someone up there,' Sam whispers back. 'He's not looking at us just yet but we can sense him, like when someone sits next to you and you can feel their body heat.'

We all freeze, unsure whether to run on to the tunnel, or back the way we've just come.

All of a sudden, we hear a whinny, then another, then a pounding of hooves.

'Hector,' Sam whispers just as I sense Zeal also bursting out of the trees among which he was standing waiting for me; through him, I know that all six of our horses and Heart are now thundering along the base of the wall. There is shouting from atop it and a gunshot cracks through the cold, still air, followed by several more.

'Our horses are giving us time,' I whisper for Belinda and Phil's benefit. 'As soon as they know we're safe in the tunnel, they'll head back into the trees. Come on, run.'

No one argues. We all pelt towards the wall, towards where I and the Sensitives know the tunnel entrance has to be. I reach the brambles first. I pull my coat sleeves down over my hands and pull the thorny stalks to one side. 'Down there, hurry.'

Jimmy disappears, followed by Belinda, Chloe, Sam and then Phil, who grabs hold of my arm and pulls me behind him. I feel for the steps that have to be there, and as soon as I gain purchase on the top two, I turn and fumble for the brambles, pulling them back across the tunnel entrance. I put my hands out and touch soil on either side. I reach out with my foot and lower myself onto step after step, all the time supporting myself in the dark with my hands against the tunnel walls until the ground finally levels out. I bend over, my hands on my knees, panting with relief.

'Everyone okay?' Belinda says in between gasps.

We all answer her and then are silent apart from the wheezing and blowing it takes us to regain our breath.

'I can't believe we made it,' Jimmy says eventually. 'And the horses are safe, they're back in the trees.'

'So either that guard needs more practice at shooting while wearing night goggles, or he was just firing warning shots,' Phil replies.

'Or his bullets disintegrated before they got anywhere near the horses,' Chloe says with a giggle.

'What do you mean?' Belinda says.

'Will and Tania can make bullets disintegrate, they did it when the guards were shooting at the horses earlier on, they're awesome,' Sam says.

'The guards were shooting at the horses earlier on?' Phil says. 'Why?'

'They saw them when they were circling the city to give us all the energy to break the rules and get out here, to them,' Jimmy says. 'And it worked, we did it! I can't believe it, we actually did it!'

'Will and Tania made bullets disintegrate? How?' Belinda says. 'And how do you know?'

'We've no idea how they did it, but they did,' I say. 'We know

because when the horses were all cantering together, they felt like
they were all different parts of the same animal and because they
were linked so closely, all of us were linked too. We could
communicate with Will and Tania as easily as we can with our
horses.'

Phil whistles. 'That sounds impossible, but something tells me
it isn't. Just when I think I have a handle on who the horses are
and what they can do, something else happens and I'm confused
all over again.'

I find myself suddenly unable to think of anything other than
being with my horse. I put my hand to the tunnel wall and feel my
way along it in the pitch black, bypassing the others. 'Come on,
let's get to our horses, everything will feel clearer then.'

The only sounds are of the six of us breathing, and the odd
curse as someone stumbles on the slightly uneven ground in the
darkness. I sense Zeal just ahead, calmly waiting for me, and fill
my heart with all he is to me.

When the tunnel begins to lighten slightly, my heart leaps. I
pick up my pace and don't slow it even when I reach a flight of
steps; going up into the moonlight is infinitely easier than
descending away from it, despite the number and steepness of the
steps. I'm gasping again by the time I get to the top, but I don't
care. My horse is standing in the moonlight that filters down
between the leaves, watching me.

His ears are pricked towards me, yet soft. His eyes appear
black in the dim light rather than the pale brown I know them to
be, but they are shining. He lets out a low whicker as I run to him
and when I fling my arms around his neck, he stands firm, as
warm, as solid as he knows I need him to be.

I breathe in the smell of him as I sob into his neck, so happy to
be with him that I can no longer hold anything inside. My grief,
my devastation, my anger, my horror, my fear – everything I have

held in check since he and Cliff left me – all come flooding out and are welcomed by him. When I have nothing left but the love I feel for him, I finally let him go. He nuzzles my hair as another nose gently wiggles on my hand.

I turn to see Heart standing behind me, alone in the night while the other five horses stand with their people on their backs, waiting. I stroke her nose gently. *Heart, I'm so sorry.*

She turns and walks away from me, and all of the other horses apart from Zeal immediately fall in behind her. She doesn't need my sorrow. She is the leader of the herd and she would have all of its members back together in one place. I waste no more time. I vault onto Zeal's back and revel in how it feels to be there again, even as I sense his weariness after his long canter around the city earlier today. Before I can ask him whether I should get off and walk beside him, he is on the move, bringing up the rear of the small herd as the horses pick their way between the trees. He will do what needs to be done. It is his way and the way of the horses. The way I will ensure we all follow.

NINETEEN

Tania

There has been laughing, shouting, even singing at one point since Pamela's students were brought out of the trees by their horses in pairs or small groups. Without exception, they are all glowing brighter.

Red and orange energy forms a burning armour around those with fire in their bellies, largely protecting them from the energy of The Old that lashes at them, leaving them free to see the regime for what it is, and to think how to resist it. The blue flecks in their energy pulsate, some of the pulses becoming small tendrils that manage to extend to their horses so that while they are near them, they are sensitive to their moods and needs. Perfect. Their time with their horses will ensure their sensitivity endures and constantly reminds them that strength is not achieved by violence.

Indigo and violet energy bursts from the Sensitives, radiating out in all directions as it reaches for and probes everyone and everything. In this environment, where they are surrounded by nature, their horses and one another, the Sensitives feel nothing but pleasure, but my heart goes out to them for the terror they feel when they are in the city. It tries to convince them it is their own when in fact it is merely latching onto the tendrils of intuition that constantly emanate from them, using them as super conduits right into their hearts and minds. Now that they can communicate with their horses from a distance, however, their connections with them will strengthen and afford them ever more protection from the energy of The Old.

Dad and I sit on a fallen tree, happy to watch the people and horses before us even as we monitor the situation in which the six yet to arrive have found themselves. When the horses and all of the Sensitives stiffen and turn to look towards the wall, we both stand up on the wide trunk. The three red-oranges nearest us all jump.

'Everything's okay,' Dad says. 'Some of the horses have just gone to help Pamela and the five with her to reach the tunnel. They'll be with us very shortly.'

A cacophony of questions disrupts the peace of the evening as the red-oranges all turn to us.

'Are they alright?'

'Who are the five with her? Who's missing?'

'Why are they late?'

'What's happened?'

'Should we go and help?'

'Is Pamela okay? Who's with her?'

The indigo-violets answer them.

'They're okay, the horses are coming back to the trees.'

'They got held up by police but it's okay, Pamela sorted it.'

'It's Belinda, Phil, Chloe, Jimmy and Sam who are with Pamela. Sam says to wait here, they're on their way through the tunnel.'

Some of the red-oranges turn back to us, and one waves at us. 'Thanks for helping us to be with our horses and each other again.

I'm sorry I gave you both a hard time when we last saw you. I still don't understand why you left us and why you came back at the moment you did, but building a tunnel under the wall like that for us all, well it's as amazing as much as it's unfathomable.'

'How did you do it?' another red-orange asks. 'I don't see any machinery here, and there are just the two of you. How did you excavate a tunnel of that length and depth in such a short time with no help, let alone do it without being discovered by the guards on the wall?'

'Never mind that,' another says. 'How did you get out here before the tunnel even existed? Who are the two of you?'

Dad joins his light flow to mine. Within seconds, the fifty-eight people and horses are bathed in white light. The indigo-violets smile, their energy tendrils ceasing their constant reaching and exploring and just floating in the love with which we bathe them all. The red-oranges all flinch then look around at one another and the light which continues to defy the darkness. Many of them lean into their horses, who stand firm, supporting them as our light probes at the shields of red and orange light that they have unwittingly tightened around themselves, until their blue flecks provide a way in and it reaches them. All of them relax.

'They're from the future.' Pamela doesn't shout as she and Zeal emerge from the trees, but her voice carries to the furthest person nevertheless. Her red, orange, yellow, green, blue, indigo and violet energy spreads far from her, reaching all of those who turn to hear what she has to say. 'Their people can do things we're not capable of dreaming about let alone comprehending, and we shouldn't try. They've built us a tunnel, the first of many they intend to build in order to ensure we can always get to our horses when we need to, as it's so important we do.'

Most stand still, shocked by her words even as they attempt to understand why her voice sounds different; stronger, more confident, more passionate than they remember. Sophie and Clare run to her and her companions, all of whom except for Pamela dismount and embrace the two of them. Pebble and Maple follow their humans so that the original eight horses and humans of the resistance stand together with Heart.

'All of us have repeatedly thanked the heavens for our horses,' Pamela continues, 'for everything they've taught us, for being the people they've helped us to be, and for the friendships we have as a result of having been drawn together by them. Thanks to them, we've become unrecognisable from who we were. We've discovered aspects of ourselves that we would never have known we possessed. We've maintained our sanity, our humanity, while everyone around us has slowly been stripped of theirs. And now we have to find a way to remain as we are even though those around us are ruled by fear, suspicion and violence. Happily for us, the horses have provided that way forward. The Way Of The Horse.' Pamela leans forward and strokes Zeal's neck before continuing.

'Our beautiful horses are sensitive to their surroundings and to one another. They know when another needs help and they give it, as they've done for each and every one of us. They know their strength is in numbers, so they stick together. They never attack but they will defend themselves and one another. Most importantly, they take abuse without ever letting it change them. Each and every horse here was hurt when Cliff and I bought them. Each of them has good reason to hate humans for the way they were used and abused. None of them do. They allowed Will and Tania to heal them and then to ride them so that we would have the confidence to ride them too, and they've dedicated themselves ever since to showing us how to make the best of ourselves.'

No one else speaks but they all move closer to their horses. Arms encircle furry necks, hands stroke velvety noses, heads rest against withers as humans and horses alike listen to Pamela's insights.

'We all see what's happening around us,' she continues, 'and who our people are becoming. There are just sixty-four of us and hundreds of thousands of them. We can't help all of them. We can't even help most of them, but we can help some of them. Thanks to our horses, we're capable of recognising those with the potential and desire to be sensitive, brave and kind. It's up to us to find ways to reach them and let them know they aren't alone, to welcome them into our family and protect them, to remind them who they really are and help them find the strength to hold on to that knowledge. It's up to us to resist the worst aspects of humanity whilst safeguarding the best, so that when the worst of humanity eventually destroys itself, the best is left still standing.'

Heads nod in the moonlight and a red-orange says, 'Hear, hear.' Another claps and yet another cheers. Then there is cheering and hugging all around even as Pamela remains sitting astride her horse in silence. The words she has spoken so far have been hers, but now she listens intently to Zeal so that she'll know what to say next.

'We are sixty-four,' she calls out. The seven standing with her all shout and gesticulate until everyone else has quietened back down. 'We are sixty-four who can never again all be in the same place at the same time. We are eight groups, each containing eight people who have learnt and grown together, and that is no coincidence. The Sensitives among you will feel the truth of my words. The rest of you, observe the friends you have come to know and love so well, and trust from their reactions that my words – Zeal's words – are true.

'Everything has an energy, everything IS energy. The number eight carries the energy of infinity and that means each group of eight is more than just a group, it's a unit of infinite strength, courage, wisdom, intuition and love – every single aspect the horses have shown us we possess – and you need only remain connected to one another for that to remain the case.

'One unit of eight is powerful. We have eight units of eight, which will give us the ability to be far more than the sixty-four we appear to be. Eight units with the energy of infinity, all working towards the same goal, will create a level of momentum that is unstoppable.'

The red-oranges look incredulous and immediately look towards the Sensitives in their groups, who are all smiling and nodding.

'We can't all meet like this again because we'll start attracting attention, and that's the last thing we need. What we can do is stay tightly connected within our groups of eight while we infiltrate the health, security, social and food production services so that we can help those who need us, recruit those who would join us, and defy those who would destroy us. The Sensitives among us can relay information within and between groups, with their horses' help. The rest of you are, as Tania has called you, Kindred Spirits. Take the sensitivity, the strength and the camaraderie the horses have brought out in you, and combine it with the fire inside you that you've always had. Help me to build a resistance that will endure through the generations. Visit your horses whenever you can and allow them to remind you of The Way Of The Horse. Any step away from it will be a step closer to insanity.'

Pamela pauses and looks around at her spellbound audience. In a softer voice, she adds, 'It won't seem like it in the days, months and years to come, but we are the lucky ones. All of the other horses who were herded out of the city have fled, knowing they can do no more for their people. Ours have stayed. They'll never leave us because they know what we're capable of and they know we need their help. But they won't live for ever. Future generations won't have their guidance, so we need to take everything they are, everything we are, and pile it into a resistance that's self-perpetuating, that's strong enough to endure on its own. The way forward for all of us, for humanity, is The Way Of The Horse.'

Cheering begins again but Pamela holds up her hand. 'One last thing. If you want to, you can be away from here right now. Your horses will carry you far away from here and you'll probably survive. Or you can stay here where life will be difficult. The choice is yours.'

Dad and I allow our light flows to fade to nothing. Each of them must make their choice unaided, uninfluenced.

'If any of us leave, our group of eight won't have the infinity energy,' a Sensitive says.

Zeal shifts on his feet as Pamela says, 'That's right.'

'I want to leave, I'd give anything to leave, but I'm staying,' the Sensitive says, her last word husky as she only just manages to get it out.

Immediately, the Kindred Spirits in her unit surround her, hugging her and thanking her for her courage. The other three Sensitives in her unit don't try to speak for fear they'll be unable to. One of the Kindred Spirits extends an arm to them, welcoming them to join the group hug, to regain the strength that their choice to stay has cost them. Soon all eight are laughing and talking excitedly, as are all of the other groups except Pamela's. They stand watching the others until they are sure no one is going to leave. Then Pamela dismounts with a smile. She looks around at her unit, who all nod to her in the moonlight.

'What are you waiting for?' Pamela says. 'Come here, you lot.' They all laugh and form a ring, each hugging the two on either side of them as the reality of what Pamela has set in motion sinks in.

The horses wander off to graze while they monitor the process going on around them, always available to help the Sensitives of the eight groups to communicate silently with one another so that ideas and information are passed quickly between groups. I smile as I sense Infinity adding her energy to that which swirls gently above each unit.

Every now and then, a unit will disperse as its members seek out the company of their horses for a while before coming back together. Some of them ride their horses gently for short periods, grounding themselves, cementing into their thoughts The Way Of The Horse that Pamela has introduced.

Our work with them is done, Dad observes. *We could disappear without notice.*

We could, I agree. *But we won't.* It is no longer my way. Dad winks at me and squeezes my hand.

We wait until Pamela and some of the other Kindred Spirits begin checking the time, conscious of not missing the window they have to get everyone from the far side of the tunnel to the cover of the piles of debris while the guards are changing.

I stand back up on my tree trunk and call out, 'You all need to head back in a few minutes, I know that.' Heads turn in my direction and there is much nudging and shushing. 'I just wanted to thank you before you go.'

'Thank us?' Jimmy says. 'It's us who should be thanking you. And you, Will.'

I shake my head. 'What Dad and I have done comes easily to us. What you're doing is difficult but you're doing it anyway. Because of you all, humanity will survive – Dad and I are living proof of that. More importantly, because of you all and your amazing, magnificent horses, there are horses in the future who are everything horses have ever wanted to be. And lastly, because of you all, I've changed and become everything my soul wants me to be. I'm sorry we left without saying goodbye to you all last time, that was down to me, not Dad. I'm honoured to have met you all and to have spent time with you and your horses. So, thank you and goodbye.'

Dad lifts a hand. 'Bye, everyone.'

We both jump down from the log as everyone rushes over to us. We are swamped in arms and deafened by all of the farewells and appreciation with which we are showered, until finally only Pamela stands in front of us. She smiles and hugs Dad, then me.

'I'll miss you so much,' she whispers into my ear.

'You won't have time to miss us, what with your new job, leadership of the resistance, and your little one on the way,' I whisper back.

She pulls away from me and holds me at arm's length, her eyes wide. They soften as understanding dawns. She pulls me back into a hug and whispers, 'I've just begun feeling nauseous, I thought it was worry. But I'm forty-three, this can't be happening.'

'It's happening,' I whisper back. 'And you'll both be fine. Want to know how I know that?'

She groans. 'I'm not sure I really do, but go on.'

'Because Dad and I are living proof. We carry your DNA, Pamela. I'm proud to know you, Gran of many generations.' It is I who pulls back from her this time. I wish it were light so I could properly see her face, but the sense I have of her is enough. I chuckle and hug her again. 'Go on, you all need to be gone. Take my love with you, okay?'

She just stands there, looking between Dad and me as if she's never seen us before. 'How can you be leaving when I've only just found you?'

Dad takes both of her hands in his. 'It only appears as if we're leaving. We'll be constantly Aware of the horses so we can heal them any time they need it, and of you and what you're doing, so we'll always be with you in a way. If you ever need us, we'll be here in person, but you won't. You're everything your daughter and your people will need you to be. I'm so glad to have known you. Goodbye, Pamela.' He hugs her for a final time.

She steps back from us both and nods slowly. Then she turns and says, 'Come on, Sensitives, Kindred Spirits, we all need to be going. Hug your horses but know you'll be seeing them again very soon.' She strides away from us without a backward glance, leading by example as we know she always will. She stops to stroke Zeal's neck, then walks on into the trees.

As the Kindred Spirits and Sensitives follow her, I sense several cats following them.

'That's nine Sensitives who won't ever be sleeping alone again,' Dad says with a chuckle. 'We'd better make doors for each end of the tunnel to stop too many cats flooding back to the city at once.' He looks at me. 'So that's two doors, then another eleven tunnels and their doors, and we're all done here. I'm proud of you, Tan.'

He isn't referring to the tunnels and doors. There was a time I would have rolled my eyes at his sentiment, but I get it now. He is who he is and he can do everything he can do, but he's also a person. And a dad. My dad. I put an arm around his waist. 'Thanks, Dad, I'm proud of you too.'

We walk arm in arm over to the horses and stand, watching them graze in the chill of the night. Without exception, they are content. They have set their humans, and by extension all humans, on the path to balance, and they are content to continue guiding and supporting them so that they stay on it.

They will help the Sensitives to become as strong and grounded in their intuition as possible so that the trait attaches to their DNA in the same way that memories can, and will spread through the generations to follow. When their descendants intuit that the time has come to begin leaving the cities, it will be the descendants of the Kindred Spirits, or the Kindred as they will become known, who will help them to leave and become the Ancients, the founding fathers of The New.

The Way Of The Horse will endure. It will ensure that the Kindred, who can leave the cities at any time, stay to resist a regime rooted in madness. It will ensure that they provide help and hope to those who need it. It will ensure that they incite protests by way of graffiti, posters and rumours whenever new controlling measures are introduced. It will also ensure that they are kind to the genetically engineered Enforcers when everyone else taunts and torments those bred to hunt and kill anyone who defies the governors. They will perish alongside everyone they have helped, but their kindness will endure, living on in the Enforcers who will eventually be free of The Old and will name themselves for those who lived in love when all around them were living in fear. Their legacy, the opportunity for humanity to begin anew, will live on thanks to the horses who stand in front of us now.

'There's no mention of them in the Histories,' I murmur. 'They've done as much for the balance of this planet as the bonded horses did, as Ember has done, but they're the forgotten horses.'

Heart wanders over to me and rests her chin on my shoulder. Neither she nor any of the others have any interest in being remembered. They do what they do because they are who they are. I stroke her between her nostrils and then when she goes back to her grazing, I leave her be.

TWENTY

Will

*T*ania and I return to The Old every day for many more weeks, until all of the tunnels that will allow the Kindred Spirits and Sensitives to reach their horses, and the Ancients of the future to leave the city, are in place. We return home only when we are exhausted, to eat and sleep, then we are straight back to The Old so that those desperate to see their horses will have a choice of ways to exit the city as soon as possible; their chances of being discovered shrink with every extra opportunity to avoid routine.

When the last door has been attached to the last of the twelve tunnels we promised to excavate, we stand back and admire our work. We both sense Lia's desperation for us to return home and have, as she's repeatedly urged us to, "a well-earned break". But my daughter and I have one more thing to do first.

I look sideways at her as I think of Maverick and our need to protect our pack, and smile as the echo of my dog bounds around us both, eager for whatever is in store and delighted as always to be included. Where before Tania would have sighed or rolled her eyes, she now smiles back and says, 'Ready?'

She's gone within a few seconds. Maverick and I, protective over her as ever, follow.

The three of us arrive in exactly the same spot we left, yet it is unrecognisable. During the two hundred years since we were last here, nature has exerted the full force of her will. We stand in a dense forest that pushes against the city wall. We sense the madness that pervades the city being held there by the tranquillity exuding from the trees that surround us, the wildlife that has flourished, and the rivers that run clear to seas that are once again full of life.

The sounds of the forest are almost deafening as birds sing and squawk, squirrels chitter while leaping between lichen-covered branches, a vixen calls to her young, leaves mutter the words of the breeze that moves them, and a myriad of animals of all different sizes, from insects and worms to rabbits and badgers, wriggle and scuttle through the dense undergrowth all around us.

Cats yet remain in the city, their skills at avoiding detection having allowed them to continue to protect all of those who have needed them through the centuries, but the horses and dogs are long gone from the vicinity.

Together, we perceive The Old from a different perspective from when we were there before.

The ways of The Old were as harmful to humans as they were advantageous to everything else, Tania observes, tracing whorls in the bark of a nearby tree with her finger.

I lean against another tree which practically hums with strength and vitality. *Imprisoning their people in the cities with their own insanity served to shield the rest of the planet from their greedy, destructive ways, so that it could recover. I never tire of seeing the perfection in life. We're part of the same energy as everything else, so when we unbalance it, we can't help but become part of the rebalancing process, whether we want to be or not, whether we're even aware of it or not.*

Tania chuckles. *Even when we're Aware of it, we can still get taken by surprise.*

I reach out a hand to her and she takes it. *It's been hard for you, but even if I hadn't known the future, even if I hadn't known who you'd become, I would still have known both.*

Thanks, Dad. Shall we go home?

She doesn't need me to answer, and fades from my embrace. I look down at where I can just make out Maverick sitting at my feet. *Come on, boy, we're not needed here anymore.*

Tania is already sitting at the kitchen table, attacking a bowl of stew when I appear beside her. The front door slams, then the kitchen door is hurled open and Delta comes flying into the room, holding a sheaf of papers aloft so that they are safe from Rebel, Ash and Chase who are leaping around her as they accompany her in. When they notice Tania and me, they race to greet us both.

Lia winces as Delta slams her papers down on the table; after all these years, she still finds our niece's lack of subtlety a shock, even knowing and loving Prime as she does.

'I haven't come round before because I know you've been working so hard,' Delta says. 'But now you've finished what you were doing, I want you to know that I've been working hard too.' She points to the pile of paper. 'That's the story of the forgotten horses. I've written it down because I find it easier to order my thoughts that way, but now I have, I'll relay it to the Keeper Of The Histories in every community so they can add it to their records. The forgotten horses will be forgotten no longer!' Her eyes widen as Tania extricates herself from Chase's enthusiastic embrace, and throws her arms around her cousin.

'Thanks, Del, you're just the best,' Tania says. 'You always have been and I should have told you before, I know that, but I'm telling you now.'

Delta smiles. 'Thank you. I just thought their story should be told, so I have, and not just theirs, but the first Kindred, the Sensitives whose DNA lives on in so many bodies of The New to this day, and Pamela – I mean, she was both, wasn't she? If she was alive now, she'd be like you and your dad, I'm sure of it.'

Tania grins. 'And when I go to help the horses and their people at the next city, you'll keep following what I'm up to so you can record their stories too?'

Delta's face falls and she scowls, making the rest of us laugh, as we have so often, at how one so beautiful can manage to look so threatening. 'You're going back?'

'Del, I have to.' Tania looks at me and adds, 'I can manage on my own now.' I wink at her and she turns back to her cousin. 'Pamela's eight groups of eight have sown the seeds in the human collective consciousness for the existence of the Kindred and the Sensitives, but it's not strong enough yet to draw those in other cities to follow their example, to know The Way Of The Horse. I'm going to have to help in far more cities before that will happen.'

Delta glares at me. 'You're not going to leave her to make a dozen tunnels at every city on her own, are you?'

I shrug. 'I doubt it, but that's up to Tania. I'll do as much or as little as she needs me to.'

My daughter smiles the most beautiful smile and squints both of her eyes almost shut.

'Flaming lanterns, give it up will you, Tan?' Delta says. 'You're super Aware, you can disappear and reappear at will, and you can travel in time. Just accept that you can't, and never will be able to, wink?'

Tania laughs. 'Does this mean I'm forgiven? You'll keep your attention with me when I'm not here, and you'll document all of the forgotten horses and their people for the Histories?'

Delta rolls her eyes. 'Where else would my flaming attention be? It's not as if I can concentrate on anything else when you're up to your tricks anyway.'

I chuckle as they continue their banter, and am just about to take a seat and eat the stew that Lia has spooned into a bowl for me, when Maverick's echo appears. The third member of our triad needs us.

Lia picks up the bowl. 'I'll put this where it'll keep warm for you, love. Take as long as you need.'

Tania blows me a kiss even as she retorts to Delta's warning that she should be more circumspect about disappearing and reappearing in front of people than she was at the city we've just left.

I wave to them both and hurry out towards the pasture with Maverick bounding in and out of visibility beside me. I smile and say, 'Hi,' to those I pass, all of whom pick up from me the reason for my hurry and refrain from delaying me. By the time I reach the pasture, there is a small crowd of people standing at the edge of it. I lift a hand to them on my way past.

'I'm glad you're here, Will,' Victor calls out, 'I wasn't sure if I should intervene.'

I shake my head. 'He'll be okay.'

Ember stands at the far side of the pasture, his herd behind him as he watches the chestnut stallion at last making his approach. One of the fillies whinnies to the young stallion, whose voice is deep and throaty as he whinnies back. A mare and several more fillies whinny and I sense the stallion's excitement rising. There's no going back for him now.

Ember arches his neck and trots straight at him. I don't want to watch what I know is coming. I don't want my strong, proud, beautiful horse to have his age and frailty rammed home to him. I want to go to him, to stand beside him and repel the stallion as Maverick and I did when wild cats threatened Ember when he was a foal. I want the young stallion to leave my boy to live out the rest of his days with his herd in peace. But I know that isn't what is best for the herd. They need a strong male to keep them together, to protect them, to sire more offspring, and they need the chestnut to prove he can be that for them by defeating Ember. So I walk slowly around the herd without interfering.

By the time I reach Ember, his fight is over and his lead mare is disappearing into the distance with all but his two eldest mares, the young stallion in place at the rear of the herd. Ember is lying flat out on his side in the grass, lathered in sweat, the bulge of his rib cage rising and falling at many times the normal rate as a result of his pain and exertion. It gradually slows as I heal his wounds and strains, assisted by the two mares standing on either side of him with their heads lowered and their noses almost touching as they shift as much of their energy to him as they can spare.

I drop to my knees beside him, tears running down my face. He's okay, he'll be up in a bit, but he's just edged a lot closer to the time he'll get up without his body. I stroke his nose and he whickers to me. Maverick's echo snuggles in between us both. My boys. Three souls who were never more than one.

Ember heaves himself onto his elbows with a grunt. I shuffle closer and he lowers his nose into my lap. I rest my forehead against his and Maverick curls around his muzzle, both of us adding our energy to that of Ember's mares. We love him. We'll take care of him. Tania will need my help in the past every now and then, but I'll never be gone for long. The rest of the time, I'll be here with my herd.

I sense Ember stir within himself. He who has incarnated with me twice over in order to support me when I was struggling, senses my intention to do the same for him. He doesn't need to be here anymore, we both know that, but he also now doesn't have a reason to leave. I'll look after him until I can no longer keep him comfortable, he'll have the company of the old mares who yet stand by him, and the shelter, protection and love of all of Rockwood.

I wipe my face as I sense him wanting to get to his feet, and shuffle back out of his way. Maverick's echo fades away but I sense his joy at yet another mission accomplished. Ember rolls, itchy now that his sweat has dried in the early evening sun. I stand up as he does, and smile as he shakes his coat free of the dust he has just rolled into it.

The two who approached some time ago and have stood waiting for this moment, now appear on either side of me.

My father puts a hand on my shoulder, as glad as I that Ember, whom he still can't help but think of as Candour, will be remaining with us for the rest of his current life.

My mother hands me the brush she has brought. I take it gratefully and use it to groom Ember until his coat almost has a shine to it. He stands still the whole while, his head lowered, his eyes closed, enjoying my attention. When I turn back to where Mum and Dad were standing, they are nowhere to be seen.

I start to walk to the village but then turn and wait for Ember, who stares at me, his orange eyes weary where once they were full of fire. I look down for Maverick and his echo bursts onto the pasture and races behind Ember, then dashes back and forth. The old stallion's eyes brighten as he senses our old friend, and his ears flick backward at the very second that I swear I hear Maverick bark.

'Are you ready?' I ask him, knowing that he is. I look past him to Maverick. 'Are you ready to run?' I definitely hear the echo of a distant bark this time as the dog who is no more answers the question that was always guaranteed to excite him.

I turn and run towards Rockwood, picking up my pace when I hear the pounding of hooves behind me. I risk a glance over my shoulder to see Ember tossing his head as he canters, like he always did when allowing Maverick to believe he was herding him. I laugh and run faster, and soon my beautiful boys are running on either side of me with the two elderly mares bringing up the rear.

We slow when we are almost upon those waiting for us at the edge of the village. In the hour or so since a herd of horses became just three, a large field shelter has been sung into existence and bedded down with straw. I wave my thanks to Victor, Ace, Prime, Delta and Ivy. A nearby water trough is full and hay has been put out in large piles to supplement the grass that has been so heavily grazed over the past weeks. Ember and his mares each stop at a pile and begin to eat hungrily.

'Thank you,' I call out to Gran and the two of her friends who I am Aware organised the hay, and to those who live in the closest cottages, who filled the water trough. 'Thank you, all of you.'

They don't need my gratitude, I know that; they are all nearly as delighted as I that Rockwood will have horses among its number for the foreseeable future.

I spot all of my family in the crowd. I wink at Lia. I smile at Eminent, glad for her that she has achieved the purpose of her trip. I grin at Tania, Delta, Amarilla, my mother, my gran and my sisters, all of whom, as well as I, chose to incarnate into bodies carrying Pamela's DNA which to this day still reverberates with

The Way Of The Horse. I reach out a hand and rest it on Ember's withers. My other hand hangs by my side, just above the echo of Maverick's head. Humanity has survived and achieved balance with its environment as it was always going to. We were never going to fail.

Books by Lynn Mann

The Horses Know Trilogy
The Horses Know
The Horses Rejoice
The Horses Return

Sequels to The Horses Know Trilogy
Horses Forever
The Forgotten Horses
The Way Of The Horse

Origins of The Horses Know Trilogy
The Horses Unite

Prequels to The Horses Know Trilogy
In Search Of Peace (Adam's story)
The Strength Of Oak (Rowena's story)
A Reason To Be Noble (Quinta's story)

Companion Stories to The Horses Know Trilogy
From A Spark Comes A Flame (Novella)
Tales Of The Horse-Bonded (Short Story Collection)

Tales Of The Horse-Bonded will take you on a journey into the lives of some of your favourite characters from *The Horses Know Trilogy*. The book is available for purchase in paperback and hardback, and is available to download for free. To find out more, visit www.lynnmann.co.uk.

A regularly updated book list can be found at
www.lynnmann.co.uk/booklist
(The QR code below enables easy access.)

The Way Of The Horse (A Sequel to The Forgotten Horses)

Nathan has survived the years since his parents' murders by visiting an equine assisted therapy centre every day, where a devoted mare provides him with sanctuary from his demons. When she and the other therapy horses are taken from the centre by the police and herded out of The City Of Glory, Nathan is ready to kill or be killed.

But then the enigmatic Tania takes his hand and he remembers another time. Another life. Then, he was one of the Horse-Bonded, one who failed to fulfil his potential. Now, he is a scientific research assistant barely clinging to sanity. The fate of The City Of Glory's citizens depends on him staying alive but in order to do that, he will need to embrace both his memory of who he really is, and the help of the horse who won't allow death to thwart them both...

The Horses Unite (Origins of The Horses Know Trilogy)

When FE88 qualifies as an enforcer of The City Of Power's rules, her life becomes marginally more secure, not least because she has the love and support of a member of the city's underground resistance to help her stay sane.

But then she discovers that the only light in her otherwise dark existence will be assigned to her as her next kill. She resolves to resist the regime that gives her no choice but to obey, and save the life that is hers to take – but is shocked to learn that it is her own life that must be preserved at all costs. Without her, the future of both enforcers and humans is uncertain. Even with her, it isn't guaranteed, for her hatred of human nature runs deep.

When the city falls, it is a horse who proves to be the two races' best chance of co-existing. If he can succeed, the pathway laid down by the horses of the past will remain open. But some tasks are too great for one horse alone…

In Search Of Peace (A Prequel to The Horses Know Trilogy)

Adam is on the verge of grief-induced insanity when a horse chooses him as a Bond-Partner and refuses to leave his side. He tries to rid himself of his unwanted companion as he has everyone else, but finds it more difficult than he could have imagined.

Just when it seems as though the horse has managed to find a way through Adam's grief and bring him back to himself, Adam rejects him in the worst possible way, resulting in catastrophe. In order to save the Bond-Partner who has tried so hard to save him, Adam must remember what his would-be saviour tried to teach him. And he must do it soon, before it is too late for both of them…

The Strength Of Oak (A Prequel to The Horses Know Trilogy)

Unloved and unwanted by her parents, Rowena is desperate for a way out of the life she hates. When a horse chooses her as his Bond-Partner, she thinks she has found one – but she soon discovers that while she can leave her family behind, there is no escaping herself.

With patient guidance from her horse, Rowena begins to accept the truth of her past, and to believe she can change. But then her past catches up with her at the worst possible moment, leaving her with a choice. She can be the person she was, or she can find the strength to be the person her horse has shown her she can be. One choice will give them both a future. The other will be the death of them…

A Reason To Be Noble
(A Prequel to The Horses Know Trilogy)

Quinta is crippled with anxiety and can barely leave the house, so she is terrified when she senses the touch of a horse's mind on her own and realises that he has selected her as his Bond-Partner. She manages to find the courage to leave her home and her village, and meet the horse whose mind calls to hers. A bond settles into place between the two of them, and Quinta's outlook on life begins to change.

With her horse's guidance, Quinta's confidence slowly increases, but she has a long way to go if she is to leave all of her fears behind, and her horse is a relentless teacher. When it seems as though he has pushed her too far, Quinta must find a way to trust that everything he has taught her still holds true. Their lives and that of a young boy will depend on it…

From A Spark Comes A Flame

When Fitt leaves Rockwood with her horse to take Awareness to the villages of The New, she knows it will be a challenge, not least because those she wants to help are terrified of her kind.

Upon arrival at the village of Bigwood, the worst of Fitt's fears about her mission are realised. She takes the only way forward that she can see, but her actions go against the advice of her horse and the cost to herself is high. It is only when the cost to the people of Bigwood is higher that Fitt is forced to acknowledge her mistake. If she can rectify it, she will discover the extent of her power. If she can't, the consequences will be deadly…

Did you enjoy The Forgotten Horses?
I'd be extremely grateful if you could spare a few minutes
to leave a review where you purchased your copy.
Reviews really do help my books to reach a wider audience,
which means that I can keep on writing!
Thank you very much.

I love to hear from you!
Get in touch and receive news of future releases at the following:

www.lynnmann.co.uk

www.facebook.com/lynnmann.author

Acknowledgments

Thank you for reading this, my eighth novel, I very much appreciate your company on my writing journey.

Huge thanks as always to my indispensable editorial team – Fern Sherry, Leonard Palmer, Caroline Macintosh and Cindy Nye – for keeping me on the straight and narrow, and to Amanda Horan for her fabulous cover design.

When I am writing, I feel a huge amount of gratitude to the horses who have influenced me so much during my life, to the dogs who have loved and accompanied me, and in this instance to a very large, very chatty and often obnoxious grey cat who barged into my life twelve years ago and has been creating chaos ever since. Hector (named after the warrior from Troy) is a force of nature who relentlessly pursues anything he desires, and frustrating as it often is to be on the other side of the equation, I admire him hugely and miss him on the odd occasion he isn't around.

Printed in Great Britain
by Amazon

30197005R00175